TAKEN

NICHOLE SEVERN

TAKEN

She knows evil inside and out.

When women start going missing in the lakeside hometown she left behind long ago, FBI agent Brie McKinney is forced to return. A necklace discovered at the primary crime scene is an exact replica to the one she wears. It ties back to her own abduction twenty years ago. And to the night her sister disappeared. As another body washes onto shore, Brie once again finds herself in the killer's crosshairs. Only this time, she's not a child. And she's not alone.

Roman Bradford has trained to be in the center of the action, to make the hard calls without emotion, but that discipline fails when the killer turns his attention to his compelling FBI partner. Unwilling to lose Brie, especially when the bond they share slides into heated desire, Roman finds himself breaking all the rules he swore to uphold to protect her. And risking his career in the process.

As Brie and Roman fight frenzied attraction it becomes clear that to unravel a web of clues a killer has left behind, she must face a horrifying truth about the night her sister disappeared—before it's too late.

CHAPTER ONE

COLD.

FBI Special Agent Brie McKinney lifted her coat's collar around her neck as she trudged through the damp sand. In vain. Neither the sun rising to the east nor the breeze coming over Lake Michigan had anything to do with the chill tunneling deep into her bones. The crime scene Ludington Police Department had already established up ahead couldn't take the credit either.

"Welcome home." Her partner, Roman Bradford, lifted the outer perimeter tape above his head to let her pass underneath, locking coffee-colored eyes on her. Seeing as how this was their first official case together, she didn't know much about him other than he'd worked his way into the bureau's missing persons division by coming up through the hostage rescue team. At six-foot-four or six-foot-five, he towered over her, but hearing the man talk in his sleep on the plane from Washington, DC took a bit of bite out of that bark. Shadows deepened along his five o'clock shadow as she passed beneath the tape. "Is it safe to say this isn't exactly the homecoming you'd imagined?"

"Not in the least." Home. She fought off the shiver prickling down her spine. Hell, she hadn't planned on ever coming back here. Or within a hundred miles of Ludington, Michigan. Big Sable Point Lighthouse demanded attention behind the floodlights, yellow crime scene tape and the handful of officers scanning the death scene for evidence. But, even after all these years, the small, grass-covered hill over her shoulder leading to the shore pulled at her.

"Special Agents McKinney and Bradford." Presenting her credentials to the officer logging visitors to the scene, Brie swallowed at the sight of Captain Greg Hobbs less than thirty feet away. The man who'd practically raised her hadn't changed in the last decade since she'd left, but she'd be lying to herself if she admitted it was good to see him. Even after everything he'd done for her, she'd never wanted to step back foot in this city. She closed in on him, Roman at her side. "Captain."

Hobbs lifted his familiar brown eyes to hers, a smile cracking at the edges of his dark lips. He set down the clipboard onto the table in front of him, all six-feet of him closing the distance between them for a hug. "Brie McKinney. Look at you, all grown up, and a special agent at that." He wrapped her in his strong, warm arms, then stepped back. "When the chief told me you were coming, I almost didn't believe it. Didn't think I'd ever see you come back here after—"

"It's been a while, hasn't it?" Heat worked up her neck, and she motioned to Roman. "Special Agent Bradford, this is Captain Greg Hobbs, Ludington PD." She shoved her hands in her coat pockets in an attempt to distract her from the captain's journey down memory lane. She wasn't here because of the past. "Seems you might've found our missing person." Brie extracted her phone and presented it to the captain, their victim's photo centered on the screen. "Ashlee Carr. Thirty-one. Missing from her home in Traverse City three months ago. We got word your Jane Doe might be her."

"That looks like our vic all right." Captain Hobbs shook his head, handing back the phone. Pointing to a couple officers and a man in civilian clothing she didn't recognize, the captain faced them again. "Witness found her two hours ago while he was out walking his dog. He put in the call to dispatch after he noticed her throat had been cut."

Her throat? Brie sank her heels a bit deeper in the sand. Damn it. Did that mean—

"She's dead." Roman shifted beside her, his clean, masculine scent fighting off the sickening odor of lake water and sand.

Most people loved the smell of the beach, couldn't wait for Michigan's bleary, January gray days to disappear. In a few weeks, families would take to the lake, soak up the sun safely ashore. Brie chanced a glance past the outer perimeter of the scene, toward the blackness of Lake Michigan that waited beyond as a kind of static filled her ears. And they'd go about their lives as if monsters didn't exist.

"Looks like our missing persons case just turned into a homicide." Roman's voice pulled her back into the moment, kept her grounded.

She breathed him in as much as she could to combat the nausea churning in her gut, tried to focus on the search of the target scene—where the body had been found—rather than the nightmares determined to break through since their plane had landed. The weight of her partner's gaze pressurized something inside of her. Right. They had no jurisdiction here anymore. Once their missing person turned up dead, the local police department would be assigned the lead on the case. As soon as they got a positive ID on the victim, the FBI was no longer involved in the disappearance of Ashlee Carr. And Brie could get the hell out of here.

"Coroner picked her up about thirty minutes before you got here." Dark circles set up residence beneath Hobbs's eyes. He'd put on a few pounds since she'd last seen him, gained a few more inches of that receding hairline. Retirement would've been right around the corner if it weren't for a high-profile case like this one. "We don't have the authority to declare time of death or touch the body until the medical examiner has had a chance to claim the remains. Otherwise I would've called and told you not to bother getting on that plane." The captain shook his head, picked up the clipboard again as cameramen and journalists started lining the outer perimeter of the scene. "Here we go again. Vultures."

"Again?" Roman straightened. "You've had another case attract this much media attention recently?"

"No." Captain Hobbs locked his attention on Brie, and every

muscle in her body strained to pull her apart from the inside. "Not recently."

"Thanks for your help." She shook Hobb's hand. "We'd like to look at what you've recovered from the scene before we officially close our end of the investigation. See if any evidence might answer for her being this far from home. Might help us build a list of suspects or witnesses involved in her disappearance."

"My guys are still searching the scene, but I'll get a log of the evidence we've collected so far." The captain nodded, glancing at Roman before focusing back on her. "It's good to see you, Brie."

"You, too." She scanned the scene as the man she'd considered a surrogate father kicked up sand and headed toward another officer. Of all the locations to dump a body, why here? Why this particular stretch of shore?

"I can practically see the wheels turning in your head. Want to share?" Roman's voice flooded through her, reaching past the tension, the anxiety of being back in her hometown, distracted her from reliving the nightmare that'd changed the entire course of her life.

She closed in on the target scene and studied the brightly-colored evidence markers where the victim would've been if the coroner hadn't already claimed the remains. She didn't have to look behind her to know Roman had followed close on her heels. Awareness of him—of every move he made—battled with her focus on the scene. She'd never had a problem keeping her head in the game during a case before, but the way he looked at her… It was as though he could see the secret she'd kept buried her entire career.

"We're fifty feet up from the shore, wouldn't you say?" She took a deep breath, forcing her shoulders away from her ears. This scene had nothing to do with the past, yet she couldn't discard the feeling the location—the exact location carved into her memories from twenty years ago—was more than a coincidence. "Even with high winds and powerful seiches, the body wouldn't have made it this far up the beach on its own."

"Someone positioned her here." Roman scrubbed a hand down his face, his facial hair bristling loud over the lapping of soft waves from the shore. Dark eyes, sharp features, muscles that stretched for days beneath his pristine suit, impossibly expressive eyebrows. Her new partner definitely fit the high-end of tall, dark, and handsome.

Which had nothing to do with this case. Brie turned back to the scene as he studied her. To prove the static in her brain had nothing to do with her new partner and everything to do with setting foot in this damn city again. "I don't think she was dumped here by accident."

"Then by arranging the body, our unsub had to have been sending a message." Roman pulled at his tie, loosening it and the top button of his shirt.

Until they had an idea of who'd been involved in Ashlee Carr's disappearance, the suspect would go by unsub or unidentified subject. First, they needed a positive identification of the victim. They'd interviewed everyone in Ashlee's life. Twice. The thirty-one-year-old single photographer took the same route to her job as every day, ate at the same restaurants weekly and visited her parents each Sunday for dinner. No boyfriend. No enemies or unsatisfied clients as far as she and Roman had been able to dig up. Nothing to suggest Ashlee hadn't just been in the wrong place at the wrong time when someone had broken into her home. Only instead of killing her, the suspect had taken her. And never made contact again.

But now, it was looking more and more like their unsub had killed his victim after all.

"Question is: to who?" Barking pulled her attention up near the black and white lighthouse, where the witness who'd discovered the body tried to control his dog as officers finished taking his statement. Brie blocked her eyes with one hand as the rising sun warmed the scene. Curling her hand around her phone in her jacket pocket, she forced herself to focus as Captain Hobbs returned with the evidence log. She reached for the clipboard he offered.

"This is everything we've collected from the scene so far," Hobbs said.

"The witness who found the body. You said he noticed the cut on the victim's neck and called police. I take it that means he had to get pretty close to her to see that." Brie reviewed the list of evidence officers had already catalogued. Locard's Exchange Principle. Any person who came in contact with the body or the evidence around it left something of themselves behind, changed the scene. Add a canine to the mix and heaven only knew how much evidence had been disrupted or destroyed altogether.

"His name's Kirk Marshall. We've taken imprints of his shoes to rule him out, but yes, looks like he and his dog got pretty close to her before he realized what he'd found." The captain twisted around as one of the journalists at the perimeter broke through the line. "Excuse me."

"How much do you want to bet the witness disturbed any footprints the suspect left behind while he was at it." Not a question. Roman's voice dropped low, and she tightened her grip on the clipboard as heat seared through her. Standing over her right shoulder, he moved into her personal space, his body heat tunneling through her coat and deep into muscle. "They collect anything that would give us an ID on the victim?"

"Nothing yet." She licked her suddenly dry lips to counteract the discomfort building behind her sternum. She'd had plenty of partners —forced herself to explore relationships—since leaving Ludington, but the pressure of having someone this close never went away. Brie shifted a few steps to her right and trailed her finger down the list of evidence. And stopped on the tenth line from the top. One second. Two. Confusion barreled through her, and right then she didn't care how close her partner had gotten. Her breath hitched, the feeling of blood draining from her face pulling at her. No, that couldn't be right.

"Brie? Everything okay?" Roman asked.

"No." She rushed past the command post the department had set up to run the search of the scene and closed in on the plastic tubs officers stored the bagged and tagged evidence. She didn't know if Roman had followed her this time. Didn't care. Evidence bag ten. Evidence bag ten... Brie flipped through the marked plastic bags with blue tape and numbers labeled on each one. Nine. Eleven. Where the hell was it?

"What are we looking for?" Roman circled into her peripheral vision, scanning through another bin beside hers.

If her heart hadn't been threatening to pound straight out of her chest, she might've stopped to appreciate his immediate support. She'd spent so long relying on herself—first as a kid facing years of trauma, working her way through college without encouragement from anyone but Hobbs, and now investigating missing persons cases for the FBI's violent crimes unit—it'd take longer than a few weeks to get used to a partner who had her back. "Bag ten. They found a gold necklace near the body. I need to see it."

"Got it." Roman pulled a bag from his bin, and the scene around her dissolved. "Is this what you were looking for?"

She couldn't think. Couldn't breathe. Couldn't command her hand to reach out and take the bag from him. Her pulse pounded at the base of her skull. Floodlights reflected off the delicate gold chain at the bottom of the plastic bag. She had to stay in control. Hundreds of people had necklaces exactly like the one in that bag, but the fact it'd been recovered on this exact beach, near a woman Brie had been assigned to find… She rolled back her shoulders. She didn't believe in coincidence. "Let me see it."

Wrenching the evidence from his hand, she pinched the plastic between her fingers. There was nothing special about the piece of jewelry, only one unique characteristic that separated it from the millions of gold bar necklaces out there, the same characteristic the officer who'd recovered the item from the scene had noted in the evidence log.

The engraved letters that spelled the name *Jessica*.

Roman closed the short distance between them, his words breaking through the static only getting louder in her head. "You've seen that particular necklace before."

Every time she closed her eyes. Brie battled to keep her breathing steady, but the weight of Roman's gaze increased the pressure in her lungs. The necklace shouldn't be here. Because… "It belonged to a victim who went missing twenty years ago." A shudder ran through her. "My sister. Jessica."

CHAPTER TWO

TOO MUCH OF A COINCIDENCE. THE SON OF A BITCH WHO'D KILLED Ashlee Carr had to be baiting them by leaving that necklace at the scene. Maybe baiting Brie.

Special Agent Roman Bradford maneuvered their rental SUV into a parking spot outside of Western Michigan University's school of medicine, thirty minutes southwest of Ludington. The medical examiner had claimed the victim's remains, but the autopsy wouldn't be conducted until the lead investigator—in this case Captain Greg Hobbs—could attend. Officially, the FBI no longer had jurisdiction even if the body were identified as their victim, but he wasn't about to walk away now.

Seeing as how a piece of evidence might connect to one of the investigators assigned to find answers in the victim's disappearance, he and Brie had come straight to the medical examiner's office here in Kalamazoo. Roman put the SUV in Park but didn't move to get out of the vehicle. Not yet. She hadn't said a word the entire drive south, but they needed to get one thing clear. "Whoever took our victim wanted your attention."

The moment he'd met Brie McKinney he'd known the truth, seen the darkness in those mesmerizing blue-green eyes. She was a survivor. Like recognizing like. The scars around her wrists proved as much, although he didn't know the whole story. Didn't need to. She tried to hide them under long-sleeve blouses and coats, but nothing escaped his attention. Not when it came to her. Slightly curled brown hair escaped from where she'd swept it behind her ear, covering the small mole on her left cheekbone, and Roman tightened his grip on the steering wheel to keep from reaching out. Thick eyebrows and dark lashes framed a gaze he'd been drawn into the moment they'd met. At five-foot-three, maybe five-foot-four, Brie McKinney packed a hell of a punch for a woman who mostly kept to herself. Intense. Challenging. And nearly impossible to ignore. But they were partners, and anything more would wouldn't just risk his career but hers as well.

"We don't know that." Brie lifted her head, setting her gaze on him. Deep red lipstick matched the polish on her nails and only added to her classic style of black slacks and a button-down silk shirt. The color suited her. Strong. Confident. In control. At least, that'd been his impression since he'd been assigned to work the Ashlee Carr case with her. Everyone had their secrets though. "Not yet anyway. There are thousands of necklaces like the one recovered at the scene, and we still haven't gotten a positive ID on the victim."

"Then let's get one." Shouldering his way out of the SUV, Roman rounded the hood as she headed for the front door. She was right. A simple gold necklace engraved with the name *Jessica* wasn't unique, but if the body was identified as Ashlee Carr, there'd be no other reason for their victim to have that specific piece of jewelry. Other than to pull them into a killer's web.

A wall of warmth slammed into him as they stepped inside Western Michigan University's Homer Stryker M.D. School of Medicine. The medical examiner's office here serviced eleven counties throughout the state, including Mason County, where their victim had been discovered. Warm, orange, accented doors, a receptionist desk, and a row of empty seating contrasted with the slight odor of disinfectant in his nose. Nothing compared to Brie's lighter, alluring perfume.

"Special Agent McKinney, Special Agent Bradford." Vibrant red hair consumed his attention as a woman in a white lab coat approached, hand outstretched. "I'm Dr. Allie Meyers, the medical examiner assigned to this case. Captain Hobbs said you'd be coming."

"Thanks for taking the time to meet with us." Roman pocketed his credentials, shaking the doctor's hand, and Brie did the same. "We understand the autopsy won't be completed right away, but we're hoping you already have an ID for our victim recovered this morning in Ludington."

"I do. Why don't we discuss the case in the conference room?" Dr. Meyers asked.

"We'd prefer to see the body, if you don't mind," he said.

"Not a problem." Dr. Meyers turned on a pair of taupe heels with red backing and led them deeper into the building. Shoving open a set of thick, double hospital-like doors, she directed them past a row of empty office chairs positioned outside what he was sure was only one of the office's many labs. The medical examiner motioned them down a set of stairs and into a large sub-basement room where temperatures dropped the deeper they went. The morgue. She pulled a pair of latex gloves from her lab coat pocket. "There's a box of gloves over there on that shelf you can help yourself to."

Crystalized puffs of air formed in front of his mouth as Roman reached for the gloves. His hand collided with his partner's as she went for the same box, and, for a moment, he could've sworn a tremor had rocked up his arm and into his chest. Her attention snapped to him, a bit brighter than before, and she pulled her hand back. Had she felt it, too? The instant hike of his pulse? Extracting two set of gloves, he handed one to her. "Here you go."

"I can get my own gloves." Brie leveled her chin with the floor as she took two gloves from the box, shutting down her expression. Out of professionalism, or to keep anyone from seeing beneath that mask she'd worn since they met, he had no idea, but sooner or later, she'd have to trust him. Otherwise, this wasn't going to work between them.

Roman shoved his hands inside the latex. The brim snapped against his wrists, and the quick sting of plastic on flesh cleared his head. "What else are partners for if not to hand you a pair of gloves to assess a dead body?"

She tried to hide the small curl of her lips as she turned away, but Brie couldn't hide from him.

Hinges protested from behind as Dr. Meyers wrenched one of the lockers open. The medical examiner tugged the drawer free. "Due to staffing shortages, we are running a bit behind schedule on our autopsies, but our pathologist was able to pull fingerprints off your victim once we brought her back from the scene this morning to start getting her processed."

Roman stepped closer to the slab, the smell of disinfectant here a lot stronger than out in the lobby. Every body told a story, and the vast design of both shallow and deep lacerations over the victim's body and the killing strike at her neck told the violent story of a woman who'd been tortured to death. He'd studied dozens of photos of Ashlee Carr over the last three months. Black and blue hues tinted the woman's skin, and her white blonde hair was darker from dirt and stringy from lake water now, but recognition flared. "You said you got an official ID."

Dr. Meyers handed him a white manila folder, but he couldn't take his eyes off the woman on the table. How long had the killer experimented with pain and blood loss before finally releasing the victim from her agony? Hour? Days? "Her name is Ashlee Carr."

His gut clenched as he reviewed the information in the file. Sure enough, they had confirmation of their missing person.

"Officers recovered a thin gold-chained necklace from the scene that had the name *Jessica* inscribed in gold." Brie's voice penetrated through the haze thickening in his head, slightly shaken, and it pulled at something inside of him. The necklace had either been planted at the scene by the killer or it'd been forgotten on that beach accidentally prior to the body dump. "Was the victim wearing it when your office claimed the remains this morning? Maybe it fell off when the medicolegal investigator moved her?"

"My investigator never said anything about a necklace, no. Everything you see here is what was attached to the body at the time our office picked her up. All I can tell you at this time is that a necklace like you're describing wouldn't have caused this bruising around her neck. Until I have the official autopsy report for you, I can't say anything more definite about how she died or when." Dr. Meyers tried for a reassuring smile, but it didn't reach her eyes. Hard to feel something as simple as assurance when constantly surrounded by the dead. "Now, if you'll excuse me. I have a lecture starting in about ten minutes I need to get to."

Roman handed the medical examiner back the file folder with a nod. "Thank you for your time, Dr. Meyers. We'll be in touch if we have any further questions."

Both he and Brie headed for the double doors and pushed through, but the tension that'd pulled the tendons in his neck wouldn't release. They had their positive ID on the victim. Ashlee Carr had been abducted from her home in Traverse City and killed. The FBI's investigation into her disappearance was officially closed, and now Ludington PD would take over solving her homicide, but his instincts screamed this was far from over. Not with the connection between his partner and that necklace officers had recovered at the scene.

Their footsteps echoed off the clean white walls as they treaded up the stairs and back into the lobby. Brie was right. He had to stay objective. He couldn't bring any theories of his own to the table. Any evidence recovered could fit an investigator's personal theory of the crime if they tried hard enough. That was how cases went cold and criminals went free.

But the fear that'd been etched into Brie's face as she'd studied that gold necklace had been brandished into his brain, and he never wanted to witness that kind of fear from his partner again.

Reaching the SUV, Roman slammed the driver's side door behind him, locking in her light, aromatic perfume as she strapped her seatbelt across her lap and chest. Silence pressed. His heart thundered behind his ears. They'd only been partnered for three months, didn't really know anything about one another, but he'd do his job to recover the victims they were assigned to find and protect his partner in the process. Even if it meant breaking the rules to do it. "You want to tell me about the necklace?"

"There's nothing to tell. For all we know it was dropped on that beach and forgotten in the last few weeks, months, or even years. Might have nothing to do with Ashlee Carr's case at all, and until forensics can pull prints or trace the purchase, there's no reason for us to still be here." The small muscles along her jaw flexed as she stared straight out the windshield. "We found our missing person. Now we go back to DC and take on the next case until we're told otherwise."

"You don't believe that. Otherwise you wouldn't be grinding your teeth right now." If there was one thing he *had* learned about Brie McKinney over the past few months at her side, it was her preference to distance herself emotionally and mentally from anything that might come close to personal. Just as she'd done on that beach this morning. She'd tried to hide it, but Roman had noted the stiff set of her lips, the small glances out across the lake. No matter how hard she'd tried to stay in control, she couldn't hide from him. "We're partners, Brie, and if I can't trust you to tell me the truth, I can't trust you to have my back in the field."

He'd learned that lesson the hard way. Secrets had a way of getting people killed. And behind those beautiful blue eyes, lay secrets deeper and darker than he could imagine.

"Everyone has something they hide from the world." She hit the release for her seatbelt and pushed out of the SUV. Pushing open the passenger side door, she set her gaze on him, voice dropping into dangerous territory. "But just because we're partners doesn't means you have the right know mine." She headed down the sidewalk.

Roman hit the pavement and followed after her, her short hair catching against the wool of her coat. He reached out, curled his hand around her arm, and spun her into him. He loosened his grip, giving her the chance to flee, but couldn't force himself to release her completely. Not when she felt so good pressed against him like this. "I'm not asking for your secrets. I'm asking for you to trust me."

The shrill sound of his phone cut through her answering silence, and he released his hold on her arm. Digging his phone from his coat pocket, he read the screen. Special Agent in Charge Mitchell Haynes, fearless leader of the FBI's missing persons division. Their boss. Roman hit the speaker phone feature as Brie swiped her hair out of her face and put a couple of feet of space between them. She was always doing that, distancing herself physically, mentally, emotionally. As though she didn't dare let anyone get close. Which he understood more than most. "Bradford."

"Bradford, tell me you and McKinney are still in Michigan." Haynes had brought him onto the team straight from HRT with two bullets to the chest. The SAC's voice had been the first one he'd heard when he'd come out of surgery, and Roman's scars burned beneath his shirt at the sound again.

"We're south at the medical examiner's office in Kalamazoo. We got confirmation the victim Ludginton PD recovered at the lighthouse is our missing woman. Ashlee Carr." Raising his gaze to Brie, he forced the tightness out of his shoulders. She didn't seem to think the necklace had any significance to their victim's case, and unless they had proof, the killer had planted it at the scene for her specifically to find, they'd follow her plan. Head back to DC. Take on the next case. His attention slipped to the small mole on her left cheek. "Next flight to DC leaves in about two hours—"

"You're staying," Haynes said.

The hairs on the back of his neck stood on end. Roman strengthened his grip around the phone. There was only one reason they wouldn't be getting back on that plane after closing a case. "Sir?"

Brie stepped into him, her attention locked on the phone. "What happened?"

Static reached across the line, but Hayne's voice registered clear as day. "Another woman has gone missing in Ludington."

CHAPTER THREE

Trust him.

They'd barely been partners for more than three months, had only worked this single case together, and Roman wanted her to trust him. The line of work they'd chosen—their partnership—required working side by side, protecting one another in and out of the field, being honest with each other concerning the case they'd been assigned. Nothing more. The only part of this relationship that mattered was that they did their jobs, and they brought victims home to their families. Like she should've done for Jessica.

Brie unrolled her fingernails from her palms as she stepped from the SUV. She couldn't focus on Roman right now, even with him keeping pace behind her up the worn, cracked sidewalk. They had another case.

Mail spilled from the brick red mailbox at the front of the matching brick home, the only sign something might not be right inside. That, and the two officers posted beside the front door. A lot of the homes in Ludington had been modeled after the typical four cookie cutter designs around the city. There were the split levels with a set of stairs leading directly up to the main level builders were convinced home buyers wanted and the rare six-bedroom ramblers, but this one seemed more familiar than most. Brie slowed for a moment. As though she'd been here before.

She flashed her credentials for the second time that day, then both she and Roman took a few minutes to don personal protection gear before they crossed the threshold. Cross-contamination between the primary and secondary scenes would become an investigator's worst nightmare in an investigation like this. And with beach sand possibly still clinging to her shoes and victim reported missing, she wasn't about to make any mistakes. She stepped into the house, taken back by the jolt of familiarity. She'd been to a dozen scenes since joining the FBI's missing persons division. Homes seemingly abandoned at the last minute, dirty dishes in the sink, the faint smell of staleness settling on the air.

Her protective equipment swished loud in her ears as she kept in line where Ludington PD officers had cleared a path through the debris littering the floor. Broken glass, furniture tipped on its side. Everything that would make a case for a struggle. Flashes from the crime scene photographer's camera flickered in her peripheral vision as she slipped her hands into a fresh pair of latex gloves. "Tell us about our missing woman."

"Chloe Francis." Captain Hobbs's deep voice reverberated through the small living room, and the battle between being happy to see him again and the reason they'd become close in the first place surfaced. Not here. Not now. FBI would take point on the woman's disappearance—at least until their victim was recovered—but working with local police would get their missing person home faster. "Thirty-five, lives alone but has been in a stable relationship for the past three years with her boyfriend, works at Ed's Diner down the street. Neighbors say they haven't heard or seen anything out of the ordinary, had nothing bad to say about her. The boyfriend called police after he hadn't heard from Chloe for two days."

"No couples dispute? Nothing to make him think she didn't just pack up and leave?" Roman moved deeper into the home, hiking her sensitivity of him into overdrive. It was only a fraction of the rush of sensation that'd hit her back in the morgue when their hands had brushed against one another. Which was insane. He'd asked her to trust him. How could she trust a partner she barely knew when she couldn't even trust herself to keep her focus centered on this case?

"Nothing he's admitting to as of right now," Hobbs said.

Chloe. Why did she know that name? It'd been close to twelve years since she'd stepped foot within city limits. The second she'd turned eighteen, she'd gotten the hell out of here, left her family behind, left Hobbs, her friends, her job at the same diner Chloe Francis worked down the street. She'd run as far from Ludington as she could get while still staying in the country and had joined the bureau soon afterward in an attempt to find the truth about Jessica's disappearance. In the end, nothing she'd done had made a difference, but Brie wasn't here to take a walk down memory lane. Picking up what looked like a recent photo of Chloe and a man with his arms wrapped around her—presumably the boyfriend who'd alerted police to her disappearance—Brie ignored the hollowness setting up residence in her gut. Their victim was a few years older, closer to Jessica's age. If her sister was alive. She rounded into the living room, and her gaze snapped to the sharp edge of brick surrounding the blackened fireplace. "We've got blood over here."

The weight of Roman's attention burned between her shoulder blades as he closed in on her. Close enough to reach out and touch. Goosebumps prickled along the backs of her arms as he studied the evidence over her shoulder. Bristles of his five o'clock shadow had grown thicker since they'd gotten on the plane to Ludington ten hours ago, exhaustion etched into his face. Cases took a toll on the agents assigned to investigate, and this one had just gotten started. "Rules out Chloe Francis up and leaving town."

"It's a good start at least." Brie rose to her feet, careful to avoid physical contact. Whatever sensations his touch had pushed through her earlier wouldn't bring Chloe Francis home, and that was all she could let herself focus on right now. Not the past. Not the necklace. Not the shocking attraction that erupted whenever Roman set those dark brown eyes on her, as though she wasn't just another partner in his world. Finding their missing person. That was all that mattered.

Giving into her need for connection, for even one night, would only end in disappointment. She didn't make connections. Not anymore.

She moved out of the way as the crime scene photographer, Captain Hobbs, and the sketch artist recorded the patch of blood, each in their own personal protective gear. From the state of the home, Brie wouldn't peg their victim well off. The floral-patterned couch had been stained over the years, the linoleum in the small kitchen peeling at the edges, laminate on the countertops. Most of the houses in this area had been built in the nineties, and this one hadn't seen any upgrades since. Nothing of value to be looted. So this abduction had been personal. Premeditated. The kidnapper would've had to have known Chloe lived alone, when she'd be home and not with her boyfriend or at work. They were either part of the victim's life or had been watching her. Possibly for weeks. "Was there a ransom note? Has the boyfriend received a call from the abductor?"

"No, nothing." Captain Hobbs sidestepped the evidence team, note pad in hand. "He says the last time he saw her though, Chloe didn't seem like herself. Kept checking the locks on the doors and windows while they were trying to watch a movie together. That was four nights ago."

Roman shifted his weight between both feet. "Sounds like she was scared."

Because someone had been following her? Watching her? Stalking her. Brie swallowed around the tightness in her throat. A feeling she was all too familiar with, even twenty years later. "Has your search team been through the rest of the house yet?"

"We've cleared those rooms but haven't done a thorough search." Hobbs turned back to the sketch artist's rendering, nodding. "Our focus is here in the living room given the state of the place. Yell if you find anything."

She motioned for Roman to follow with the crown of her head as she slowly headed away from the chaos of the target scene. Her heels sank into dingy carpeting, and the past rushed to meet the present. Laughter echoed in her head, then the shattering of glass. Brie froze in front of the family photo hanging to her right in the center of the hallway wall. She'd broken the frame of a photo exactly like this as a kid while running through the house. Reaching up, she feathered her glove-cased fingers over the scars on the photo. Where glass had cut into it. She blinked to clear her head. Chloe hadn't been acting herself the past few days. Maybe Roman had been right. Something had scared her. "There are three bedrooms with windows down this hall, one bathroom with a window over the shower, and a door to the garage. Chloe's abductor could've come through any one of them to get to her."

Roman's body heat tunneled through her coat from beside her, fighting back the chill setting up residence at the base of her spine. But there was no use. There was something about this case. Something she couldn't see yet. "And you know how many points of access this house has because…"

Eight thousand people lived in Ludington, MI, the absolute definition of a small town. Everybody knew everybody, got into their neighbor's business, attended each other's bar-be-cues, helped raise the neighbor's kids. But what were the chances of two women turning up missing and Brie having been assigned to both cases in a town she vowed never to step foot in again?

"I've been in this house before." She lowered her hand to her side. Her heart threatened to beat straight out of her chest the longer he studied her. She battled the tremor working down her back and forced herself to take a deep breath. "When I was a kid. I used to come here after school before my parents got home from work. Chloe Francis was my sister's friend. Her mom would watch us until it was time to go home for dinner."

Up until Brie and Jessica's entire world had been ripped apart.

"First the gold necklace at the primary scene, now another tie to your sister." Hiking his arm above his head, he leveraged his weight against the wall. "Can't be a coincidence."

She didn't believe in coincidence either. They were investigators. They had to let the evidence tell the truth and not fall prey to their own theories. And, as far as she could tell, the body recovered on the beach and their current missing persons case weren't connected. Brie swiped her tongue across her bottom lip. His gaze shot to her mouth, and tendrils of electricity lightninged through her. "We should search the bedrooms. Whoever abducted Chloe would've been watching her, getting close to figure out her schedule. Might've even broken in to find out more about her."

"Lead the way." The deep promise of unbreakable loyalty resonated in those three simple words, and every cell in her body stood at attention.

How was it he could affect her like this? As though his voice was the key to unlocking years of suppressed desire and biological drives. Hell, she'd dated a few times, experimented with the idea of getting married, settling down, having kids, but none of those relationships had gotten past a few dates. Not with her career goals. Not with her need to find the truth. And not with the secret she'd been forced to carry.

Brie headed straight for the back room. Chloe's old room if she remembered right, only the white twin bed frame had been replaced with a queen-sized mattress, fresh, white decor had been chosen over the pink and purple unicorns, and there wasn't a teddy bear in sight all these years later. She maneuvered around the bed, the sound of Roman's protection gear swishing to her right. She and her sister had spent a lot of time at this house when they were growing up. Chloe had never really been her friend, but she'd gotten to play with her and Jessica every once in a while. She hadn't thought about or seen Chloe or this house for years. Not since the funeral. "No signs of a struggle in this room."

"The window has a new lock on it." Roman pointed above the bedframe. "The white paint on the frame is chipping, but this latch is silver, and there are no scratches on the surface. No sign of wear."

"The boyfriend told officers Chloe had kept checking the windows and doors while they were watching a movie a few days ago." Instinct prickled down her spine, and Brie tapped her pen against the notebook in her hand. "Most people check locks once before going to bed then don't think about it again. But she kept going back to ensure they were secure." Studying the room, she spotted the small garbage can beside the door and glanced inside. Bingo. She pulled a handful of old, painted latches from the bottom. "This wasn't the only window latch she replaced."

"Something scared her enough to change all the locks," he said.

"Or someone. Civilians aren't trained in situational awareness, but they can still feel if someone is watching them or has been inside the house." The hairs on the back of her neck rose on end, and she set the old latches back in the garbage bin to distract herself from the sick feeling in her gut. "They notice when something has been moved or if some of their personal effects have gone missing. If our unsub has been in here, Chloe would've felt it."

Roman pulled back his shoulders, a darkness consuming his gaze. One step. Two. Her blood pressure spiked as he stared down at her, but she wouldn't step back this time. To prove his proximity didn't control her. "Sounds like you have personal experience in that department."

The air conditioning kicked on overhead, and sunlight glinted off something metallic swinging at the corner of her eye. Something hanging from one of the nightstand lamps. Ice worked through her veins as she maneuvered around him. A hint of engraved lettering pulled her closer to the necklace hanging from the lampshade on the nightstand and urged her to run as fast as she could at the same time. She had to see, had to make sure. Gravity cemented her feet in place as she swept the necklace into her palm. *Jessica.* The world tilted on its axis, and she let the piece of jewelry fall from her hand. No. The cases weren't supposed to be connected. They weren't supposed to be personal. She shot her hand out, fisting her fingers in Roman's shirt as black spiderwebs worked in from the edges of her vision.

"Brie?" Concern plunged Roman's voice into dangerous territory a split second before he clamped one hand over hers and kept her upright with the other beneath her elbow.

"It's him." Her voice broke. "It's the Dream Catcher."

CHAPTER FOUR

Four women.

The National Missing and Unidentified Persons database—NamUs—had now linked four women to their investigation, including Ashlee Carr and Chloe Francis. Every one of them had been taken from their homes within the last year. All women in their thirties. All women having the same gold necklace engraved with the name *Jessica* logged as evidence in their abduction investigations. But only three of them had been confirmed deceased. Chloe Francis was still out there.

Controlled chaos buzzed around the police station as Captain Hobbs called in off-duty officers and volunteers. It was all hands-on deck for the search, but Roman only had attention for Brie.

She hadn't moved from in front of the murder board she'd constructed in over two hours, precariously balanced on one end of the conference table. Photos of the crime scenes and their victims had been strategically placed, starting with the first from nearly a year ago on the left side and ending with their most recent abduction. Hair pulled back away from her face, Brie gave him a perfect view of her face as she chewed the red polish from her thumbnail. Exhaustion had set up residence beneath those guarded blue-green eyes hours ago. When was the last time she'd slept? Twenty-four hours? More?

"You can't help Chloe Francis running on fumes, Brie. You need to eat, get some sleep." He set her coffee order beside her and took a drink from his own. Hot liquid stung the back of his throat, but not enough to pull his attention from the board.

"I need to find the link between these women." She latched onto the to-go cup and brought it to her perfect red lips. A stain remained behind from her lipstick as she set it back onto the conference table, eyes never leaving the white board. "If we can uncover a connection, we have a chance to find him before it's too late for Chloe. We can stop him from taking another victim. We need to dig into their lives, as far back as we can."

"Hobbs has guys working on it." But no matter how many times they'd tried to connect the dots to the two earliest cases they'd found, there were no obvious ties between the victims. Nothing but the gold necklaces that'd been recovered from three death scenes and an abduction scene. The killer's signature.

Roman settled right beside her. "Anything new?"

"He changed his M.O. with Chloe." *Motus operandum*, a killer's habits, the way he gained satisfaction from each kill. "The necklaces were recovered with the first three bodies, but Chloe was different. He left hers in her bedroom, right where he knew we'd find it. Like he's taunting us, like he wants us to know it's him."

Not them. Leaving behind necklaces on the bodies of his victims, their unsub wanted only one person's attention on this case. Brie's. Why else use a piece of jewelry exactly like her sister had worn before she'd been taken? Roman had read the police report as they'd left Chloe Francis's house to regroup at the police station, learned how her sister, Jessica, had been taken from her home in the middle of the night when she was thirteen years old. Brie had been ten at the time, asleep in the next room. No leads. No ransom note. No answers all these years later.

It's him. Roman couldn't purge her words from his head. Brie had described how Chloe Francis must've felt being watched, how she would've known if someone had been in her house. His partner had acted as if she'd lived through that exact experience herself. And now they had evidence to link these cases. "You believe these abductions are tied to your sister's case."

Not a question.

The slight narrowing of her eyes was the only sign she gave she'd heard him, as though having any kind of response—emotional or otherwise—would be seen as weakness. Living up to those damn rumors Roman had heard whispered around headquarters behind her back. But what the other members of their division might view as sociopathic tendencies, he saw as a familiar fight for survival. A determination to stay in control, to protect herself, and carry her fellow investigators with her strength when the team's cases took too big of a toll.

"My sister was wearing a necklace exactly like the ones recovered from these scenes the night she went missing. My parents gave it to her when she turned ten, and she never took it off." She kept her voice low, steady, and swiped her thumb across the lipstick stain on her coffee cup. Her hair escaped from behind her ear, but she didn't move to fix the soft curls. Shoving away the from the table, Brie closed in on the white board. Twenty years since that night. But, still, the pain was evident in the tension between her shoulders and neck. "It doesn't make sense. Jessica was thirteen when she was taken. All these women are in their thirties."

"Our suspect has already changed his M.O. by leaving the necklace in Chloe's home rather than with her body." Roman followed in her steps, re-centering his grip on his coffee. "You know as well as I do these guys run off of the rush, the feeling of domination they get by hurting their victims. He could be changing up his game to keep the chase exciting. Hell, he might've switched his preferences to older women so his prey could actually fight back."

There was only one other option.

"Or he wants me to know he's still out there." Her words barely registered above the buzzing of officers beyond the conference room door.

"Why you?" he asked. She'd been ten years old when her sister had been taken, barely old enough to understand the chances of Jessica making it home alive.

Brie faced him, a new kind of determination etched into her expression. And damn if that wasn't the sexiest thing he'd ever seen. "Back at the medical examiner's office, you asked me to trust you, and you're right. We're partners. If we can't depend on each other, we're never going to find Chloe Francis alive or any of the other victims we're assigned after this case."

"Okay." Roman folded his arms across his chest, and settled back against the table.

"I know you read the report on my sister's investigation. I had a friend in the IT department set up an alert on my phone whenever that file is accessed from the bureau's servers." She dropped her gaze to the coffee cup in her hand. Brie fought for that legendary control then set her blue-green eyes on him. "But, the truth is, nothing written in that file is accurate."

Surprise charged through him, pulling the muscles down his spine tight. He unfolded his arms. Roman lowered his voice, closing the distance between them to prevent officers around the station from overhearing their conversation. He chanced a glance toward the captain as he directed volunteers in the bullpen. "Hobbs was the lead detective on Jessica's investigation. He wrote that report. That case made his entire career. And you're telling me he falsified everything that happened that night?"

She notched her chin level with the floor. "Yes."

"Shit." What else had the captain falsified to push himself up the career ladder? How many other cases would come into question once Brie's confession went public? Roman ran one hand through his hair. Hell, the district attorney's office would have to go through Hobbs's past cases, reinvestigate every piece of evidence, interview witnesses. He froze. Brie could be implicated, charged as Hobbs's accomplice. She'd lose everything, and he'd…lose another partner. "Why are you telling me this?"

"Because it might save Chloe Francis's life." She shot her hand out, wrapped those long, delicate fingers around his arm, and his heart jerked in his chest. Swiping her tongue across her bottom lip—a nervous habit he'd noticed the first week they'd been assigned as partners—she dropped her voice. "He did it for me, and I'm trusting you with this information because you're my partner."

Heat tunneled through his shirt sleeves the longer she held onto him, fighting for his brain's attention. Already, his new partner had started unburying his protective side, something he wasn't sure he'd ever feel again. "Tell me exactly why the lead detective on your sister's case would falsify his report of her abduction and essentially make the case unsolvable."

"My sister wasn't the only one who was taken that night." Brie released her grip on his arm, putting her guard back into place. But he caught the flex of small muscles along her jaw, the way she'd swallowed to keep the tremor in her voice at bay. "I felt him for weeks. Watching me when we walked to school in the morning, every day we left Chloe's house to go home for dinner. I'd come home to my stuffed animals rearranged on my bed or my window unlocked when I could've sworn I'd locked it before bed the night before. I told my parents, but I was ten years old. They thought I was looking for attention."

Ringing filled his ears, his fingers curling into fists. The statements her parents had given to police all those years ago hadn't said anything about suspicious activity leading up to Jessica's abduction. Blood drained from his face as realization hit. Roman forced himself to breathe. "But you weren't."

She brushed her hair back behind her ear. Florescent lighting reflected off the small line of unshed tears in her lower lash line. "I woke up below deck of a boat. Jessica was unconscious next to me." Those beautiful blue-green eyes grew distant. She shook her head. "I tried to wake her up, but she never moved. I found a small piece of glass under the leather seat he'd set us on and cut myself free. But before I could get Jessica loose, he came down into the galley and lunged for me. I still had the glass in my hand." She darted her gaze around his body as voices outside the conference room grew louder. "I stabbed him and ran, but I couldn't get to my sister. I had to leave her there with him to get help. I went overboard, screaming, trying to keep my head above water, but nobody came, but eventually, I got myself to shore."

Air knocked from his chest. His stomach surged, and it took every ounce of control he had left not to reach out for her. "The same beach where Ashlee Carr's body was discovered this morning."

"Hobbs found me when he responded to some teenagers defacing the lighthouse with spray paint. I don't know how long I'd been out there. He wrapped me in a blanket he had in his car because I couldn't stop shaking, carried me off the beach, made sure I had something in my stomach before he took me to the hospital." Her gaze shifted back to him, and Roman's entire world shattered. "I told him everything, but when it came time to write up his report, my parents begged him to leave me out of it. They didn't want the police's investigation into Jessica's disappearance to be divided. They wanted my sister back. So I gave him this in hopes it would help find her."

Brie dropped her chin to her chest, bringing her hands up to unclasp a thin chain buried beneath her silky white blouse. She offered it to him, her fingernails sliding against the over sensitized skin of his callused palms. He suppressed the shiver tingling across his shoulder blades and uncurled his fingers. A gold necklace. Engraved with the name *Jessica*. "I ripped it off of her before I stabbed him so I could prove she'd been taken, too. The only person who knows about that necklace other than my parents is the Dream Catcher. He's back. And I don't think he's going to stop abducting and killing these women until he gets what he wants."

"You." The one who got away.

Roman couldn't keep his distance any longer, pulling her into his chest. The muscles along her spine stiffened at the contact. Pressing his chin against the crown of her head, he closed his eyes, memorizing the way she felt in his arms, the way her scent tickled the back of his throat, the erratic beat of her heart against his chest. But he couldn't stop the swell of rage exploding through him at her admission. She'd given him a glimpse of what scared her most in the world, and he'd never forget it. Never forget the fear etched into her perfect features.

"He's never going to touch you, Brie. We're going to find him. Together."

He closed his hand around the necklace. That was what partners were for, even if it meant breaking every damn rule standing in his way. He'd trace the necklace purchases across the entire country, interview the witness all over again in the two prior cases, go back through the evidence. Roman would find the bastard before their suspect ever had a chance to come near her or take another woman. He'd saved countless lives as part of the bureau's hostage rescue team, but he'd been trained in death.

And the hunt had only begun.

CHAPTER FIVE

SHE COULD STILL SMELL HIM ON HER.

With most of the hotels close to the primary crime scene closed for the season, they'd been left to rent one of the beach houses backing up to the cliffs along Michigan Lake. Four separate bedrooms, three bathrooms, twenty-two hundred square feet of planked hardwood floors, floor to ceiling windows looking out over the lake, and gorgeous views breathtaking enough to almost make her forget Roman had hugged her back at the station when she'd told him the truth.

Brie hauled her duffle bag onto the bed, caught the flutter of birds in the pine trees at one end of the property when the motion-censored flood lights lit up through the window above the headboard. She hadn't really had a choice. These cases—the necklaces discovered with the victim's bodies—it was all connected. All pointing to what happened the night she and Jessica were taken. She would've had to tell him the truth sooner or later. Fingering the chain beneath her blouse, she swallowed the sudden dryness in her throat. But that hug... She'd exposed her darkest secret—something she was sure he'd take to their boss or the Chief of Ludington Police—but he'd simply wrapped his arms around her and promised to help hunt their unsub down. Together.

His clean, masculine scent resurrected as she unzipped her duffle for a change of clothes. After the day they'd had, the hundreds of miles they'd driven, exhaustion pulled at her, but for the few brief moments he'd held her in that conference room, the nightmares hadn't existed. Her mind had gone completely blank. There'd been nothing but Roman. Strong, trustworthy, loyal. The kind of man who'd go down with the ship if it meant saving everyone else before considering his own safety. Brie dropped her hand away from her necklace. When was the last tine she'd felt that kind of peace?

Three knocks had her spinning toward the bedroom door.

"Captain Hobbs is working on tracking those necklace purchases." That voice. His voice. Smooth, deep, capable of pulling the rug out from under her while keeping her upright at the same time.

The knot of anxiety tightening in her gut released as dark brown eyes settled on her. Nothing would happen between them. Nothing *could* happen. The moment they took their partnership to that next level, the bureau would have them reassigned. They could be removed from the missing persons division or fired altogether. And she'd worked too damn hard to put her career at risk over an affair that wouldn't last longer than one night. Because with the darkness in her past—the hollowness that'd become part of her—that was all she had to give. She'd trusted him with the secret she and Captain Hobbs had carried for the past twenty years, but at the end of the day, all she had was herself. And that had to be enough. "Any hits?"

"Nothing yet. Turns out the manufacturer made over ten thousand in the last decade alone with the name *Jessica* stamped in the gold. It's going to take some time to narrow it down to a single suspect." Of course it would. Which meant holding up in Ludington longer than they'd anticipated. Meant seeing people she'd tried to forget existed. He closed in on her, every step gained hiking her awareness higher. He'd changed his clothes, exchanged the suit for jeans and a T-shirt, and she couldn't help but admire the bulky muscle vying to escape from beneath the fabric. Hints of a tattoo peeked out from the left sleeve. Hostage rescue. She'd recognized the same design on a few other operators back in Washington. "Tell me what's going through your head, Brie."

She busied herself unpacking and refolding her personal items onto the thin gray quilt stretching over the queen-sized bed. Not the way her name left his mouth. Not the way her insides coiled as he scanned her over. Damn it. She couldn't let him affect her like this. Not with Chloe Francis still out there. Not with multiple death scenes tying back to her sister's necklace. She couldn't afford to make a mistake with this investigation. She was stronger than that. Had to be. Taking a deep breath, Brie shut down the reactive part of herself as she'd done so many times before when she'd lost sight of the objective. Solving the case. "Are you worried I won't be able to do my job because this case is getting personal?"

Everything about this case had worked beneath her skin since the moment she'd stepped back into this city, but she'd be damned if she let anyone see the results. Especially Roman. Most agents in her situation would take a step back, inform the special agent in charge about the conflict of interest, and get themselves reassigned. She wasn't most agents. Pulling her shoulders back, she set her hands on her hips and faced him. If the man who'd taken her sister was the one behind these abductions, it was her duty to find him.

"Personal attachment can alter the course of a case." Veins popped from beneath his skin, and she bit back the urge to run her fingers over the mountains and valleys they created across his arms. "I'm not going to fill the team in on the fact our unsub seems tied to your past, but I need to know you won't let your own need to find answers interfere with our investigation."

"Haven't you heard what they say about me around the office?" Cold-blooded. Emotionless. Not capable of understanding what victims and witnesses had gone through for their files to wind up on her desk. A sociopath. Roman held his ground as she stared up at him. Pressure built behind her sternum, but she wouldn't be the first one to flinch. None of the nicknames and taunts her colleagues thrown her way had ever bothered her. The truth was, she knew exactly what the families of victims had gone through, how gut-wrenching it was to lose the people closest to her so violently, how the simple act of burying an empty casket was supposed to bring closure. What it felt like to lose people she trusted. And Brie would never let herself feel that way again. "I don't have personal attachments."

"I don't believe that," he said.

"Believe whatever you want. Doesn't change the fact that I'm back in Ludington for only one thing: to do my job." And to bring the man who'd destroyed her life to justice. She turned away from him, grabbing a change of clothes off the bed before heading toward the attached bathroom. As soon as she'd showered, eaten, and gotten a few hours of sleep, she'd head back to the primary crime scene. With or without him—

Strong fingers wrapped around her arm, spinning her into his chest. Her vision blurred as Brie threw one hand out for balance and hit nothing but soft cotton and hard muscle. His lips crashed down on hers, one hand pressing her flush against him. After that initial punch to the gut, everything inside her released. Melted, for the first time in years. Her heart threatened to beat straight out of her chest as he kissed her harder, deeper, wilder than she'd ever been kissed before. She opened her mouth wider.

Her grip flexed in her clean clothes. And the pain inside…stopped.

His tongue slipped past the seam of her lips. Nothing soft or hesitant. The aftertaste of mint exploded through her mouth as he battled her for dominance. But everything she'd kept inside—the emptiness she'd bore over losing her family, the rage that burned whenever she considered how she could've saved Jessica that night, the insecurity of realizing no matter how hard she tried, she'd always be branded a victim—she pushed it into this kiss. And Roman met her at every stroke, shouldered the emotions she'd kept buried. No one had ever kissed her quite like this, and for a split second, she never wanted it to end. Never wanted to leave the illusion of safety she felt with his arms around her.

But it was just that. An illusion. Because outside these walls, monsters waited. Perpetrators didn't care about her past. They wouldn't wait for her to work through whatever mental crisis decided to rear its ugly head after they'd recovered those necklaces. Brie tightened her hold around the fresh set of clothing in her hand and broke the kiss, forcing herself back into the moment. She rolled her lips between her teeth and bit down to center herself. Ninety thousand people in the United States alone went missing every year. And it was their job to bring those victims home. Nothing could get in the way of that. She swiped her fingertips across her mouth as her lips stung from his kiss. "That was..."

"Personal?" His words rumbled in his chest, vibrating through her.

She cleared her throat and stepped out of his reach as heat climbed into her cheeks. Brie raised her gaze to his, locking down her expression. She had to focus. Every day Chloe Francis was missing was another day they'd lose at finding her alive. "Our victims are counting on us to do our jobs, and I don't think that will be possible if we turn this into more than it is."

"By all means, tell me what this is, Brie." Muted light from the lamp on the bedside nightstand cast shadows across his face, but dark brown eyes burned bright with desire. How easy it'd be to ignore reality for a few hours, to stay in the center of his attention. Out of all the men she'd gotten involved with over the years, she wouldn't have to explain herself to Roman. She wouldn't have to hide the skeletons she kept buried from her colleagues, her friends. He understood. He'd already dived headfirst in the realities of the their world and fought to keep that darkness from affecting innocent lives. One night with him would be easy. Simple.

"A mistake." And a hell of a one at that. Her stomach twisted as that heat in his gaze cooled. "One that can't happen again. We're partners, and that's all we're ever going to be."

Roman lowered his chin a fraction of an inch, barely visible, but everything about him—every move he made, every word out of his mouth—registered high on her radar, as though she'd been specifically tuned to his frequency. Which didn't make sense. Not after all the work she'd put into keeping her distance, all the time she'd spent protecting herself. Hiding. The space she'd put between them disappeared as he moved in. "You want me to pretend that kiss never happened? That you don't smell and taste exactly as I'd hoped? That you weren't kissing me back with just as much as I was giving?"

"We don't have a choice." She held her ground—to prove she could—and ignored the sharp tug inside. Peppermint lingered on her tongue, but she had the feeling she would be tasting him long after this case was finished. "The bureau has rules about this kind of thing. You said it yourself. Personal attachment alters the course of a case."

"I always read the rules before I break them." His voice graveled.

One breath. Two.

"It's late. There's nothing more we can do for the case tonight." Brie thumbed her fingertip over the collar of her sleep shirt, every cell in her body still reeling with pleasure from his kiss. They couldn't cross this line. No matter how much she wanted to forget the nightmares waiting outside these walls. They would lose everything. "We should get some sleep and head back to Chloe's house when the sun comes up."

A few hours of sleep. That was all she needed to get him out of her head.

"I'll take the first shift and secure the perimeter." Roman shoved his hands into his pockets, his arm hitting the grip of his weapon still in his holster. He nodded with one of the sexiest closed-lipped smiles in existence, and the backs of her knees tingled in response. What other weapons did he intend to pull out of his arsenal tonight? "Goodnight, Brie."

"Goodnight." She forced herself to stay rooted until he closed the bedroom door behind him, then a few seconds more. His heavy footsteps retreated across the hardwood floor of the hallway. After a few deep breaths, Brie headed into the attached bathroom and twisted the shower spray on. Within minutes, she'd discarded her clothing and washed the nauseating scent of the beach from her skin. Bits of sand escaped down the drain, but no matter how hot she'd made the water and how hard she scrubbed, she could still feel it clinging to her. It'd taken three days to get rid of the sand caked to her when she'd clawed her way to that damn beach that night, but thankfully, with Ludington PD taking over the death scene, she'd never have to step foot on that shore again.

She pressed her hands into the cold white tile against one wall. No.

She hadn't cried then, and she wouldn't cry now. Wrenching the shower knob off, she stepped onto the bathmat and reached for the nearest towel.

And froze.

"Roman!" Steam furrowed around her as she reached for the weapon she'd left on the back of the toilet. The bathroom door was cracked. Hadn't she closed it before she'd gotten in the shower? Securing the towel tight around her, she read the message overlapping her reflection on the bathroom mirror again and swung open the door.

I've missed you.

CHAPTER SIX

HER SCREAM WRENCHED HIM FROM THE FRESH SHOE PRINT OUTSIDE THE house's back door, the only entrance that led straight to the cliffs. Withdrawing his weapon, Roman pumped his legs hard then slammed through the front door. Pain rippled through his shoulder and into his chest, but he kept going. And he wouldn't stop until he found her. "Brie!"

"I'm fine." She stood in a pair of old sweats and a stained oversized T-shirt, weapon drawn, at the center of the main living space. Tendrils of wet hair played around her shoulders and face, the soft patter of water hitting the floor barely registering over the pound of his heart behind his ears. "He was here."

Shit. He tightened his grip around the gun. "There's a fresh footprint out the back door. Bastard must've broken in while I was searching the perimeter at the front of the house. Timed it perfectly."

"He left me a message on the bathroom mirror while I was in the shower." She ran a hand through her damp hair. "I've cleared the bedrooms, but he couldn't have gotten far after he left the message. I was only in there for about five minutes."

Movement through the window to his left registered in his peripheral vision.

"He's still here." Brie ran straight past him for the front door. Straight toward the threat. She disappeared out of sight as she made a hard right.

"He's headed west toward the cliffs!" But the son of a bitch wouldn't get that far. Someone had threatened his partner, and Roman wouldn't let him get away with it. He sprinted to the back of the house and out the back door, gun in hand. Moonlight played over the slightly damp grass as a shadowed figure raced toward the stone fire pit set just before the cliff. He hadn't surveyed the terrain this far from the house yet. If their perpetrator knew this area better than they did, there were a dozen places the unsub could disappear in the blink of an eye. Not happening. Roman pushed himself harder, his lungs burning with the hint of humidity in the air. "FBI! Put your hands on your head!"

A second shadow stood out against the backdrop of open lake over the cliffs, her petite frame familiar. Brie. She ran faster than he thought possible, but before she had the chance to reach out and grab their suspect, the son of a bitch vanished. "Roman, stop!"

Roman pulled up short as the grass disappeared out from under from his feet, and he hit the ground hard. Oxygen crushed from his lungs. His heart fought to catch up with the rest of him as he chanced a look below. One more step and Brie would've needed a coroner and a body bag to get him back up. Off to his right, a set of wooden stairs cut into the edge of the cliffs, but they'd been impossible to see until he was right on the edge of the drop off. He hauled himself to his feet, but it was too late. Their unsub had already made it down the cliffside, the growl of a boat engine echoing off the rocks and sand below.

"Damn it." They'd lost him. He motioned to his right with the barrel of his weapon and compressed the safety. "What the hell are the stairs doing all the way over there?"

Heavy breathing cut through the lapping of water against rocks as Brie slowed to his side. Hand on her hip, she bent at the waist to catch her breath, then straightened. "We need to call this in. Bring in Captain Hobbs. Get the forensics guys out here. We can pull the suspect's prints off the mirror."

"Brie, stop." His muscles pulled tight with battle-ready tension at the sight of blood across her right foot. She'd gone after their suspect barefoot. No telling what she might've stepped on during her pursuit around the property. Crouching beside her, he rested one hand on the back of her calf and hiked her sweatpants a bit higher. Lean muscles flexed at his touch, but he pushed the satisfaction to the back of his mind. She'd been injured. Now wasn't the time to focus on how he reacted to her. Roman straightened. "You're bleeding. We need to get you inside and take a look. And don't even think about telling me you're—"

"I'm fine," she said. "Doesn't even hurt."

That was the adrenaline, but sooner rather than later, the endorphins from their chase would wear off, and she might not be able to make it back to the house on her own. Damn her incessant need to prove she was stronger, faster, and more self-reliant than anyone else. He holstered his weapon, and positioned his arms behind her knees, catching her with his other arm before she hit the ground. "We're doing this."

"I can walk on my own." She shoved against him, but he only held her tighter.

"For all you know you could've stepped on a hypodermic needle or a broken bottle, and you still have debris in the wound." He set her flush against his chest and started back across the stretch of grass between the cliffs and the beach house. Hints of her sultry scent teased his nose through the breeze coming from the lake, more pronounced than earlier in her bedroom. Shampoo? Body wash? Whatever the hell it was, he filled his lungs until he couldn't hold another breath of air and hung onto it as long as possible. Made it part of him. Brie had set the rules between them after he'd nearly devoured her on the spot back in her bedroom. They'd never be anything more than partners. But rules were meant to be broken. "You know as well as I do Haynes won't let you do a damn thing on this investigation if you get an infection. This is happening whether you like it or not."

"What happened to reading the rules before you break them?" Moonlight highlighted her brilliant smile as he rounded the property to the front, and he nearly stumbled at the sight. The back door was closest, but he couldn't risk disturbing the evidence where their perp had broken into the house. The bastard had come for Brie.

"This doesn't count. As long as you're my partner, your safety comes first." Twisting to his side, he carried her up the porch and through the still open front door and flipped on the lights. He set her gently on the navy-blue sectional in the front room, her fingers sliding down his chest as she studied her injury. Nerve endings fired beneath his skin as she trailed those long red nails over his sternum, and he locked his jaw against the urge to ask her to do it again. "I spotted a first aid kit under the kitchen sink when we first searched the house. I'll be right back."

Long fingers wrapped around his arm as he turned away, away from the sudden physical attraction that had taken him by surprise. "Roman, wait."

The raw edges of his nerves burned at the simple mention of his name on her lips. If he hadn't been checking the perimeter in an attempt to distract himself from the taste of her in his mouth, the unsub who'd broken in would've never gotten close to her to leave that message. Hadn't worked. The moment he'd penetrated the seam of her lips, she'd branded him. And he had the sense there was nothing he could do to get her out from beneath his skin. Not matter how much he wanted to..

"Is it going to be awkward between us now?" Bright blue-green eyes searched his.

"You mean because I know how much you love romantic comedy movies?" he asked.

"Tell me how you know that." She pushed to her feet and pointed one long, deep red tipped finger at him then sat straight back down. Her adrenaline had started wearing off, the pain evident in her expression, and he stepped forward to help her sit back down. "I've been trained in interrogation. I will torture you."

Roman leveraged his weight into the arm of the couch, leaning into her as much as he dared without closing that small space between them completely. Her sharp exhale hit his over-sensitized skin. She was just too damn beautiful when she got confrontational for him to give up so easily.

"Sorry. There's nothing you could do to make me give up my source, but if it makes you feel better, it wasn't anyone on the team." He straightened. Heading for the kitchen, he couldn't hide the smile pulling at one corner of his mouth. The teasing flirtation had come naturally, and he'd only gotten started breaking through that invisible guard she'd kept in place since the beginning of their partnership. He didn't have a source. She'd forgotten to log out of her streaming subscription on their shared laptop during Ashlee Carr's investigation. But the chance of seeing that gut-wrenching smile again was enough for him to want to keep this game going. Roman grabbed the first aid kit from beneath the kitchen sink then paused to message Captain Hobbs to let him know about the break in tonight. With a body and a missing person on their hands, he doubted the captain would have anyone to spare for at least twenty-four hours. He and Brie would have to collect the evidence themselves, but not until he had a look at that foot. He rounded back into the living space, setting sights on her.

"This isn't over." She crossed her arms over her chest as he took a seat on the couch beside her then bent at the waist and softened her voice. "I will make you watch every single romantic comedy in existence with me until you tell me the truth. I'm talking all of them. Starting with Pretty Woman and ending with this year's Hallmark Christmas movies. Don't test me."

A laugh escaped his chest. She was good, but did she really think she could break him?

"I've negotiated hostage situations, rescued politicians from overseas, brought down terrorists, and run manhunts all over the country for HRT. Give it your best shot, cupcake." He lowered his voice to match hers as heat exploded through him. Then again, maybe having this woman break him wouldn't be so bad. "Now give me your foot."

"Why? Do you have a medical degree in addition to your masters of criminal justice from UCLA?" Brie relaxed back against the pillow at her back, hauling her injured foot into his hand. Smooth skin caught on the calluses of his palms, and he snapped his gaze to hers. Red toenails. An exact match to the polish on her fingers. "That's right. I did my homework on you, too."

"Was that before or after you watched something called A Christmas Prince for the fifteenth day in a row?" Her digging into his past didn't surprise him. They were investigators. Every agent had to know what they were getting themselves into with a new partner. He popped open the first aid kit and started cleaning away the dried blood from the arch of her foot with an alcohol wipe. The weight of her attention increased the pressure in his chest, but he'd trained himself to work better under stress. First, having to force himself to focus on homework while his parents screamed at each other in the next room when he was a kid. Second, during his stint in special forces, then as part of the bureau's hostage rescue team. This interrogation of hers was just another challenge in a long line of instances determined to unsettle him. He held onto her ankle gently as he repositioned her foot so he could get a better look at the injury. War. Death. Murder. He'd seen it all but having Brie's gaze centered on him rocked him like nothing else ever had.

"I like happily ever afters." The softness in her voice pulled him from assessing the damage. "When we're assigned a new case, our victim has already gone through the worst day in their life, and there's no guarantee we can do anything to bring them home. We deal with so much darkness and death, at the end of the day, it's nice to be able to guarantee a happy ending. Even if it's not real." She sat up a bit straighter, surveying her injury, but the way her tone softened suggested she hadn't told him everything. This wasn't just about the victims they were assigned. "What's the damage? Am I going to live?"

Roman blinked to clear his head. She was right. There weren't a whole lot of happily ever afters in their line of work. Not for their victims. And, hell, not for the two of them, but after everything Brie had already been through—after how much she'd suffered—she deserved to be happy. He feathered the pad of his thumb over the protrusion of bone on the side of her ankle. She deserved someone she could rely on. Trust. Someone who'd have her back no matter the situation—in the field and out—and sit beside her with a romantic comedy on the TV every night or a romance novel in her hand every morning.

But she'd made it clear it wouldn't be him.

Just as well. Trusting in—relying on—the wrong partner could be deadly. He set her foot on the couch, handing her the first aid kit. "Shallow lacerations, most likely from the rocks. Nothing a few bandages, a couple ibuprofen, and ointment can't fix."

"Good." Brie ripped open two large bandages from the first aid kit and applied them to the bottom of her foot. Standing, she tested the pain and shifted her weight between both feet. "We need to get our equipment from the SUV and start gathering evidence in case Captain Hobbs doesn't have anyone from forensics he can spare. The longer we wait, the higher chance there won't be anything left to recover."

That bastard had targeted Brie, thought he could take her from him.

Shoving to his feet, Roman fought the urge to reach out, but he was only so strong when it came to the woman standing in front of him. He wouldn't let the son of a bitch have her. Ever. Smoothing his knuckles along her jawline, he stepped into his partner. "He's not going to touch you again, Brie. You have my word."

CHAPTER SEVEN

I'VE MISSED YOU.

 The steam had evaporated from the bathroom, but the message remained behind more clearly than before. Brie swabbed a section of the last letter from the mirror. If their suspect had written the message with his bare finger, the lab would be able to pick up DNA, transferred fibers, something to lead them to their unsub's identity.

 Distracting herself with collecting evidence had worked for the past hour, but now that she and Roman were almost done and one of Captain Hobbs's officers had arrived to secure and transfer the evidence back to the police station, she couldn't ignore the truth for much longer.

 The Dream Catcher had come for her.

 The muscles around her spine straightened a bit more. He'd gotten within three feet of her, and she hadn't sensed it, hadn't known the man who'd ripped away her childhood had stood on the other side of the thin shower curtain. Hadn't noticed the change in temperature when he'd opened the door. She sealed the swab into an evidence bag and labeled it clearly. If Roman hadn't been securing the perimeter, would their unsub have finished the job he'd started all those years ago? Would he have tried to kill her right here in this bathroom?

Brie pressed her back teeth together and gripped the edge of the counter through her latex gloves, not really seeing the design in the granite. They had to find him, before he took another victim, before he destroyed another life, and to do that, she had to think like him. She had to give into everything she'd tried to bury the past twenty years.

"I've got Hobbs's officer logging everything in the front room, and I gave him my statement. He'll need yours too while it's fresh." Roman leaned against the door frame, muscled arms crossed over his chest. "Brie?"

"He wanted me to know it was him. That's why he left the message on the mirror. That's why he's leaving the necklaces with his victims." Her eyes shifted to his reflection, and she held onto the evidence bag tighter. Swallowing around the hint of peppermint still at the back of her throat, Brie removed the invisible dam she'd constructed over the years to keep the darkness at bay, and she let it all flood back. Just for a moment. "He wants me scared like I was when I was younger, but he has no idea how far I'll go to make him pay for what he's done."

"How far is that?" His voice penetrated the ice flooding through her veins.

She stayed silent. He'd asked her if she could keep herself emotionally detached from this case. Admitting the break in had gotten to her would only end with her reassignment and maybe losing him as a partner altogether. She didn't want either of those things. Because, in the end, she was the only one who could find their suspect.

Every agent on their team were some of the finest investigators the bureau had ever employed, but they didn't know killers like she did. They didn't know how long the Dream Catcher watched his victims before making his move. How he liked to drug them with a mild sedative while they were sleeping so they wouldn't fight back. How his gravelly voice echoed off the interior of a pitch-black boat. Captain Hobbs had done her parents a favor all those years ago leaving her name out of the reports after he'd recovered her on the shore, but that one favor had manipulated an entire abduction case in her kidnapper's favor. No evidence had been recovered aside from the necklace she'd taken off her sister that night. No profile had been built without Brie's statement. No body recovered to autopsy. And her abductor had gotten away with it.

This was her chance to make things right, to bring a killer to justice. Brie forced herself to hand over the cotton swab to Roman before she destroyed the evidence in her too-tight grip. "Did you find anything new outside?"

He stared down at her as though he could see straight into her head, read her thoughts. Taking the bag from her, he unfolded his arms and pulled back his mountainous shoulders. Not to intimidate her, to reassure her, just as he'd tried to do after carrying her into the house. "I recovered a few hairs in the footprint outside the back door. Hobbs's guy will be running them to the lab as soon as we're wrapped up here."

"Chloe had long blonde hair." Leaving necklaces for Brie to find, breaking in, writing the message on the mirror. Their suspect wanted to be noticed. Transplanting the victim's hair onto another scene would fit into that plan.

"These were short and dark, probably belonging to some kind of animal, but we should know for sure in a few hours. Along with Ashlee Carr's autopsy report." He shifted his weight. "You're dead on your feet. I'll tell the officer we're through for the night, and we can stop by the station to give your statement in the morning."

"No. It's my fault he's still out there taking these women." A wave of exhaustion pulled at the backs of her eyes. He was right. Between recovering Ashlee Carr's body on the beach thirty hours ago, Roman's mind-altering kiss, and the break in, her energy reserves had hit empty. There wasn't a damn bit of good she could do for the investigation until she got a meal in her stomach and some sleep, but he deserved to know the truth. "My parents begged Hobbs to keep me out of those reports, but I could've said something. I was just too scared."

"You were ten years old, Brie. You couldn't make sense of what was happening at that age. And right now, the best thing you can do for Chloe Francis is take care of yourself." He moved deeper into the small space, crowding her. Everything about Roman Bradford set her on edge. From the foot of height and the sixty plus pounds he had on her to the way his eyes darkened whenever he leveled his gaze with hers.

It'd be so easy to use those differences between them to intimidate her, to overpower her, but that wasn't the partner she'd come to know over these last few months. She might've led the charge after their suspect on foot, but he'd run straight out the rear door to back her up. Ready to confront their suspect. And that was what she needed most right now. Someone she could rely on. Someone who'd be honest with her, no matter how hard the truth would be to hear. "You have a chance to make it right."

"What if I can't?" She snapped her attention up. Every cell in her body vibrated on the brink of losing control, as though she'd shatter into a million pieces right here. She'd relied on no one but herself since getting herself to shore that night. The minute her parents had discovered why she'd survived and Jessica hadn't, they'd turned their backs on her, blamed her for leaving her sister behind. They'd stopped loving her. Brie swallowed around the tightness in her throat. She couldn't go through that again. She and Roman had already failed to find Ashlee Carr in time. She couldn't shoulder losing another victim. "What if we don't find Chloe in time, and he gets away with another murder? What if the bureau finds out what really happened all those years ago, and I'm pulled from the case?"

"Forget all of that. None of it matters. The only thing you have control over is making sure this bastard doesn't hurt another victim by bringing him to justice." Roman set the evidence bag on the counter, wrapping strong fingers around her arms. His body heat tunneled through her loose T-shirt and sweats, brought her back from the edge. "You know this guy, Brie. You're the only one who's escaped him as far as we know, and that makes you the perfect agent on this case. You can do this."

The muscles along her jaw relaxed the longer he held onto her, grounded her. She nodded, hiking one hand to her hip as she swiped the back of her other hand under her nose. She took a full, deep breath for the first time since discovering the message on the mirror. "You're right. Thank you."

"Anytime." He slid his hands down her arms then stepped back, and a part of her begged her to follow. "Now please tell me you know how to cook because we've had nothing but fast food for the last two days, and I don't think my stomach can handle another french fry."

A laugh bubbled up her throat. If she didn't have this small release, she feared she might break apart right here in the bathroom. Collecting the bag from the counter, she flipped off the light and moved into the bedroom. She'd have to clean the mirror later, after the swab had been processed at the lab and the scene cleared. "It's a wonder you've lived this long in the field. I'm practically made of french fries and hamburger meat."

"Heaven help you." That mesmerizing smile of his drilled straight through her before Roman headed back into the living room, and her fears disappeared to the back of her mind.

A few minutes later, they'd handed off the last of the evidence connected to the break in over to Captain Hobbs's officer and were left alone once again. Nervous energy skittered down her spine under the weight of Roman's attention as she collected ingredients from the refrigerator. Onions, a selection of colorful peppers, mushrooms, chicken. Thank goodness the owners who'd rented them the home had stocked the fridge and pantry. Spices tickled her nose as she pulled them from the spice rack positioned in the corner of one counter, but failed to overwhelm his clean, masculine scent as he moved behind her. "Want to grab me a cutting board?"

"Already on it." His voice sounded much closer than she anticipated, but Brie refused to turn around as he reached past her to set the board down on the counter in front of her.

"Thanks." A tingling sensation climbed across her shoulders as he settled against the edge of the counter to her right. Hand tight around a blade she'd pulled from the knife block, she forced herself to focus on slicing through the chicken breast and not the tip of her finger. He'd already cleaned and bandaged her foot after they'd chased after their suspect. She wouldn't give him another reason to touch her unless absolutely necessary. "If you're going to stand there, you might as well pick up a knife and help me with these vegetables."

"I can do that." He gripped another knife and centered the peppers on his own cutting board. "Okay, I take it back. Tell me what I'm doing here."

Another laugh surprised her, this one with more humor behind it. Wiping her hands on a dish towel, she maneuvered beside him. Her arm brushed against his, and she paused. Odd. She couldn't remember the last time she'd laughed like that. "Didn't they teach you anything about knives in the military?"

"Mostly how and where to stab people," he said. "Not how to cut them into edible sizes. That was a different class."

"Great visual. Thanks for that." Brie reached across his midsection and positioned her hand over his, guiding the knife cuts through the orange bell pepper. Hard muscle pressed back against her forearm, and her blood pressure hiked into dangerous territory. "Okay, can you feel the blade sliding across the board like a boat rocks back and forth? That makes it easier to cut the pepper in long, thin slices like this."

"Yeah." His voice lowered into the same pitch as it had when he'd kissed her.

Awareness of how close they'd gotten rushed through her, and she took a step back to prepare the rest of their meal. Brie cleared her throat to counteract the heat exploding at the center of her core. This wasn't like her. She had control. She didn't let her desires get the best of her. "Good job. You can cut the rest of the peppers after that one."

They finished preparing the fajitas in silence then doled out their creation onto flour tortillas from the pantry, every part of her attuned to him. Without a dining room table, they relaxed back on the couch with their plates where he'd bandaged her injury a mere hour before.

Her heart pounded loud behind her ears as he took the first bite of chicken and onion. Smokey flavors played across her tongue, but none of it outweighed his taste still at the back of her throat. Within minutes, they'd cleared their plates, and Roman collected them to take the dishes to the kitchen sink. "I'll take care of these. You should get some sleep."

The thought of going to bed now... Alone...

"I know what I said earlier. About us crossing that line." She wanted his touch right then. Wanted him to make her forget about the past, this case, the fact her nightmares were real. She'd tried to ignore the attraction between them from the minute he'd been assigned as her partner and followed the rules. She still was. She just…needed him. Needed his warmth. There was no denying the desire flaming into her neck and face when he looked at her, how she'd held her breath when he'd cleaned the blood from her foot. No one had ever been able to pull her body out of the constant rigidity that'd plagued her all these years as he'd done with that kiss. "Will you please watch a movie with me until I fall asleep?"

"Sure." Setting down the plates on the end table beside the couch, he moved in close, close enough for her to touch. His gaze burned as he positioned himself beside her on the couch. "What are partners for?"

The couch dipped under his weight as he slid beside her. He hit the remote to scan for a movie, but she didn't care what they watched.

His body heat pierced the ice coursing through her. It'd been so long since she'd let someone get this close, and, for the first time since she'd escaped her abductor's hold, she felt safe. Cared for even. Curling her legs into her chest, Brie let heaviness consume her inch by inch. "I'm going to find him this time, Roman. I'm not going to let him get away."

CHAPTER EIGHT

She was asleep in his arms, and his control had already started splintering.

Roman pressed the power button for the TV, driving them into darkness. The movie they'd chosen had ended a while ago, but he hadn't been able to stop himself from memorizing every freckle, every laugh line from the low light the post credits gave off. Sleep didn't come easy anymore. Not since his HRT days. He needed to see the threat coming. Now more than ever. Moonlight cast dark shadows across her cheekbones through the bay windows looking out over the lake. Just like the moon, Brie kept part of herself always hidden, a maze with no escape, but secrets had a way of getting people killed.

"No!" She jerked upright beside him, the muscles along her spine tight under his touch. Her rough exhales reached his ears through the dark, and he automatically secured her against him. "Roman?"

"I've got you, cupcake." Hell, how his name on her lips gutted him. Even more so when shaken with panic. He smoothed his hands down her back, the damp cotton of her T-shirt sticking to his fingers. Sweat. After everything that'd happened over the last thirty-six hours —finding those damn necklaces, discovering a familiar victim had been abducted, and the break in all connecting to her past—he'd forgotten about the nightmares. A half dozen previous nights' screams echoed through his head as he rubbed small circles into her spine, a combination of perfume and soap overtaking his senses. Three months they'd been assigned as partners. In that short time, he'd heard her screams from the other side of the wall of their hotel rooms every single time they'd overnighted it in the field, and there hadn't been a damn thing he could do about it. Until now. The evil she'd met as a kid had returned, but Roman would make sure she didn't have to fight it alone this time. "It was a bad dream. You're safe. I'm the only one here."

"I'm okay." She buried her nose at the tendon between his neck and shoulder. Right where he needed her to be. But tightness still gripped her hard. Her pulse thudded in her chest, practically trying to escape her small frame. Loose curls shifted across her cheek as she slid back onto the couch, more than a foot of space between them now. She smoothed her hand down her face. "We should check in with the captain. See if anything came up during the search for Chloe."

Disappointment burned hot beneath his skin. Would she ever trust him? Or would her past make it impossible for her to rely on anyone but herself? "You know you chew the inside of your mouth when you lie."

Both of their phones pinged with alerts from the small, circular coffee table a few feet away, screens bright. Roman hit the switch to the lamp beside the couch before checking the message.

Brie reached for hers, swiping her thumb across the glass. "Dr. Meyer finished with Ashlee Carr's autopsy. She included the toxicology report, too." Settling back against the couch, she ran a hand through her short, mussed hair, and damn, if that wasn't the sexiest thing Roman had ever seen. "Cause of death was asphyxiation as a result of blood in the respiratory passage when the murderer cut Ashlee's throat. Looks like a thin blade, possibly a fishing knife could be the murder weapon, which would make sense if the Dream Catcher is responsible. He would've brought her onto his boat. Fishermen need knifes for cutting rope and cleaning fish. Stands to reason he'd use something he's familiar with. The medical examiner recovered evidence from the marks around the victim's wrists and ankles, too. Blue nylon strands."

"That doesn't give us much. Nylon is in everything from rope and fabric to pet collars, but the color narrows it down considerably." He collected the backpack he'd set beside the front door when they'd first arrived. She didn't want to talk about what kept her up at night, and he'd respect that choice. For now. Unpacking his laptop, Roman logged into the federal NamUs database. The chance they'd be able to connect any other cases with a few fibers of blue nylon were slim, but he'd take that shot. He brought up the two prior cases they'd already tied to their current search for Chloe Francis, each linked by gold engraved necklaces recovered at the body scenes. "There weren't any fibers found from the two other victims, but both women were killed in the same manner as Ashlee Carr. The killing strikes angle slightly upward toward the right ear, making the killer a little taller than them both and right handed. He killed them from behind, maybe by surprise, or to keep his identity hidden."

But that knowledge didn't bring them any closer to a suspect.

"Positioning the bodies in well-visited areas, leaving minimal evidence, killing sporadically over the last seven months instead of by some internal need for release." Brie tapped the top of her phone against her chin, eyes locked on the floor but not really focusing on anything in particular. "Our unsub is a killer, but he's not a sociopath. He has control. He planned every one of these murders beforehand by stalking his prey, getting to know them, getting close to them, and so far, this guy is very good at what he does."

"So are we." He'd been partnered with one of the best investigators the bureau employed. They wouldn't fail the victims involved in this case. Not with Brie on their side. Bringing killers to justice was their job, but more than that, he'd joined the bureau to protect those who couldn't protect themselves. Roman ran a search for similar cases through the federal database, adding in the blue fibers recovered by the medical examiner. No hits, but that didn't mean their suspect hadn't made a mistake all this time. "We're going to catch this guy, Brie. We're going to stop him. And he's going to pay for what he's done."

If it was the last thing Roman did, he'd make the son of a bitch answer for his sins.

"I hope you're right. Because as of right now, we have nothing but four necklaces available at any mall in the country and a few blue fibers we can't trace." Hopelessness carved shadows into her expression as she scrubbed her hands down her face. She settled her elbow into the couch's arm and placed her temple at the base of her palm. "I always knew he'd find me, but I thought I'd be more prepared when he did." A humorless laugh escaped up her throat. "Then again, how prepared can you be for something like this? I'm an FBI agent, for crying out loud. I've been trained to find people. That should've been enough, but he's just as out of reach as he was when I was a kid."

Roman could read between the lines. "You've been hunting him."

"Not at first." She turned that brilliant blue-green gaze on him, her expression locked down as though she were afraid she'd confessed too much, exposed herself more than she'd intended. "I forced myself to focus on getting my life back until I could graduate high school, then did the same all throughout college. Almost worked, too. I thought I'd convinced myself what happened all those years ago didn't matter, that I could be happy. I could move on, start my career at the FBI, maybe find a guy to who'd make breakfast on Saturdays and read me the highlights from the newspaper before starting our day together."

His gut hollowed at the imagery of Brie falling for some other man. Someone who wasn't him making her smile, making her call out his name between the sheets, giving her everything she deserved and more. Roman reviewed the case file on the screen, not really reading the report. Throat tight, he blinked to clear his head. She'd made the relationship between them clear. And it'd never include those things she'd said. Once they crossed that line, there'd be no going back, and he wasn't about to risk their partnership for mere desire. "Sounds nice."

"It was a fantasy. A lie. No matter how hard I tried, the Dream Catcher was always there in the back of my mind. And he always will be. At least, until I catch him." She played with the edge of the bandage wrapped around her foot. The vulnerability in her voice vanished as she straightened, her attention centered on the reports lighting her screen. "But I haven't come close to finding him. There was never an M.O. to follow thanks to me. I didn't even know where to start, and by the time I did, too much time had passed. All the evidence was gone. The marinas around the lake had purged their records. None of the victims' families would talk to me. There was nothing to go off of other than what little I remember, and unfortunately, memories aren't evidence."

Piece by piece, Brie was trusting him with secrets she'd held onto for over two decades, and he couldn't hold back anymore. Threading his fingers through her hair, Roman waited for her to pull away, like she always did. But Brie didn't move. Every cell in his body fired with awareness of how dangerous getting this close to her would be—for both of their careers—but right now, he didn't give a damn about any of that. She was all that mattered. "But the necklaces and nylon fibers are."

"Yeah, well, I'm not sure either of those things are going to help find who took my sister. Killers escalate. They get smarter, more obsessed, more violent, but they don't change their victim profile." Brie shook her head, rolling her bottom lip into her mouth. "The man who took Jessica preferred girls, and all these victims we've connected to the case are women. The only thing I can be sure about is somehow our killer knows about my past. He's doing everything in his power to use it against me, to distract me from recovering our vic." She leaned into his hand, her cheek pressed against his palm. "And, damn it, it's working, Roman. By leaving those necklaces at the crime scenes and placing Ashlee Carr on that beach, he's shifted my focus from finding our victim to making me believe this is tied to Jessica's killer."

It was possible. But why target her in the first place? They'd both been assigned Ashlee Carr's case before their victim had turned up on the shore yesterday morning, and Roman had plenty of secrets of his own he'd kept buried. No. This ran deeper than a murderer simply trying to distract them with smoke and mirrors to avoid getting caught. Their killer had made this case personal for Brie. The spider had pulled her into his web and was waiting for her to make the next move.

"Captain Hobbs fabricated those case reports, but I doubt he told anyone in fear of losing his job." Besides, Roman had noticed how much the captain cared for Brie as he'd wrapped her in that hug down at the primary crime scene. Hobbs wouldn't have put her at risk by letting the truth slip. Not without a good reason. "How could our unsub have discovered the truth of what happened that night unless he'd been there?"

"I don't know." She leaned forward, pulling out of his grasp, and his body agonized with the loss of her skin against his. "I only remember one abductor that night, but my head was fuzzy, and I was scared. He wore a mask, so I didn't get a good look at him, but in order to take me and Jessica from the house at the same time, I thought maybe—"

"He had a partner." It would fit Brie's theory. Because she was right. Killers didn't change their M.O. on a whim, but this investigation wasn't like any case he'd worked before. Whoever'd abducted these four women had left necklaces with three of the bodies when he was finished with them. Except for Chloe Francis, who was still missing. The necklace had been discovered at the victim's home. That, coupled with the change in age preference of his victims, rooted this new angle deeper. Perhaps the original killer *had* preferred girls over women, but the partner developed his own tastes and had struck out on his own. Serial killing teams were rare but not unheard of in bureau history. "That gives us two different killers. Two different M.O.s. Two paths to follow. So the question is which partner took you and your sister, which abducted Chloe, and are they still working together?"

"Whoever's doing this doesn't fit into the normal parameters of a serial killer. All of this—the necklaces, placing Ashlee Carr's body on that beach, abducting Chloe—he's doing it to get my attention." Brie shoved to her feet. "We need to get back to Chloe's house. She's our priority."

Baggy sweatpants hung off her hips, her oversized T-shirt hiding the lean muscle and small frame underneath, and his core ignited at the thought of kissing her again. He needed to shut that line of thinking down right the hell now. How many times did he have to tell himself nothing could happen between them? Not now. Not ever. No matter how much he wanted to break the rules, risk it all for one more taste of her. Her eyes glittered at him, a fire burning in those irises that chased back the shadows of the last few hours. She'd been forced to confront the nightmare of her past, and the break in had hit too close to home, but the woman standing in front of him in her pajamas wasn't a victim. She was the agent who brought victims home, and he had every reason to believe she'd do the same for Chloe Francis and any other victims they were assigned in the future.

"You're right. Our vic has been missing for two days, and the autopsy report says our killer kept Ashlee Carr alive for three." Roman stood, his control back in place. "We're running out of time."

CHAPTER NINE

"Something's happened." Four Ludington PD patrol units surrounded the house as she and Roman pulled to the curb. Brie pushed out of the vehicle, hand on the butt of her weapon, and squinted against the sun's sudden brightness. She hit the sidewalk and jogged toward the front door of Chloe Francis's home, neighbors already making their way onto their lawns for early gossip. "FBI! Go back inside your homes!"

The medical examiner had narrowed Ashlee Carr's captivity to three days. Was it already too late for Chloe? Had the unsub added one more kill to his list? Ragged carpeting threatened to trip her up as she entered the home, Roman's footsteps loud behind her.

"Don't tell me to calm down." A single male voice echoed through the house. "He took her, and you're not doing a damn thing to find him!"

Unholstering her weapon, Brie fought back the tension climbing up her spine at the sight of six armed officers in a semi-circle with their weapons drawn. All focused on the single Caucasian man with the gun in his hand. Electric blue eyes came into focus first, centering on her as she pushed through the line of officers. A few days of beard growth, unkept brown hair. Dried blood on his hands. Pure, unfiltered anger registered in the dark circles beneath the gunman's eyes, in the way he adjusted his grip around the gun. She scanned him for injuries, service weapon raised, but couldn't locate the origin of the blood. "Sir, what's your name?"

"You." The gunman took a step forward, the vein near his right temple more pronounced. "You're the one who did this. He took her because of you!"

"One more step toward her and I'll put a bullet in you before you have time to raise that weapon." A chill slithered down her spine at the tone in Roman's voice. Dark. Dangerous. And absolutely deadly. She'd never heard him talk like that before, as though he'd tear anyone who threatened her apart limb from limb with his bare hands. "Now take a damn breath, focus on me and tell me your name."

Brie glanced at her partner at the change in his demeanor. He was trying to build a rapport with the gunman, figure out what the man wanted. Build trust. Display empathy. Like the good hostage rescue negotiator he'd been before transferring to missing persons.

One breath. Two. The gun twitched in the man's hand as he shifted his attention toward her partner. Three distinct lines set up residence between his eyebrows, aging him almost instantly. A softness replaced the anger in his expression but didn't smother it completely in those light blue eyes. "Ben...Ben Carlin."

Recognition flared at that name, and Brie released a slow breath. She loosened her grip around her weapon but wouldn't lower it yet. Not until they'd diffused the situation. Any fast movements, any trigger to set him off again, and Ludington PD would be adding one more body to their already heavy load. "You're Chloe's boyfriend. You reported her missing yesterday."

"This is your fault." Ben fastened that darkening gaze on her through his eyebrows. Muscles flexed along the man's jaw, the gun still in his bloody hand. "You were the one who was supposed to die. Not her. Chloe never hurt anyone, and now she's paying for something you did."

Air rushed from her chest. Her stomach hollowed. She couldn't breathe. Couldn't think. He thought Chloe being taken was her fault.

Gravity pulled at her until blood drained from her face. If Brie had died like her abductor had intended that night, would Chloe Francis have been targeted in the first place? Would any of these women have been targeted? But…information about what happened the night she and Jessica were taken—that she'd been the only one to escape her kidnapper—wasn't public knowledge. How could Ben Carlin blame her for something he wasn't supposed to know about? "How—"

"Okay, Ben, we need you to keep calm, remember? I'm going to have all these officers holster their guns and leave the room so we can talk. Just you, me, and my partner." Roman held up one hand, palm faced toward the gunman. Slowly, the officers followed his orders and backed toward the front of the house, leaving her and Roman alone with the suspect in the matter of minutes. "See? It's just us now. I need you to drop the gun and slide it over to me. Then we can talk."

Fire simmered beneath the surface the longer Ben stared at her. Sweat built along her sternum when he didn't respond right away, and Brie gave into the possibility she'd have to pull the trigger, that she'd have to take down an innocent man who only wanted the person he loved most in this world to come home safe. She understood that desperation, the hole that'd been left inside her when police hadn't been able to bring Jessica home, but any apology would seem insignificant compared to what Ben had already endured. "Chloe's kidnapper contacted you."

That was the only way Ben could've learned about her past. The suspect raised the gun and took aim. At her. She constricted her finger around the trigger of her service weapon, held her breath. Her instincts screamed warning a split second before a gunshot exploded in her ears. Blood sputtered across the gunman's shirt, and before she could take her next inhale, Ben collapsed, hand over his right shoulder.

"I warned you, Ben." The bullet had gone into the gunman's arm. Ripping the weapon from Ben's hand, Roman yanked his uninjured arm behind his back. In the blink of an eye, Ben Carlin's face met the old carpet and his wrists had been cuffed behind his back with a scream. Roman pressed one knee into the man's spine and handed her the suspect's gun. "How did he contact you? When?"

Heavy sobs wracked through the gunman's body, blood spreading across his long-sleeve shirt. "I got it this morning."

"Got what?" Roman asked.

"The box on the counter," Ben said.

A plain brown box demanded attention in the corner of her vision, and Brie holstered her own weapon, Ben's gun heavy in her hand. The small package had been left on the kitchen counter, bubble packaging splayed around it. Nothing unusual. Except Ludington PD hadn't released the crime scene yet. She would've remembered that box from hers and Roman's initial search yesterday afternoon. Officers had been stationed around the perimeter to prevent anyone from disturbing the scene. The hairs on the back of her neck rose on end. Glancing back to Ben's blood-crusted hands, she rounded into the kitchen. "Roman, the blood."

Two officers moved in at Roman's signal to take custody of the gunman. She surrendered the weapon to another officer holding an evidence bag and motioned toward the box. She dug into her jacket for a pair of latex gloves, the snug fit against her wrists shoving that dark void of guilt for Chloe's abduction to the back of her mind. For now. "This package wasn't here yesterday, and there's no postage on the outside. I'm willing to bet our kidnapper came here and left it for us to find."

"But Ben found it first." Roman nodded toward the box. "Ladies first."

"Can't say chivalry is dead." Brie pulled back the four corners of the small box. Four years working in missing persons. Four years of crime scenes, violence, blood, but the air still rushed from between her lips as she studied the contents of the package. She swallowed the bile working up her throat, but she had a feeling nothing would distract from the nausea churning in her gut. White tissue paper. Blood. A note. And a single finger in the bottom of the box. "The killer has never sent body parts of his victims before."

"He's changed his MO twice already. It's like he's purposefully trying to throw us off now. Or this came from the partner." Roman maneuvered one corner of the box out of his sight line to get a better view of the appendage inside. "I think you were right. This isn't an ordinary serial killer. He's highly intelligent, extremely organized and meticulous. I wouldn't be surprised if he has knowledge of crime scene analysis and police investigations, too, to avoid being apprehended this long. He's planned every detail of his kills. And he's staying one step ahead of us."

Brie unfolded the crisp white note. *Help me.*

"We need to get this to forensics to run a print. Something on the finger might be able to tell us where she's being held before it's too late." The sickening hollowness in her gut already had an idea of who the finger belonged to. Chloe Francis. Why else leave it at her home for the victim's boyfriend to find? Brie folded the cardboard flaps together to hand the finger off to Ludington PD, but something still wasn't adding up. She stopped before the front door, studying Ben Carlin as EMTs loaded him into the back of an ambulance. "There's nothing else in this box, but Ben blames me for what happened to Chloe. He said I should've been the one who was taken."

"Your abduction isn't public knowledge thanks to Captain Hobbs." Roman shifted his weight between both feet, mere inches from her, and her nerve endings fired in rapid succession to the point her skin tingled as he looked at her. "How did he know you were on the killer's mind?"

Her thought exactly.

"He said, 'I got it this morning,' but maybe Ben wasn't talking about the package. The only way he could've found out about me was if the killer contacted him directly." She watched the emergency techs hike their gunman into the back of the ambulance, the box still in her hand. The bottom had grown soggy from the amount of blood, and she searched the porch for the spot their unsub might've set it down to be found. Her small exhales crystallized in front of her mouth as freezing temperatures charged through the open front door, but she wouldn't give into the shiver climbing up her spine. There. A light square outline of reddish-brown liquid about the same size of the box. She motioned to the evidence. "Ludington PD hasn't released this crime scene yet, so Ben had no reason to come back here. I think our killer led him here."

"We need to talk to Ben," Roman said.

Brie notched her chin level with the pavement. Setting down the evidence, she raced across the front lawn full force toward the ambulance. Frozen grass crunched beneath her boots, her lungs burning as she pulled up short of the vehicle's bay doors. The entire neighborhood had journeyed to their front lawns to see what was going on, but she didn't have time to worry about them right now. Chloe's life was still at stake. "How do you know I was supposed to take Chloe's place, Ben?"

An EMT to her stepped into her peripheral vision. "Agent McKinney, your questions will have to wait. This man has been shot. He needs to get to the hospital—"

"We're doing this now." Roman positioned himself between her and the technician, shutting out the world, giving her a chance to end this nightmare once and for all. He'd shot Ben to protect her, put himself at risk of being taken off the case.

"How did the killer contact you this morning?" Cold worked into her fingers from the ambulance door, but she only strengthened her hold in an attempt to steady her nerves. Whoever had taken these women wasn't fitting into the box she'd created for him inside her head, wasn't following any kind of pattern. They needed something—anything—to get one step ahead.

"I'm not telling you anything." Ben latched onto his injury, closing his eyes tight against whatever pain EMTs hadn't yet been able to dim. "This is happening because of you, and the second I get the chance, I'm going to make sure you pay."

Brie shot her hand out to stop Roman from advancing on the gunman. She swallowed to combat the dryness in her throat as his heart pounded beneath her palm. This wasn't about her past. Wasn't about the need to bring her sister's killer to justice, or even get her own revenge. This was about bringing Chloe Francis home safe and stopping what happened to her from happening to anyone else. She softened her voice. "You're right. I should've died the night he took me, but I didn't. I escaped. So that makes me the only person who can find her, Ben. Give me a chance to find her. Please."

Impossibly blue eyes studied her, and she pushed as much honestly into her expression as she could manage. She'd told the truth. Her experience with this particular killer gave her an advantage over any one else on her team. Kinsley Luther and Aiden Holloway might be the best agents she'd ever worked with, but Brie was the best option to find Chloe. Despite the hatred simmering in that gaze, Ben Carlin would have to come to terms with that on his own. Digging into his pants pocket with one bloodied hand, he extracted his phone. "He sent me a video. It's already cued up."

"I'm going to do everything I can to find her. You have my word." Brie hauled herself into the back of the ambulance and took the phone. "You can take him to the emergency room now. Thank you," she said to the EMT.

Warmth speared through her thick coat as Roman huddled over her shoulder. A small white triangle appeared over the black screen, and Brie glanced up at her partner. A thousand possible endings to this case played through her mind as he steadied dark eyes on her, but no matter what happened, they were in this together.

She pushed play.

CHAPTER TEN

He couldn't watch the video again.

The projector flashed blue right before the clip from Ben Carlin's phone cued. They were back in the Ludington police station conference room, Captain Hobbs, an officer whose name Roman didn't know, Brie, and Special Agent in Charge Mitchell Haynes all the way from Washington, DC himself highlighted by the screen's dim glow. He and Brie had watched the video back at Chloe Francis's house, but this case had just gone straight to hell. Roman caught sight of the murder board partially hidden behind the projector screen. Four women taken, three murdered, and now their killer was mailing body parts. Hell, they needed the extra manpower on this one.

Heavy breathing echoed from the sound system speakers above, then an ear-piercing scream as a woman was pulled into frame by her hair, but Roman forced his attention to Brie. To the way she refused to blink in order to memorize every moment, how one corner of her mouth twitched as their masked killer came into the darkened frame, then as she shifted her gaze to him when their unsub took the victim's left hand and removed the finger with what looked like a boning knife from a fishing boat. Only problem was they couldn't positively identify the victim as Chloe Francis or confirm the location where the video had been recorded. Not until the tech department ran their protocols, which would take hours, maybe days. Could've been a basement, but poor lighting and the fact their killer had taken center stage hid the victim's face. Then the bastard had called out Special Agent Brie McKinney specifically.

The truth had come to light. Brie's connection to the unsub was out in the open.

"He goes by the Dream Catcher. His original M.O. targeted young women, girls as young as seven years old as far as I've been able to find, all along the east shore of Michigan Lake. He watches them for weeks up until he finally strikes. He drugs them, takes them from their homes to his boat out on the lake, and they're never heard from again. Only now, it seems his tastes have changed, or he's brought on a partner, which would explain the difference in M.O. between each case." Her attention flickered back to the video, then to Captain Hobbs. "I believe he's taking these women because of me."

Silence descended. Thirty seconds. More.

"Everybody but Bradford and McKinney get out." Special Agent in Charge Mitchell Haynes rose out of his chair and hiked his jacket out of the way, both hands on his hips as Hobbs and his officer stood to leave the room. Gray eyes scanned the floor as Haynes shook his head. A five o'clock shadow and tussled brown hair evidenced the amount of sleep their boss had already lost on this case, but Haynes would never let something as simple as sleep affect his job. He ran the entire violent crimes division for the bureau. He wasn't some pencil pusher like most of the division heads back at headquarters. Mitchell Haynes had built this team from the ground up with the best investigators he could find. Including Roman. "I'd like to think you were planning on filling me in on your secret before Chloe Francis turned up dead, Agent McKinney."

Brie pulled back her shoulders, every bit the confident, strong, and decisive woman Roman had come to know over the last few months. Come to respect. "Sir, I can explain—"

"Pretty much explains itself. You obviously have a personal connection to this killer and forgot to fill in the rest of your team. We all have our secrets, and I don't expect my agents to tell me everything, but, damn it, Brie, you should've come to me with the truth. We could've gotten ahead of this." Haynes pressed his index finger into the gleaming surface of the conference table. "If we can't work as a team, our victims pay the price. Understand?"

Pressure built behind his sternum as Brie lowered her gaze to her lap, expression hard. And if he hadn't memorized every small change in her features, Roman never would've caught the exact moment a coldness crept into those beautiful blue-green eyes of hers. "Yes, sir. Understood."

Scrubbing one hand down his face, Haynes secured the other on the back of his vacated chair. "Now this guy's already abducted four women, and from what you've told me, there's no pattern to suggest he's going to stop once he's finished with our latest victim here." The special agent in charge faced the projector, the video paused on an agonizing shot of the victim struggling for freedom. "So we go on the offense, do whatever it takes to bring this bastard down."

Roman's gut told him where his boss was going with this.

"We're not using Brie's connection to lure this psychopath in." Roman sat forward in his chair as a combination of disbelief and rage took control. Haynes couldn't possibly support putting one of their own in danger. "We have evidence. Captain Hobbs is tracing the necklace purchases, officers are still searching Chloe's home—"

"The necklaces are a dead end." Her voice remained even, no hint of the woman whose armor had cracked a fraction after the break in, and his gut clenched. "There are too many to trace, and the lab is overwhelmed with this case. It'll be weeks before we get results on evidence recovered from the primary scene and the beach house after the suspect broke in. Assuming our killer and the man who left that message on my bathroom mirror are one and the same, he's already got a head start." Brie kept her focus on the projector screen as though to prove the last forty-eight hours hadn't shaken her deep into her core, but Roman had seen the truth. Behind that invisible wall she'd built there was a woman who'd asked him to stay with her so she could fall asleep on the couch, who'd threatened to make him watch every romantic comedy in existence until she got what she wanted, a woman whose breath had quickened when he got near, and who'd given up a piece of her tightly held control and trusted him with the truth. Like hell they were going to use her as bait. "All we know for sure is whoever abducted those four women—whether he has a partner or not—thinks he knows me, and he's not playing by traditional serial killer rules. We need to do the same. I'm willing to take the risk if giving him what he wants gets us closer to finding Chloe."

"We're not talking about a fueled helicopter stashed with cash, Brie. What if what he wants is *you*?" The question left his mouth as a growl. Because if he lost her... Roman forced himself to push that thought into the dark box he kept at the back of his mind. Pain spread through his knuckles as he pressed his hand hard against the table to regain an ounce of control. No. Not happening. "You've seen what he does to his victims. You've already lived it and barely escaped with your life. I'm not about to put you in danger on the off chance this bastard doesn't see through our plan and takes the bait." How could she consider putting her life at risk like this? He'd run countless tactical missions as a hostage rescue team operator. His unit had been trained to adapt to situations based on changing intel, extreme climates, and hostage negotiation breakdowns. There had to be another way for them to bring this guy out into the open. "We have other options."

"I'm not ten years old anymore, Roman, and I'm not helpless. Besides, Ben Carlin was right. I'm the reason Chloe was taken in the first place. I'm not going to let these women pay for something I'm responsible for." Her dark eyebrows drew inward, creating a single ridge at the bridge of her nose. Lips parted, she let her chest rise on a shaky inhale. "I'm going to be the one to make it right."

She wasn't responsible for any of this. Couldn't she see that? Even if she hadn't managed to escape the monster who'd taken her all those year ago, the son of a bitch would've kept hunting. That was what killers did. They destroyed lives, giving into that dark need for violence until they were captured or killed. "By putting your life on the line?"

No answer.

"Then it's settled." Haynes gathered the case folder from the conference table then headed for the door. "I expect a brief of your operation in my hands within the next hour. Whatever you need—manpower, firepower—you name it, you'll have it. Let's bring Chloe Francis home." Haynes pointed to Roman with the file in his hand. "Bradford, you're taking a back seat on this one until we can close the investigation on the shooting that occurred at the crime scene this morning."

"There is no investigation," Brie said. "It was an honest shooting. Ben Carlin raised his weapon to take a shot at me. If Roman hadn't interfered, you'd have another body on your hands."

"I believe you, but standard procedure demands every agent involved in a shooting during a case to surrender his or her weapon until we get a clear picture of what happened. You know that." Haynes held out his free hand, that dark gaze apologetic. "I'll get you back on the case as fast as I can."

"My partner was being threatened. I knew exactly what I was doing." And he knew he'd be taken off the investigation the moment he'd pulled that trigger, but he wouldn't have changed a damn thing. Roman unholstered his weapon, released the magazine, and cleared the chamber before setting it all on the table. "Who are you partnering with Brie until I'm cleared?"

Because there was no way in hell he was going to let Haynes send her after their unsub alone.

"Agents Luther and Holloway are already on their way," SAC Haynes said. "Their plane from DC landed fifteen minutes ago."

Roman studied the wood grains of the conference table. Holloway was a good agent, one of the best on the team. The guy had spent five years serving his country with the army's special forces before joining the violent crimes division. He'd neutralized terrorist activity in the most extreme conditions, trained militaries in friendly countries around the world, and had gotten more suspects to break under interrogation than any other soldier in the service. If Roman had had a say in his replacement to partner with Brie, Aiden would've been at the top of his list. The former interrogator would do whatever it took to protect her. And, as for Kinsley Luther, the team's profiler studied killers for a living. She'd narrow their suspect list and help bring their unsub out of the shadows. "Good."

"McKinney, I want that operation plan in one hour." Haynes collected Roman's service weapon from the table and walked out the door.

His ears rang. What was he supposed to do now? The thought of going back to the beach house alone—without his partner—pooled dread at the base of his spine. He and Brie had been a team since the moment he'd been transferred in from HRT. Their lives had revolved around one another, around their cases on a daily basis to the point he'd become attuned to her every movement, every shift in mood. If he hadn't pulled that trigger, Brie wouldn't be sitting across the table from him, but her in the field—being used as bait—without him at her back didn't sit right.

"There's nothing you could've done to talk Ben down. You know that, right?" The projector screen flashed blue as Brie pulled the connection from Ben Carlin's phone and placed it back inside the evidence bag. "He blames me for what's happening to Chloe. I don't think you could've said anything to get through to him after what he's been through."

Memories of his last night in HRT raced across his mind. Deep woods. Him approaching his teammate's cabin. Gunfire and blood. Roman forced himself to breathe evenly as images of his former partner on the ground—three bullets in his chest—pounded at the back of his head. He'd been reassigned to violent crimes after pulling the trigger that night, but just as he'd come to accept the consequences of his decision then, he'd do the same now.

"If it's guilt you're worried about, you've got nothing to worry about." Roman sat forward in his seat, his empty shoulder holster brushing against his rib cage. "My team was the most important element of my job when I was assigned to HRT. I trusted them, and they trusted me. Because if I couldn't depend on the agents beside me, I couldn't do my job efficiently. The same holds true today. I did what I

69

had to do when Ben Carlin raised his weapon to protect my partner, and I wouldn't hesitate to do it again."

She studied him through a strand of dark hair caressing one side of her face, long fingers stretched across the table alongside the evidence bag seam. Her eyes narrowed at the edges, and a chasm in the invisible barrier she'd built in front of Haynes spread deep enough for him to see through once again. "I never said thank you. You saved my life back there, and it doesn't seem fair you're being pulled off the investigation for it."

"I gave you my word." Roman stretched his hand across the table. He brushed his fingertips against hers as cold from the conference table surface burrowed through his button down shirt, but, in only a fraction of a second, disappeared as his body reacted to her. Didn't matter if they'd been partners at the time, or if Haynes reinstated him back onto the case down the line. Roman would've pulled that trigger, no matter the situation. To protect her. She could hide behind the bureau's rules, shut him out again, bite back with that challenging brightness in her gaze, or straight up partner with another agent on this investigation. None of it mattered. Because Roman wasn't going anywhere. "I'm not going to let anything happen to you."

The conference room door swung open, hitting the door stop hard. Both Brie and Roman pulled their hands back and shot to their feet as SAC Haynes and Captain Hobbs filled the doorway.

"Agent Bradford, I'm pushing back your review and reinstating you to this case." Haynes tossed Roman his badge, but the hardness etched into their boss's expression said the next words out of his mouth would change the entire course of this investigation. "We just got word Chloe Francis is alive."

CHAPTER ELEVEN

THEY HAD A WITNESS.

Brie studied the officers bagging evidence found on their victim from the hospital room doorway. Clothing. Scrapings from beneath her fingernails. Hairs. Anything that could give them an idea of where Chloe had been held for the last three days. Their missing victim had walked into the emergency room of her own accord, bruised, battered, barely conscious. She'd been starved, dehydrated, and tortured with what looked like a similar weapon used on Ashlee Carr. No eyewitness accounts of which direction she'd come from or how far she'd had to walk to get here, but she'd escaped. Survived. Brie shifted her weight between both feet. Not all of the killer's other victims had been so lucky.

"How long will she be unconscious?" Bright florescent lighting and the smell of disinfectant hiked her heart rate into overdrive. Brie had been in plenty of hospitals since Captain Hobbs had brought her to this exact location after finding her on that beach, but no amount of control could fight back the last memories of that night. Every muscle in her body ached in remembrance. It wasn't about the physical pain. This place would always be a reminder of when her parents had blamed her for Jessica's disappearance.

"We were forced to sedate Ms. Francis in order to treat her injuries, but she should come around within the next hour or so. You can talk to her then, but you'll only have a few minutes. The drugs we're keeping her on for the pain are pretty strong, so she may be in and out of consciousness for a while." The doctor assigned as Chloe's physician reviewed the paperwork attached to the metal clipboard in his hand. "She's lost a lot of blood, especially from a deep wound in her left side, but we were able to stop the bleeding and stitch her most serious injuries before she went into shock."

They'd found a survivor. They had another chance to bring the Dream Catcher down, but Brie had worked enough of these cases over the course of her career to understand exactly what Chloe's escape meant. The predator hadn't gotten what he'd wanted.

And he wouldn't stop until he did.

She inhaled on a shaky breath, the tips of her fingers urging her to reach out toward the partner she'd come to rely on over the past two days. She curled her fingers into her palms. They might have recovered Chloe, but this investigation wasn't over. Their unsub would take another victim as soon as he had the chance. That was how killers worked.

"Did she say anything? What her abductor looked like, where she'd been held, smells she remembers?" Roman stood tall, shoulders pulled back, that dark gaze centered on their victim, with his expression unreadable. From what she'd seen back in Chloe Francis's house, the hostage rescue team had lost one hell of an operator. Because no matter the situation, he'd proven himself her calm in the middle of a storm over the last few days, a safe haven. "Anything that could give us an idea of who took her?"

Brie blinked to clear her head. They were partners. They relied on one another to cover each other's backs and get the job done. Nothing more. Once emotion got involved, the chances of making a mistake increased. As did the chance of losing him to another team—another partner—entirely. No. She wasn't going to take that risk.

"Nothing we were able to make sense of at the time," the doctor said. "She was delirious from blood loss and trauma, and first responders found a contusion at the crown of her head. It's amazing the got herself to the ER at all."

Folding her arms across her chest, Brie settled her weight into the doorframe of Chloe's room. Stab wound, head injury, lacerations over nearly every inch of her body. Nobody had seen which direction their victim had come from before she'd walked through the emergency room doors, as though she'd appeared right out of thin air. What if Chloe hadn't gotten herself to the hospital after all? At least, not alone.

"And what about her hand?" Roman's deep rumble calmed the overwhelm of buzzing in her ears. "Is there any chance you'll be able to reattach the finger?"

"Finger?" the doctor asked.

Brie straightened a bit more, shifting her attention to the physician. It would've been kind of hard not to notice an appendage missing from their victim, even in the chaos of trying to stitch Chloe's other wounds. "Her abductor cut off and mailed a finger to Chloe Francis's house this morning for us to find. We'd just assumed it belong to our vic."

"I don't know what to tell you, agents. Ms. Francis has all of her fingers and toes, so whatever body part you recovered, it isn't from her." The doctor lowered the clipboard to his side. "Now if you'll excuse me, I need to check in on my other patients. I'll be back in about an hour to review her vitals." And with that, he strode down the corridor.

"If that's not Chloe's finger, who the hell does it belong to?" Roman asked. "And why send it to her house? The bastard's never done anything like that with the other victims."

"He's doing what killers do best." Brie twisted her gaze upward, noting the thicker patches of her partner's beard. With everything that'd happened in the last two days, he hadn't had a chance to shave, but if she was being honest with herself, it looked damn good on him. "He's toying with us, trying to control us."

"Still think we're dealing with a serial team?" he asked.

"I don't know, but there are too many inconsistencies between all four victims for this to be the work of one perp." The shadow of a man on those cliffs, the message he'd left for her, the break in, all of it rushed to the front of her mind. "If we're dealing with the same killer who abducted me and Jessica all those years ago, he'd be quite a bit older now. Might not be able to move as well as he used to. It's not a long shot to imagine he picked up an apprentice along the way to assist if his victims started fighting back."

"We weren't chasing an old man last night," he said. "You and I were both running as fast as we could to apprehend him, and he still got away."

Her thoughts exactly.

"A partner explains the sudden shift in M.O. since Jessica's disappearance. Would explain why the original killer took such a long cooling off period. The change in age preference, leaving the necklaces with the victims, cutting off and mailing body parts. He's either going out of his way to throw us off and confuse us, or he's teamed up with a partner and planned every single move from the beginning to draw us in closer." Draw *her* in closer. She dug her fingernails into her arm. Closing her eyes against the pulsing ache at the base of her skull, she took a deep, cleansing breath, and refocused. She wasn't responsible for her sister's disappearance. She knew that, but being here, and with so many pieces of this case tying back to that night, it wasn't hard for her to imagine all of this happening because she'd escaped her abductor. Just as Ben Carlin had accused her. "Or maybe I'm playing right into the killer's mind games trying to connect these cases to my sister's kidnapping because that's what he's wanted from the beginning. Maybe I'm only seeing the evidence I want to see, and I'm completely missing something that is right in front of us."

Brie snapped her mouth closed. She hadn't meant the words to slip out, but it was too late. She'd revealed her deepest, darkest secret to a man she was supposed to stay professionally detached from. Her fear of being controlled again, harmed, manipulated. She shook her head to counter the heat working into her neck and face. She'd always been able to keep an emotional distance with her previous partners and the rest of the violent crimes division, but Roman… He'd put her safety first during the standoff with Ben Carlin and bandaged her foot after they'd chased their suspect to the cliffside. He'd watched a movie with her so she could fall asleep after the break in and supported her theory of the connection between these cases without hesitation. Would anyone else on her team have done the same?

"I don't believe that." Roman wrapped a strong but controlled grip around her arm, his thumb scorching a path back and forth through her blazer. She tensed for only a moment this time. She didn't like getting close to anyone, least of all physically, but his touch triggered a sense of calm, drowning the shame attached to her vulnerability. Within two breaths he'd eased the tightness in her chest. "If there's one thing I know for certain about this case, it's whoever's doing this is targeting you. Leaving the necklaces with the victims, Chloe's connection to your missing sister, the killer's message on the mirror. There's not a bone in my body that believes you've been compromised, or that you've altered the course of this investigation. It's all tied to you, but no matter what happens, I will always have your back, partner."

"Thank you." The fear that'd bubbled to the surface vanished at his words, and for the first time since watching the video from Ben Carlin's phone, she was able to breathe without constriction. But with that release came the sudden awareness of how much she enjoyed his touch, enjoyed the way his thumb stroked over her jacket, how his rhythmic movements chased back the uncertainty.

"Now this is where you promise to always have mine." A smile creased the laugh lines around the edges of his eyes and mouth, and her insides twisted. That dark gaze lightened as he dropped his hold on her, but his body heat held to her tight.

"I promise." A powerful burst of laughter rocketed through her, and the endorphin release in her central nervous system kept surging. Because of him.

A moan registered from the hospital bed, a slight shift of movement pulling her focus back into the room. "We need to review the surveillance footage in the emergency room around the time Chloe came in." Brie nodded toward the hospital bed, arms folded across her chest. "That woman was tortured for three days and hit over the head. Hard. After all that blood loss, do you really think she knew where she was going or that she walked through those doors on her own?"

"I'll get security to show me the footage." Roman unpocketed his phone and brought it to his ear. "Should answer our question as to whether our killer let her go or if there's another witness out there."

"Let me know what you find out." If their unsub had brought Chloe to the hospital, why send that video to Ben Carlin or mail the finger to their victim's house if he intended to let her go all along? Brie chewed on the end of one thumbnail, bits of nail polish breaking over her the tip of her tongue. Chloe was coming around. Everything about this case suggested the killer was tied to Jessica's disappearance, but Chloe had been chosen as his messenger for a reason. Not Ashlee Carr. Not the two women taken and killed before her six months ago. And the woman in the hospital bed was the only person who could tell them why. "I'm going to talk to her."

"I'll meet back up with you as soon as I've reviewed the footage." Roman nodded then turned and strode down the hallway.

She stared after him. One breath. Two. Her feet remained cemented to the floor as Roman's shoulders flexed beneath his button-down shirt. She wasn't exactly sure when it'd happened, but there was no denying it now. An invisible bond had been forged between them over the last few days, and everything she'd believed to be true about that connection now came into question. It manifested in the way her breathing changed when he neared, how her awareness of him had intensified the longer they were partnered together, how even right now she couldn't stop thinking about that delirium-inducing kiss they'd shared back at the beach house. No matter how many times she'd told herself having a relationship with her partner—with anyone—was another form of manipulation and control, her gut said Roman would never hurt her. She'd mastered being alone over the years, but with him…there was a chance she didn't have to anymore.

Brie slipped inside their missing victim's hospital room, wiping her damp palms down her slacks. Monitors beeped steadily from beside Chloe Francis's bedside, the scent of antiseptic stronger in the patient's room than in the hallway. She kept her footsteps light and voice low as she approached. This woman had been through enough. Brie wouldn't make this harder than she had to. "Chloe, I'm Special Agent Brie

McKinney. I've been assigned to your case. I know you're in a lot of pain right now, and we'll get that taken care of as soon as we can. I just wanted to ask you a few questions while you were awake."

"I know who you are. I…remember your name." Blonde hair streaked with blood and grime slid along Chloe's neck as she shifted in the bed. An IV tube pulled at thin skin along the top of the woman's hand as she tried to brush it out of her face. "Is she here, too? The other woman?"

Brie's instincts prickled.

"What other woman?" She checked the amount of pain medication still in the clear bag above the bed, but she wasn't a doctor. No telling how much morphine Chloe had already been administered, or if anything she said wouldn't be influenced by the medication. "Was someone else with you when you were being held?"

There hadn't been any other reports of a missing woman in the area. She and Roman had reviewed every incident—twice—when searching for similarities between cases all over the state. Brie straightened a bit more as a combination of confusion and fear took hold. "Chloe?"

Tears slipped down pale skin peppered with a few freckles at the bridge of Chloe's nose and toward battered, swollen lips. Sobs wracked through the victim's chest as Chloe ripped her arm away and brought one hand over her eyes. "He wanted me to tell you I wasn't the only one he took."

CHAPTER TWELVE

Damn it, he was a glutton for punishment.

Nothing could happen between him and Brie without opening them both up to a world of pain. And she'd been through enough. The attraction was there. Hell, how could it not be? The woman hiked his blood pressure higher every time she looked at him, heated him from the inside with a single touch, and sent jolts of electricity down his spine when she took charge. But no matter how much he wanted to break the bureau's interpersonal relationship rules and memorize every inch of her body with his mouth, she didn't trust him. Not completely. The walls she'd built to protect herself had been standing for so long, he wasn't sure they'd ever come down.

But he'd wait. For now.

Roman slid his attention between live feeds on the hospital's monitors as the head of security cued the footage from the time Chloe Francis walked through the emergency room doors. Fingers gripped around his two-way radio, he leaned over the large desk housing an entire arsenal of keyboards and monitors. Cool temperatures kept the stacks of servers from overheating on the other side of the room and limited the movement in his knuckles after a few minutes, but it was the fact he'd left Brie on her own when there was a killer still out there that kept his sense of urgency raw. "Bring up the feeds from outside the ER doors. Five minutes before the victim arrived."

"You got it." The security guard shifted the mouse across the screen, and within a minute had the footage front and center on the largest monitor. Standing, the guard pulled out the rolling office chair and offered it to Roman. "Be my guest. Just let me know when you're finished. I'll be right outside."

"Thanks." He took a seat, setting the radio beside the keyboard as the door to the dark office closed behind him. The soft hum of electricity and whirling fans filled his ears. The camera focused on Chloe Francis's hospital room fed into the monitor on his left, Brie's outline clear in his peripheral vision. The door to the patient's room had been left open, showing Brie still interviewing the victim. She'd worked this job for almost five years, trained with the best at Quantico in weapons and close combat maneuvers, and been recruited into the missing persons division by Special Agent in Charge Haynes himself. He noted the guard outside of Chloe's room and forced himself to get his head back on the case. Even with a killer out there, possibly targeting her, she could handle herself.

Roman hit the space bar on the keyboard to replay the security footage of Chloe's arrival. Brie had been right. Something wasn't adding up. He'd trained in the most extreme conditions and tested his endurance during nearly every operation he'd been assigned with the hostage rescue team, but he'd still have difficulty finding his way with Chloe's injuries. Three days of torture, blood loss, and a head injury? There weren't a lot of civilians who could survive that, let alone get themselves help. Someone had to have seen or helped Chloe get to the hospital.

The footage played across the monitor. Soft drops of rain clung to the outdoor camera's lens, but twenty to thirty seconds before their missing person stepped through the emergency room door, an older vehicle—a four-door sedan, brown with a few rust stains on the passenger side door—pulled to the curb. A single outline of a shadowed figure rounded the hood from the driver's seat, face and arms covered with what looked like a dark hooded sweatshirt, dark pants, and black boots. In four steps, the shadow wrenched open the passenger side door, spilling Chloe Francis onto the sidewalk.

Hell. Brie's suspicions had been right. There was a witness out there. Someone who knew what'd happened to their victim. Or the bastard who'd taken her had come out into the open. He'd have Ludington PD send out a BOLO for the vehicle. They had to find that car.

Roman palmed the two-way radio and compressed the button along the side. His phone vibrated across the desk, and he relaxed his grip until the static cleared. With a single glance at the monitor to his left, he confirmed Brie still inside the victim's room, and the guard stationed outside. He swiped this thumb across the glass when Aiden Holloway's name lit the screen. "Give me something I can use."

"Reports from CSU good enough? Unfortunately, you're probably not going to like the news." The former interrogator's voice barely registered over the servers and fans surrounding the security monitoring desk. Holloway waited a beat as Roman stepped into the hospital corridor, his fingers thawing with warmer temperatures. The head of security nodded before locking the server room behind them and heading down the hallway.

With him temporarily back in the field, he was surprised Holloway and his partner hadn't followed them to the hospital. The man had spent years abroad, training military personnel, responding to terrorist activity, doing recon work. There wasn't a patient bone in the soldier's body. Holloway was constantly on the move, always vying for the next case. And Kinsley Luther wasn't the kind of doc who worked up killer profiles from behind her desk. She liked to get her hands dirty, to be in the field with the rest of the team and get as close as possible to their suspects. "Tell me what you have."

Rustling reached through Holloway's side of the line. "The only footprints recovered from the scene at the beach belong to the witness who found her—Kirk Marshall—and his dog. Your killer was either very careful, or—"

"The witness compromised the scene when he found her." That was what Roman had been afraid of, but without their witness, who knew how long it would've taken law enforcement to find Ashlee Carr's body. "What else?"

"The medical examiner also recovered a few strands of animal hair on the victim. Canine. Specifically a German Shepard," Holloway said.

"Kirk Marshall had his German Shepherd there at the scene while he was giving his statement. Stands to reason he left more than his own footprints when he found our vic." Damn. None of this identified who'd left Ashlee Carr on that beach, or who'd taken Chloe Francis. Roman glanced down the hall toward the victim's hospital room and narrowed his eyes. He could've sworn there'd been a security officer standing guard outside of Chloe's room a few minutes ago. And hadn't the door been open? He put one foot in front of the other, heading back toward Brie's last location. "Any luck with the necklaces recovered from all four scenes?"

"None. Every mall in the state carries that brand, and there are too many to narrow down. Even if our guy had purchased and engraved them in bulk, as of right now, it's a dead end," Holloway said. "But the medical examiner was able to narrow down the kind of sedative your unsub injected into Ashlee Carr in her toxicology report. We also compared it to the two other women you've connected to this case, and we found a match. Phenobarbital."

"That's not something you can get at any mall." Hadn't Brie said she'd been drugged when her and her sister had been taken? If the original abductor was involved in these last four cases, stood to reason he'd stick to at least part of his M.O. with Ashlee Carr and Chloe Francis. Both victims had needle marks in their necks, as though they'd been continually drugged every few hours. Lucky for them, federal law required all medical providers and pharmacists to keep records of prescription drug orders. Narrowing down which pharmacy filled the injectable phenobarbital order wouldn't take much time. They just had to pick up the paper trail. Roman slowed as he closed in on Chloe Francis's room. Warning exploded through him, his free hand raising to the butt of his Glock. "I'm going to have to call you back." He ended the call and shoved his phone back in his slacks, unholstering his weapon.

Pressing his shoulders against the wall beside the now closed hospital room door, he slid the side of his head across the drywall and craned his neck back to get a better look inside. Chloe Francis lay in the hospital bed, eyes closed, but where— A pair of low heels registered from beside the bed—unmoving—and every cell in his body caught fire. Scanning the rest of the room through the small window, he shouldered his way inside, gun raised. Clear. "Brie."

The heavy room door slammed closed behind him, and he lunged to his partner's side. Unconscious. Pulling her into his chest he swiped at the blood trailing down the side of her face from a cut at her temple. Damn it. He should've been here with her. Should've known the bastard who'd targeted her might come after her in public. A moan escaped her throat, tightening the muscles down his spine. He checked the rest of her for injuries, but couldn't find any. Whoever'd attacked Brie couldn't have gone far. The security guard, the one missing from his post. He listened for the machines beside Chloe Francis's bed then noticed the battery packs littered across the floor. No power. Was their victim even breathing? Roman unpocketed his phone and hit Aiden Holloway's number, not waiting for the agent to speak when the line picked up. "Alert Ludington PD of an attack at Spectrum Health. We've got one agent down. I need a medical team to Chloe Francis's room. Now."

He discarded the phone to the stark white linoleum beside him. He wasn't leaving Brie. Not with the chance the attacker was still in the building. He slid his fingers down her cheek. "Come on, baby. Open your eyes."

Baby? Hell, she wasn't going to appreciate that when she woke up.

She blinked up at him, the corners of her eyes narrowing as though she were trying to see him clearly. The injury to her head hadn't started swelling, which meant she'd probably suffered a concussion during the attack. Her pupils were dilated, but that wasn't a sure sign of head trauma. Just the simple fact she'd encountered their killer could've triggered her fight-or-flight response. Pure, unfiltered fear erased the confusion from her expression. Brie straightened, her fingers fisted in his shirt. "Roman, he was here. He…he attacked me from behind. I didn't have the chance to turn around." She pressed the base of her palm into one eye socket and the other into the floor. "Chloe said something...before he hit me."

"You're bleeding. I need you to stay still until you get checked out." His name on her lips started a chain reaction inside he couldn't control, but now wasn't the time to get lost in the pure pleasure of it. He tightened his arms around her as shouts echoed from the hallway. The hospital was going into lockdown. The son of a bitch wouldn't get away that easy.

Medical personal barged through the door and surrounded Chloe Francis's bed in a rush. The doctor they'd met before barked orders as nurses maneuvered around the bed. "Get those machines back up and running. Now!" A nurse wheeled in a bright red cart with an array of drawers with yellow labels, a monitor, and first aid kit. A crash cart. "Agents, we need you to give us some space."

"She needs to get checked out, too. The attacker hit her in the head." Roman helped Brie to her feet, keeping one hand beneath her elbow in case she collapsed again. Her sultry scent fought to drown the antiseptic odor in the room, but he had the feeling not even her perfume would erase the burn in his lungs. Lowering his hand to her waist, he held her tight against him as he led her out into the hallway. The door shut firmly behind them, silencing the chaos of high-pitched keen from the revived machines and the doctor's directions. Their killer had taken a big risk coming here. He studied his partner as she ran a hand through her blood-crusted hair. And he'd taken an even bigger risk touching Brie. Heat burned through him, fingers curling into fists. The bastard would pay for that. Rounding in front of her, he cut off her view of their victim's room. He couldn't keep himself from touching her, even if he'd wanted to, and slid his hands to her hips to help lower her to the floor. He invaded her personal space as a combination of concern and rage took control. "Tell me you're okay."

The more details they had, the faster he'd get to tear the bastard limb from limb for putting his hands on her.

"Honestly, I think my ego is more bruised than my head." A slight smile stretched her lips thin as she settled on the floor, but it didn't reach her eyes. Then disappeared altogether. She looked up at him as she lightly feathered her fingers over the wound. "He was right there, Roman, and I didn't see him coming. And now our victim's life is on the line." Brie shifted her gaze to his left arm as though she could see through him into Chloe Francis's room. "She was supposed to be safe here. She trusted us to keep her safe, and he walked right through that door to get to her."

Two security officers in uniform approached. "We've got the entire hospital on lockdown, Agent Bradford. Nothing yet."

"There was a guard stationed at this patient's room up until a few minutes ago. Where is he?" Roman turned toward the officers. It couldn't be a coincidence the guard had disappeared mere minutes before he'd found Brie on the floor.

"No one has been assigned to guard this patient, sir," one guard said.

"Then I'm going to need to see the surveillance footage from that camera again." He pointed up at the round, black orb attached to the ceiling then faced Brie as the officers rushed away. "We've been underestimating this guy from the beginning, but we will find him. He's already made a mistake."

"What do you mean?" she asked. "What mistake?"

"You were right. Chloe didn't walk into this hospital on her own. Someone left her at the curb, and she stumbled her way through the emergency room doors," Roman said. "And I know for a fact there was a security guard stationed outside of this room while you were interviewing the victim."

She smoothed her expression as realization hit. "He was there. Listening."

"If Chloe escaped her captor, he'd need to make sure she didn't reveal anything that would give him away as a suspect." They'd been underestimating this unsub since the beginning, but it wouldn't happen again. "The bastard was smart. He dropped her off at the curb, then came back, got her room number, and posed as a security guard until he could tie up the loose end. The only question is why. Why let her go in the first place?"

One breath. Two. Why wasn't she saying anything?

The hospital room door swung open, and Roman pulled his shoulders back as he waited for the news on their witness. A low electronic keen followed the doctor and two nurses into the hallway, then abruptly ceased, and his stomach dropped.

The doctor who'd been trying to save Chloe Francis's life shook his head.

"She didn't escape. He brought her here, and I know why." Brie leveled her chin parallel with the floor as the last of the nurses covered the body with a crisp white sheet through the doorway. Blood visibly drained from her face, gutting him from the inside. "He let our victim go to make sure I got the message."

CHAPTER THIRTEEN

"Thanks, Aiden. Let me know if you find anything else." Brie slid her fingertips along the freshly stitched sutures at her right temple with her free hand. Her head pounded in rhythm to her heart beat, slow and steady, as she ended the call with the team's interrogator, Aiden Holloway. After being evaluated by Chloe Francis's physician for a concussion, she and Roman had returned to the beach house. They'd checked the perimeter, scanned for listening devices, and secured every door and window, but still, the part of her that couldn't stop blaming herself for Chloe Francis's death said it wasn't enough. Roman had been right. They'd underestimated this killer from the beginning, and now four women were dead. With another possibly missing. "Aiden checked local reports and reached out to police departments statewide. There are no other recent reports of a missing woman with our abductor's M.O."

"But Chloe was sure there was another woman being held with her?" Roman double clicked his laptop's touch pad as he hunched over the device on the opposite end of the living room couch.

Come on, baby. Open your eyes.

Brie held her breath as his plea echoed in her mind. She'd been hit pretty hard, to the point some of the details with her interview with

Chloe had been compromised, but Roman's voice had tugged her from unconsciousness. She strengthened her grip on her phone as she studied the sharp, handsome angles of his face. She'd never forget that. His concern. The slight hint of panic as he'd pulled her into his arms.

Every word out of his mouth urged her to believe he actually gave a damn about her. That she wasn't just another partner. But that didn't change the fact she wasn't the woman for him, the woman for anyone. On top of that, there were still rules against partner relationships within the bureau. Personal attachment led to risks. Risks endangered lives and assignments. And the moment they crossed that line, their partnership would be over. Their careers would be over. And she'd never find out what happened to her sister. Not without his help. Was her need to feel wanted—loved even—that out of control she was actually considering taking the leap with him? Brie leaned on the wall beside her as emotion rushed through her. They had two bodies—women they'd been assigned to find—in the morgue. She had to focus. "She looked me right in the eye and asked me if the other woman had made it out, too, but there's always the chance whoever she is, she hasn't been reported missing yet."

"We'll have an ID on the bastard who attacked you soon enough. The video file from security at the hospital is downloading now. Bad news is, Aiden sent the M.E.'s files from the evidence we submitted as part of the break in. The swab you collected only contained traces of artificial leather. Most likely from a pair of gloves. No DNA. So even if we identify the guard who disappeared from outside Chloe's room, there's no tying him to the break in. We need something more concrete." Back lighting from the laptop screen highlighted the shadows under his eyes as he looked up at her, but she'd profiled him enough to understand Roman didn't stop when he got tired. He'd only stop when the job was done. And this nightmare was far from over. She had to admire him for that. No matter how many turns this case took, or if she were to be taken out of the equation, she trusted Roman to find their killer. "What else do you remember from your interview with the victim?"

She rubbed small circles into the base of her skull, trying to chase back the pain piercing all the way up through her right eye. She mentally reached for the memories buried under a thick layer of blackness when she'd gotten cold clocked from behind. She didn't even remember falling. Only darkness. "I was standing next to her bed. I think I reached out for her arm when she started crying, but I didn't want to scare her after what she'd been through. She told me she knew who I was after I introduced myself, then that she wasn't the only one he took." Exhaustion pulled at her, and Roman shifted the laptop beside him on the couch as she sank to the couch, one foot tucked under her opposite knee. Pressure built behind her sternum as he closed the space between them, sinking to a crouch in front of her. "I think there was more to it, but...I don't remember anything after that."

In her next breath, he'd wrapped his large, callused hands around hers in her lap, his grip a bit too tight. The small muscles flexed along his neck, and she wanted nothing more than to smooth her hands over the valleys and ridges he created by locking his back teeth. "I should've been there. I could've stopped him—"

"No." She squeezed his hand. "He was watching us. He knew we were there and still got exactly what he wanted. There's nothing we could've done differently. As long as he's one step ahead of us, we're only playing catch up." Flashes of broken images lightninged across her mind. Chloe had said something else, before Brie had been hit from behind. Why couldn't she remember? Friction heated the over sensitized skin between her index finger and thumb as Roman massaged the pressure point there. Her insides clenched, his clean, masculine scent bringing her to the edge of reason. She should pull away, remind him they wouldn't be anything more than partners as long as they were working this case, but she couldn't force her body to obey. With a few simple strokes, anxiety had drained from her shoulders and neck and soothed the pounding at her temple. One touch. That was all it'd taken, and she'd caught fire. He'd chased back the pain, the guilt, the hollowness that'd been carved into her soul since she was ten years old. Seemed impossible. How could he affect her so strongly when she'd succeeded in keeping everyone else at a distance her whole life? "Roman..."

"Careful, partner." He was reminding her of the rules she'd set between them. But his stare physically brushed across her skin as though he'd touched her, a tingling sensation in its wake, and her pulse quickened in response. "I only have so much control when it comes to you."

"I could've died tonight." She'd kept everybody in her life at arm's length once she'd left Ludington in an attempt to protect herself from being hurt—rejected—by the people who were supposed to care for her, but after what they'd been through the last two days, the isolation had become too much. The numbness had spread to the point she wasn't sure she remembered how to let someone in. But with Roman? She wanted to let him in. She wanted to trust him. "So I don't want your control. I want you to kiss me. I want to feel."

Rolling to his knees, he settled his weight against the edge of the couch and crushed his mouth against hers. No hesitation. Holding nothing back. It was passion, desperation, desire, and anger burning through her that fed into the kiss, and she never wanted it to end. His fingers threaded through the hair at the base of her neck, pulling her closer, as he swept his tongue into her mouth. She should slow down, think this through, but she'd done enough thinking over the course of this investigation. Heated sensation climbed from her toes to the crown of her head, and she wanted nothing more than to enjoy it while it lasted. She pressed her body to his, wrapping her arms around his neck as he knelt in front of her. Her breath heaved in and out of her lungs. Her own control had splintered the moment she'd woken up in his arms on that hospital room floor. What was it about him that broke past her defenses when so many others had failed?

"You taste exactly as I remembered." He kissed a trail from her mouth down the front of her throat, tugging her hair down between her shoulder blades. Her automatic response urged her to drop her chin, to contain the vulnerability sliding through her, but Roman would never hurt her. Not like so many others had when they realized she couldn't give them what they'd wanted. She closed her eyes at the feel of his tongue tracing the outline of her collarbones, fighting back a shiver. A growl vibrated through his chest and down into her core. "Like vanilla. My favorite."

She overlapped his hand with hers at the back of her neck, her fingers following the pattern of tendons and bones shifting beneath his skin. She'd been careful. She'd watched her thoughts, her actions, told herself nothing could happen between them. Every moment of every single day they'd been partnered together had been a new lesson in control. But now… She needed Roman more than she'd ever needed anyone before. If for one night, she needed to feel more than the pain permanently lodged in her chest. "You have on too many clothes."

"Once we cross this line, there's no going back, Brie." He pulled back, enough to ignite the rejection she'd held onto for so long. Targeting her with that dark gaze, Roman loosened his grip in her hair, and her insides lurched. "I can never go back. Tell me to back the hell off now if you plan on labeling this a mistake in the morning." His voice dropped into graveled territory, primal, dangerous. "Because I want to make one thing clear: what happens between us will never be a mistake."

"I…" She didn't know what to say to that. Air caught in her throat. Her pulse ticked at the base of her throat in an unsteady rhythm. He'd done that to her. He'd torn down the reigns on her control with nothing more than his fingers in her hair and his mouth pressed against hers. When was the last time anyone had ever made her feel this way? When was the last time she'd given into someone like this? No. This wasn't a mistake. This was everything she'd been missing since her life had been ripped apart, and Brie only held onto him tighter as the invisible weight she'd carried evaporated. In the same moment, the cobwebs sticking to the edges of her mind dissipated as he waited for her to answer. "He wanted us to know."

Confusion deepened the lines at the edges of Roman's eyes. "What?"

"Chloe." Then the son of a bitch had killed her. Brie leaned into him. And she'd have to live with that guilt for the rest of her life. For not being fast enough, strong enough. For not being the protector their victim had needed her to be. "I think he wanted us to find her. That's why he sent the video to Ben Carlin. That's why he left the finger at Chloe's house, but the analysts and the lab weren't moving fast enough for him, so he brought his victim to the hospital. He used Chloe Francis to send us a message."

He wanted me to tell you I wasn't the only one he took. That's what Brie hadn't been able to remember. The entire situation had been a set up.

"What message?" Roman rocked back on his heels again but kept his grip on her.

"That Chloe was just the bait." The hairs on the back of her neck rose on end, chasing back the heat Roman had generated moments ago. As much as she wanted to ignore everything outside these walls and drown in his touch—in him—something else was going on here. Something she couldn't see yet. "Maybe it's not about the women he's taking now. They're pawns to him, a small part of his overall plan."

In her experience, there were two types of predators. Tigers were known to be fast, strong, deadly, stealthy if needed, but they struck the weakest and smallest of the herd out of a need for food. Snakes on the other hand blended in to their surroundings. They charmed their prey, calculated their strike in advance, and had the patience to wait until the timing was right. Unlike the tiger, their desires didn't control them. And they didn't control their unsub either.

"So what does he really want?" Roman asked.

"I don't know." And that was what scared her. Her phone pinged with an incoming message from the small circular coffee table, and she maneuvered around him to reach for it. Sliding her finger across the screen, she read the message from Aiden Holloway. Then read it again. Blood drained from her face. Her heart thudded hard at the site of her injury, and she shook her head as though that would help the words make sense.

"Brie?" Brown eyes leveled in her sightline, a callused hand framing one side of her face, and she forced herself to shift her attention to the man kneeling in front of her.

"They identified the owner of the finger sent to Chloe Francis's house with an old set of prints." Nausea churned in her gut, drowning the desire she'd felt less than a minute ago. She handed Roman the phone, the forensic report bright on the screen. Her mouth dried at the news, but no amount of swallowing helped the information sink in. Her voice broke. "It belongs to Jessica."

CHAPTER FOURTEEN

Her sister was still alive.

Roman had no idea what was going through Brie's head, but the sweat beading at her hairline despite the dropping temperatures outside and her frantic collection of gear didn't scream good news. "Brie?"

"I need to find her." His partner dropped the magazine from her bureau-issued Glock, checked the rounds, then slammed it back into place and holstered the weapon in the holster at her hip. Sliding her arms into her blazer, she slowed her pace and faced him. Challenging him to stop her. "He took her twenty years ago. The police never recovered a body, but I'd accepted she was never coming home. That she was dead." Color drained from her face as her bottom lip wobbled. "She's been out there, all this time, wondering if anyone was going to save her, scared out of her mind. And I did nothing about it."

"The killer sent your sister's finger to pull you into his sick game. You know that." And he wasn't going to let the son of a bitch win. Roman understood the desperation burning in her gaze all too well, the feeling of worthlessness and guilt. The nausea-inducing thoughts that replayed over and over in his head. Could he have done something different? Would he have been able to save his former partner if he'd made another choice that night? But none of it made a difference. It was in the past. He couldn't change a damn thing. All that mattered now was Brie. He closed the distance between them, her alluring scent more pronounced as adrenaline from that kiss sharpened his senses. "He's planned this from the beginning. If you charge out there like this, you're going to get yourself hurt or killed. And I can't let that happen."

The tendons along her neck tensed, attention locked on his chest. "Everything about this case has linked back to her. The necklaces, the location of Ashlee Carr's body, Chloe Francis's abduction. All of it." Brie raised her gaze to his. "This was what he's been trying to tell me, Roman, why he used Chloe to deliver his message. He wanted me to know he still has my sister, and I'm going to bring her back. With or without the FBI's support."

Or his.

"All right. We'll find your sister. Together." Not because it was part of the job, although that was what had brought them together in the first place, but because Roman feared he'd do anything for the woman standing in front of him. A savage storm sprinted across her expression, but it was the fearlessness in her body language that settled his doubt. She wasn't charging into danger on a whim or without considering what would happen to her career at the end of this. She'd planned on confronting her abductor from the start and become a queen who'd turned her pain into power. Only this time, she wouldn't be alone. Mere inches separated them, and Roman ate up the space in his next breath. The butt of her weapon prodded his ribcage, but all he could focus on was her. Intelligent, courageous, confident, vulnerable. Hell of a deadly combination. He lowered his voice. "But I'm not finished with our earlier conversation."

She scanned his face, rolling her lips between her teeth. With a nod, she replaced the distance he'd closed between them and shouldered the gear she'd collected. "We should head back to the station. The team might have more information that will lead us to Jessica."

Right. The case—finding her sister and the bastard who'd held her hostage all these years—had to come first. He knew that, but the need coursing through his veins had long taken control over him when it came to her.

"I'm not afraid to wait, Brie." Her footsteps on the hardwood echoed loud in his ears, and he twisted his head over his shoulder to follow her retreat. "But I'm not going to wait around for something that's never going to happen."

She slowed, fingers wrapped around the front door knob. Her head dropped toward her chest before she slowly turned to confront him. Two steps. Three. Pressure built behind his sternum as she set her hand over his heart, the lighting overhead gleaming off her chipped red nail polish. Brie stared up at him, one hand tight around the duffle bag, then raised up on her toes and pressed her mouth to his. An explosion of want ripped through him hard and fast, but all too soon, she'd sank back onto the four corners of both feet. "I never said I was finished with you either, but let's be honest with each other, Roman. If anything were to actually happen between us, we both know it'd burn out fast." Brie smoothed a wrinkle in his shirt, then swiped her thumb across his bottom lip. "And it wouldn't be fair of me to make you believe otherwise."

His heart jerked in his chest, right beneath her hand, and there was no chance she hadn't felt it. "What the hell does that mean?"

"My parents live in Ludington." She stepped back as though she were just as surprised by the words as he was, then took a visible deep breath. "They're in their fifties now, but healthy, happy, from the looks of it last time I checked, but I haven't spoken to them in two decades." Her voice grew detached, cold, brittle, as though she were reading from the newspaper instead of reliving a piece of her life. "Captain Hobbs took me in after finding me on that beach because they couldn't stand to look at me once they realized Jessica wasn't coming home. They blamed me, said I should've fought harder to get her out of there. That they wished my sister had been the one to come home." She steeled her expression, closed off any hint of vulnerability. To him of all people. "They walked away from me. So I numbed myself to make the pain go away."

"They left you?" What kind of parents abandoned their ten-year-old daughter who'd just survived an abduction? Rage exploded through him at the thought of that small girl in the hospital. Alone, confused, rejected, wondering what she'd done to deserve that kind of hell, but the more he tried to envision it from her point of view, the faster the disbelief inside turned to anger. The urge to punch something nearly overwhelmed his control, but fear at the intensity building inside of him kept him in check. He had to breathe. Had to think. He hadn't suffered an incident like this since discovering his last partner had betrayed the entire HRT team, since before he'd learned how to channel all that pent up rage.

"Now you know." Brie cleared her throat, a single nod ripping her gaze away from his. Her voice softened, and the heat bubbling to the surface eased. "When I said nothing could happen between us, it's not because of the bureau's rules or anything you did. It's because I'm not going to let anyone hurt me ever again. I'm not going to give myself to someone just to have them walk away. I won't be manipulated by the promise of something more." She wiped the back of one hand across her face. "But you deserved to know the truth. There is no real future with me, Roman. So whatever is going on between us, it's not going to last—"

He wrapped his arms around her and pulled her into his chest in an all-encompassing hug. Tension thickened the muscles across her shoulders and down her spine, but he hadn't been able to stop himself. He just had to hold her. Reassure her. Comfort her. Protect her. Anything that would help chase back the pain and numbness. If only for a few seconds. Brie slowly relaxed into him, the duffle bag sliding to the floor. She tucked her face against his chest, igniting the heat they'd shared a few minutes ago, but he wouldn't push her for more than this. Her reasoning for keeping him at a distance was solid, but he couldn't ignore the sickening disappointment they'd never have more. Which meant his emotions had already been engaged. Releasing her, he maneuvered her back at arm's length, fingers still wrapped around her biceps. "I give you my word, Brie. I will never hurt you, and I will kill anyone who tries."

She bent to collect the discarded gear then those blue-green eyes locked on him, and the past, the investigation, the threat waiting outside these walls disappeared. There was only Brie. His Brie. "You have no idea how much I wish that was true."

Roman didn't answer. He followed her out the front door toward their rental SUV, locking the deadbolt and setting the security alarm behind him. Sand crunched beneath his shoes as they treaded down the stone walkway, the rolled-up sleeves of his button-down shirt tight around his forearms. Darkness had fallen, the horizon of Lake Michigan nothing but a sea of black at the edge of the cliffs. The old wooden stairs leading down the shore weren't visible from this angle at the front of the house. The son of a bitch who'd left Brie that message on the mirror had known exactly where to dock his boat when he'd broken in to the house, known precisely where the stairs were to be able to find them in pitch dark. Roman slowed before he reached the vehicle, studied the landscape for a few moments longer. Their unsub had either staked out the house before he and Brie had landed in Ludington, which didn't add up since they hadn't reserved the property until they'd confirmed Chloe Francis's disappearance. Or… "He's local."

"What'd you say?" Brie slammed the back passenger-side door closed, her gear secure.

"There's no way the perp who broke in would've seen those stairs this late at night, which means he knew this area." Gripping his phone, he hit a recent number in his phone app and brought it to his ear. There'd been two elements in common with the first murder scene and the break in. He just hadn't seen it until now. "Holloway reported the crime scene unit had recovered canine hair matching a German Shepherd breed on Ashlee Carr's body that morning at the beach. We assumed it was cross-contamination from the witness who'd called 911, but I found animal hair inside the footprint at the back door that night, too. Can't be a coincidence."

"You think we're looking for a local who owns a dog." Brie sidled up beside him.

"One we might already know." The other end of the line picked up as Roman turned back toward the house. "Dr. Allie Meyer, please." He disengaged the house's deadbolt and the security system, Brie close on his heels, and headed straight for the crime scene report from the beach. Soft music played in his ear as he unburied the file from beneath their case stack on the kitchen counter and spread it out over the granite. The photo. It had to be here somewhere.

"Dr. Meyer," the woman on the other end of the line said.

"It's Special Agent Bradford." Roman pinched the phone between his shoulder and ear as he shuffled through the stack of photos taken at the crime scene on the beach. Both he and Brie had reviewed them a half a dozen times, digitally and in print, but nothing had connected any of the other scenes. Until now. He set the phone on the counter and hit the speaker function to loop Brie into the conversation. "The two hair samples collected from Ashlee Carr's body and the break in at the beach house. Were you able to match them?"

"Actually, I was about to send your team the final report." Dr. Meyer paused, and his heart shot into his throat. "The hairs match exactly. Both samples came from a German Shepherd, older based on the slight whitening at the base of the hair. DNA's a match."

Roman pulled a photo from the stack of crime scene photos, the weight of Brie's proximity pressurizing the air in his lungs. Son of a bitch. The scene was exactly as he remembered it. The handful of evidence markers where Ashlee Carr's body would've been had the M.E. not claimed the remains before they'd gotten on scene, Ludington PD and Captain Hobbs working around the target scene on the perimeter. And there, in the top right corner of the photo, their suspect. "Go ahead and send the report. Thanks." He ended the call with the medical examiner then handed the photo off to Brie. "The bastard was there all along, admiring his handiwork."

How had he missed it? The evidence had been there right in front of him.

Her breath rushed out of her as he maneuvered around her and sat on the couch in front of the laptop. "The blue fibers found on Ashlee's body. They came from—"

"A dog leash. Ludington PD took his shoe prints at the scene to rule him out as a suspect, but there was a reason they weren't able to find the killer's." Roman cued the hospital security footage from outside Chloe Francis's room and hit play. The black and white video lacked sound, but Roman didn't need to hear the unsub's voice to confirm his theory. The security guard posted outside of their victim's room had donned a non-descript baseball cap to hide his face from the camera, as though he'd known exactly where it'd been installed, but there was no mistaking the height, the build. The killer had been there, in the background of their investigation, this entire time. Roman brought up the National Law Enforcement Tracking System—NLETS—and typed in their witness's name. A split second later Kirk Marshall's face filled the screen. He turned his gaze to Brie. "Guess what our new suspect does for a living?"

CHAPTER FIFTEEN

"A VETERINARIAN WOULD HAVE ACCESS TO THE PHENOBARBITAL OUR killer used to sedate his victims." Brie stared out the tinted passenger side window of the SUV. Rain slithered in rivets diagonally across the glass, heavy clouds throwing the entire east side of Lake Michigan into a sea of darkness, but it was the endless acres of forest surrounding the road that pooled anxiety at the base of her spine. Captain Hobbs had already sent out a all-points bulletin for their witness but came up empty at his veterinary office and his home. However, they couldn't ignore the mortgage statement for a cabin on Hamlin Lake in Kirk Marshall's name, less than three miles south of the beach where they'd recovered Ashlee Carr's body. And now she and Roman had become part of the team searching the state park, the surrounding cabins, and any boats docked at the marinas along the shore.

The suspect's face had burned itself to the back of her retinas since seeing it for the first time in the NLETS database. Mid fifties, white hair and beard, receding hairline, deep nightmare-inducing green eyes. He fit the height and build of the security guard outside of Chloe Francis's hospital room, but the crime had only been partially recorded by surveillance. No confirmation of the killer's ID despite being able to piece the rest together. The guard had been the one to knock Brie unconscious a split second before he'd closed the door to the room behind him to kill Chloe Francis, all without showing his face to a single camera. In or out of the hospital.

Had it been Kirk Marshall? Was he the man who'd taken her that night all those years ago? She swallowed back the sudden tightness in her throat, forcing herself to breathe evenly. They had a name, a lead. She should've felt relieved, but the thought of Jessica still out there, of being alone with a psychopath all this time… Her lower lash line burned with unshed tears. Brie swiped her tongue across her bottom lip and leveraged the uninjured side of her head into her palm against the window, but not even the cold glass kept the anger at bay. Police had never recovered her sister's body. She should've kept looking. "Coming forward as a witness was a smart move."

"Gave him the opportunity to stay close to the case, manipulate the investigation, too. He could've given officers any story he'd wanted back at the scene to throw us off." Roman kept his eyes on the road, his woodsy scent filling the small interior of the vehicle. It fought to counteract the weight crushing her from the inside, but she couldn't ignore the truth. Everything that'd happened in this investigation connected back to her. To that night.

The rage she'd witnessed from her partner earlier at the mention of her ugly past had drained from his features, leaving nothing but clear brown eyes and a smooth, handsome expression. In those few intense moments he'd held her, their partnership had changed. It hadn't been about lust or desire like before. Simply one friend comforting another, yet somehow those short seconds in his arms had meant more to her than anything physical that could happen between them. And she'd never forget it.

She studied him out of the corner of her eye.

Roman had sworn never to hurt her, and her partner wasn't the kind of man to ever break an oath. But the thought of relying on him for more than having her back in the field—of seeing him as more than her partner—scared her straight to her core. "It also excluded him from being considered a suspect. At least until now."

Silence settled between them. Empty. Exhausting. They'd been running off adrenaline for so long, they'd never had the chance to just…be. The heavy pings of rain rang loud in her ears as she searched the road ahead. It'd been a long time since she'd come out here. Ludington State Park had been one of her family's favorite weekend spots. Camping, boating, swimming, picnics, laughter and smiles. She and Jessica had spent some of their best summers memorizing every trail, preserving every rock for their shared collection. A smile pulled at the corner of her mouth but vanished a few moments later. They'd been happy once. Look where she was now. "You never told me why you transferred from hostage rescue. According to your file, you were one of their top operators with a line of promotions ahead of you. What changed?"

Roman pressed his shoulder blades back against the seat, never taking his gaze off the road. The slight tightening of his knuckles against the steering wheel drew her attention from his face. "I trusted someone I shouldn't have." A quick glance in her direction was all it took before her insides heated again. "My partner."

Her heart fluttered. She'd read his file, but most of it had been redacted toward the end. No mention of a partner. And now his policy concerning trust between partners had started to make sense. "I'm sorry. I didn't know."

"Team is the most important element in HRT. You trust them, they trust you." His shoulders rose on a deep inhale. "My unit came up as selectees together. We ran overseas missions, took down terrorists in the middle of the night, pulled bullets from each other if we had to. We ate, lived, and slept within mere feet of each other for years. Every single one of us was loyal to the unit. I considered them family, more so than the one I was dealt growing up." His Adam's apple sank then hiked back into position as he swallowed. "We'd all been trained to plan and spot the threat, but none of us saw the threat from one of our own until it was too late."

Brie straightened a bit more in her seat. "What happened?"

"I confronted my partner about a piece of evidence I suspected he'd planted to secure a guilty plea from a suspect we hadn't been able to get answers from." His voice dropped, the betrayal evident in the undertones, and air caught in her throat. "With the help of one of our undercovers, we knew our suspect had built an RDD and set it to detonate during a political rally scheduled a few hours later, but we couldn't prove it. We'd searched this guy's clothes, home, a storage locker, his car, his family's houses. Came up with nothing. No radioactive material. No explosives. My partner lost it, got rough with the suspect, and I had to ban him from the interrogation. Twenty-four hours later, our experts came back with a report of traces of dynamite on our suspect's clothing that hadn't been reported before."

"Did you test your partner, too?" she asked.

Roman shook his head. "We got back to the states a few days later. I drove up to talk to him about what the hell happened in that interrogation, and I caught him burning his clothes and destroying the evidence at his family cabin. I'd never considered the connection until then." The edges of his eyes creased as he stared out through the windshield, patterns of rain streaking across his face. "He told me to walk away, ignore what I'd seen, but I couldn't. I joined the FBI to fight for justice, to do the right thing, and he knew that. Next thing I knew, he'd pulled his weapon on me, fired two rounds, and I shot him in self-defense. Right in front of his family." A rough exhale escaped his chest as he tugged the edge of his collar down. Two raised mounds of scar tissue cast shadows across his skin. Bullet wounds. "I couldn't trust my team after that, so my section chief suggested I put in for a transfer to missing persons, and here we are."

The soft pattering of rain on glass and metal filled the interior of the SUV.

But she couldn't let the conversation stop there. He'd revealed a piece of himself, trusted her with his greatest fear. Brie reached across the center console, setting her hand on top of his right thigh. Thick tendons of muscle hardened beneath her touch as he shifted his gaze to her. "You can trust me. No matter what happens."

Her heart pounded hard behind her ears, an internal reaction exploding throughout her system the longer he studied her. Did he believe her?

"I do," he said.

"Good." She nodded, turning her gaze back to the road. They were supposed to be searching for their suspect, and the outline of something ahead caught her attention.

"Wait. Slow down. I see something up ahead." She straightened a bit more, trying to see more clearly through the rain lashing across the windshield. Reflective red plastic brightened as they closed in on the dark shape ahead. Taillights. The hairs on the back of her neck stood on end. Her fingers tingled to wrap around the grip of her weapon. They still had more than a mile of road before they hit Kirk Marshall's cabin or any others for that matter, and she'd spent plenty of time memorizing this road as a kid. This stretch wasn't used by tourists and visitors compared to those nearer the campgrounds and resorts. No reason for someone to leave their car here other than engine trouble. Or to abandon it. "What kind of car did you say showed up on the video of Chloe Francis being left at the emergency room?"

"Four door brown sedan, rust stains on the passenger side door." Roman lifted his foot from the accelerator, and the SUV slowed to a roll. He stared at the dark, seemingly empty car and shoved the SUV into Park. "Exactly like that one."

Tendrils of steam rose from the hood as temperatures dropped. The engine was still warm. Unbuckling her seatbelt, Brie shouldered out of the SUV and hit the dirt. She hefted her jacket behind her holster to expose the butt of her weapon as she tracked Roman's path around the hood of their rental. Rain pelted off the sedan in thick sheets, and she narrowed her eyes in an attempt to see more clearly, but the rain was too heavy. "License plate is missing."

Her partner rounded to the driver's side door as she took up the rear. Roman unholstered his Glock and took aim as he searched both the front and back seats, tendrils of his short hair sliding down across his forehead in streaks. "VIN number under the windshield has been scratched off, too."

Her heels sank deeper into the mud and loose gravel as she motioned to him with her chin. Tension radiated down her back as he ripped the driver's side door open. One shot. That was all it would take to end their partnership. It was a risk they'd each taken on when they'd joined the bureau, but the thought of losing him—after everything they'd been through—settled at the front of her mind. Unholstering her weapon and a flashlight, she gripped the cold steel of her weapon in one hand and positioned the flashlight beneath the her wrist with the other in support. He'd made her a promise to protect her, and she'd sure as hell try to do the same for him. That was what partners were for. "Anything?"

"Clear." He rested one hand against the car's hood, his button-down shirt contouring all the ridges and valleys beneath the thin fabric, and she diverted her gaze to keep her head in the game. To prove she could. "The hood is still warm. If our suspect is the one who left the car, he can't have gotten very far on foot in this weather."

Brie rounded to the passenger side of the vehicle. He was right. It'd already been raining steady for over an hour. The road was slick with mud, the grasslands soaked. It'd be hard for Kirk Marshall to make it to his cabin on foot. She stopped at the edge of the road where a fresh set of foot prints cut through the dirt. She brushed soaked strands of hair out of her face and dislodged rivets of water from her mouth. The longer it rained, the faster their evidence disappeared. She stepped around the shoe prints, following the vanishing canyons into the wide expanse of trees on the other side of the road. Pure darkness stared back at her from the woods. "Looks like that didn't stop him from trying." She pointed to the prints with the barrel of her weapon. "Put the call into Haynes. This is officially a manhunt."

CHAPTER SIXTEEN

HE WAS BACK TO BEING AN HRT OPERATOR, HUNTING THE TARGET with little intel, impaired vision, and a team he could trust. A partner he could trust.

Roman maneuvered through the woods in a slow rhythm beside her, one step at a time as mud and rocks threatened to trip them up. Special Agent in Charge Haynes had immediately sent backup their way, but Aiden, Kinsley, and the rest of the team were at least another twenty minutes out. If they wanted to intercept the bastard who'd already killed four women and taken another, he and Brie had to move now. Rain pounded on his forearms as they ventured deeper into the wilderness, his senses on high alert. This was what he'd been trained for: the hunt.

"No cell service out here." The soft click from locking her phone's screen barely registered over the patter of rain bouncing off dead foliage and trees around them. Brie pocketed the device, her exhales crystalizing in front of her lips as she swept her flashlight out in front of them. Temperatures had started dropping the second they'd left the warmth of the SUV, but if there was one thing he'd learned about her over the course of this investigation, it was that nothing would stop Brie from finding her sister. She'd been waiting for closure more than half her life, and he had the feeling nothing short of bringing the son of a bitch who'd taken her and Jessica to justice would relieve her of that nightmare. "Looks like we're on our own."

"We stick together. No matter what happens, understand?" Their killer had already made a point of targeting Brie in his sick mind games. She'd trained for this, but Roman wasn't about to leave her unprotected either. The simple truth was, he'd never told anyone else— not even his most trusted HRT teammates—what'd happened that night with his last partner. He'd been required to inform his section chief, asked to provide proof of his teammate's betrayal and a statement to the investigating team, but outside the responsibilities of his duty as an operator, he'd kept his mouth shut. He'd already lost everyone he'd cared about. He wasn't about to lose anyone else.

"I understand," she said.

"Everything this guy has done had been about you." Roman fought the heavy feeling pressing against his chest as he slid his fingers between her arm and ribcage and pulled her into him. Muted blue eyes narrowed on him in confusion, but she didn't push back. He wasn't sure when it'd happened, when he'd started falling for her, but he had enough self-awareness to know it was already too late. She'd gotten under his skin, become part of him, and there wasn't anything he could do to purge her from his system. Blood rushed between his ears with the intensity of an airplane engine. Hell, there wasn't anything he wanted to do about it. "You're the key to him getting what he wants, but I give you my word I'm not going to let that happen. Use me as a shield if you have to, and get yourself out of here if I'm taken out. Promise me."

An audible breath rushed from her lungs. Her delectable mouth worked to form the words. "Roman, I—"

Gunshots exploded from the right. Years of training kicked in, and Roman lunged, throwing his partner to the ground in an attempt to cover her body with his. Bark exploded above their heads, raining down in shaved slivers. Rocks cut into his palm as he homed in on the slight movement of shifting branches across the small clearing and fired back. One bullet. Two. Adrenaline dumped into his bloodstream, hiking his pulse into overdrive. A growl escaped from his chest. The son of a bitch had taken a shot at them. At Brie. He rolled off her then hauled her to her feet. Every protective instinct he owned urged him to charge the suspect—end this nightmare once and for all—but that raised his chance of taking a bullet and would leave Brie vulnerable. Not happening. Bringing down a middle-aged veterinarian wouldn't be too hard, but he'd treat this assignment as any other he'd executed for HRT. With caution and respect. He was in unfamiliar territory, and there was no telling how far a target would go to achieve his mission. "Keep low and stay behind me."

"No argument here." Brie stayed close on his heels, her shallow exhales loud in his ears as they forged a path forward.

No movement from the bushes where the shots had originated, but Roman wouldn't let his guard down. Not until they had the bastard in cuffs. They'd lost the element of surprise, but there were only so many places a man like Kirk Marshall would go when cornered. Crouching behind one of the larger trees in the park for cover, he released the magazine from his weapon and counted thirteen rounds. Brie settled beside him, her gun pointed at the dirt, and a hot fist clenched in his gut. Even soaked to the bone, the woman had a way of spiking his blood pressure into dangerous levels. "You good?"

"Yeah. Good." Nodding, she plastered her hair back away from her face. The rain wasn't letting up, which only complicated following their suspect's tracks. Didn't matter. They couldn't turn back now. Jurisdiction aside, he and Brie were in this until the end. "Thanks for making sure I didn't get shot."

"Couldn't take the chance of losing another partner. Brass might suspect something was up." He scanned the trees ahead. Every second they wasted surveilling was another chance their killer would get away, but they couldn't go in blind either. Not with innocent lives at risk. "Could affect my future promotions."

"Jerk." A burst of laughter escaped up her throat and heat surged through him. Damn, he loved that sound, loved being the one to make her laugh, but now wasn't the time to think of all the ways he'd work to hear it again. Drops of water flittered across her mouth as she spoke. "There are three campgrounds ahead, a boardwalk, and the Lost Lake Trail in this area in addition to the cabins lining the shore, giving Marshall any number of places to lay low until backup arrives. Tourist season dies down the beginning of November, but we can't assume there aren't civilians in those areas, even with the freezing temperatures."

She strengthened her grip around her weapon as tremors ran up her hands, and Roman wanted nothing more to take them between his to warm her up, but they were in the middle of an assignment, and time wasn't on their side.

"Serial killers aren't willing to die for their cause. They'll do anything to avoid capture and arrest." He searched past the bushes where the shots had come from, and lead sank in the center of his gut. "Which means if he does find civilians out here, he's likely to take a hostage so he has a chance of escape."

But Roman didn't negotiate with killers.

"Or he'll run straight back to the location he's keeping Jessica and disappear." Her wide blue-green eyes locked on him, and Brie shoved to her feet. In a flash, he had his hand wrapped around her arm and her chest pressed against his, the erratic beat of her pulse strong at the base of her neck. "I can do this. I *need* to do this. Please don't try to stop me."

"I read your file, too, and studied all your past cases. I couldn't stop you if I tried, cupcake." Roman lowered his mouth to hers, but didn't close the small distance between them, giving her the choice. Her shallow exhales spread across his over sensitized skin. "His specialty is mind games. He's counting on your guilt to get the best of you, Brie. He wants you to react emotionally to take the advantage from us. Don't let him get in your head."

"How could he when you've already taken up so much space?" She smoothed her hand across his jaw, the bristles of his beard echoing in his ears, and planted a chaste kiss against his mouth. Not long enough. Not even close. "Let's move."

They jogged in the direction the shooter had disappeared, low hanging branches cutting across their faces. Thirty feet past the tree line, they'd picked up the trail of fresh prints in the dredging mud. Hurried. Messy. Panicked. They were on the right path. His muscles burned as they picked up the pace, ice working down his throat and into his chest. Even out of the hostage rescue team, he'd kept in top shape, but the temperatures out here didn't discriminate. Brie's strangled breathing evidenced exhaustion, and soon the chance of hypothermia would become a reality. Without cell service or GPS there was no way Ludington PD or the missing persons team would be able to provide back up this deep in the woods, but they had to keep moving. They couldn't let Kirk Marshall get away with murder.

The trees ahead thinned, and both he and Brie broke from the woods into what looked like a small backyard for one of the rental cabins. Patches of dirt and dying grass stretched across the landscape, a pale staircase taking up a large section at one end. The white-planked, two-story home offered views from every angle imaginable on the property. Perfect to see who was coming and going from the safety of the cabin. The footprints they'd followed from the wilderness led straight to the staircase, and every cell in Roman's body screamed to take cover. They'd tracked their killer. "Head to the south side. There are no windows on that end."

They moved in tandem, guns drawn, then he spotted it. The camera mounted beneath the roof's ledge to make up for lack of visibility on the sound end of the cabin. He reached for Brie and pulled her deeper into the trees, his heart in his throat. Her drugging scent mixed with the atmospheric smell of rain, an addictive combination. Adrenaline had driven his life since the day he'd turned eighteen and joined the military, but nothing made him feel more alive right now than having Brie within his reach. The weight of her gaze had him nodding toward the corner of the cabin where the camera would most likely be blind. The lower level of the structure—most likely the basement—had windows every two or three feet. If the front of the cabin matched the back, they'd be able to slip into the basement through one of them without being seen. Two steps. Three. Pressing his spine back against the siding, he twisted his attention around the corner, Brie at his side. No other sounds above the pounding of rain registered, but that didn't mean they were safe. Or that they hadn't been spotted. In two quick moves, he'd removed the screen from the nearest window and slid the glass along the grime-filled track.

They were in.

A rush of warmth slithered along his exposed skin from inside. Roman took position as lookout as Brie climbed through the window. He knew the law. They didn't have a search warrant. They didn't have back up or cell service to figure out who owned the home before conducting their search. But that wouldn't stop him from saving an innocent woman's life. Nothing would.

Roman ducked beneath the window's frame and stepped down inside to the basement. Light-colored wood paneling surrounded them, old furniture scattered throughout the main living space. Worn orange carpet, a brick fireplace and mantel, and an old black and white TV said the place hadn't been updated since the seventies. He cleared the room, keeping his movements slow and his head in the game.

His partner stood in front of the wooden bookshelves that'd been built straight into one end of the room, her shoulders tense despite the fact she'd lowered her weapon to her side. Strands of short wet hair spidered down the back of her jacket, dripping onto the carpet.

Swinging his weapon up, he sidestepped to her position, clearing the short, darkened hallway leading into what he assumed was the rest of the second level of the home. "Brie, we've got to move."

"They're his trophies." There was something guttural, almost traumatized, in her voice, and an explosion of protectiveness rocketed through him. He chanced a quick glance to the items peppered across the dusty shelves as she studied them, one by one. Newspaper clippings, jewelry, a stuffed bear, a single lock of light blonde hair. Too many to count.

A ball of lead settled in his gut. More than the five victims—four women and one thirteen-year-old girl—the FBI had linked to their unsub. Son of a bitch. How many other victims had the bastard gotten a hold of? How many—if any—had survived as Brie had? Soft squeaking raised his focus to the floor above them. "We have to get out of here."

"Not yet." His partner snapped a latex glove over her free hand, reaching for something out of his line of sight. Sunlight glinted off the tarnished gold metal as she pulled the thin chain from the shelf. The item came into focus. The movement above stopped, but Roman couldn't focus on that as he beat down a surge of nausea. A gold pendant, similar to the necklaces recovered at each of the four victims' crime scenes. Only this one had a different name engraved into the gold. Briohny. Her hands shook as she held it up. Brie licked her lips as though her mouth had gone dry, blue-green eyes darting to his. "We found the Dream Catcher."

CHAPTER SEVENTEEN

SHE HADN'T GONE BY HER FULL NAME IN YEARS. THE TENSION UNDER her ribs wound tighter, suffocating, nauseating, but she forced herself to set the necklace back in its place on the shelf to preserve the evidence. It was exactly like her sister's, given to her by her mother the gynecologist to celebrate her transition into womanhood, just as Jessica had received hers.

The man who'd abducted her had kept it all these years. She'd found him.

Her gloved hand brushed against the stuffed teddy bear set off to the side of the arrangement of jewelry. She fought through the horror setting up residence at the base of her throat. At one trophy per victim, they were looking at more targets than they'd originally attributed to the Dream Catcher. Six shelves. Each stocked and organized. Her voice barely registered over the hard thump of her heart behind her ears. "There are so many of them."

"Too many," Roman said.

Their killer had to be highly intelligent, extremely organized and meticulous, possibly had knowledge of crime scene analysis and police investigations to stay at large this long. He'd made everyone around him believe he was like them. For years. They'd brought their family pets to him, trusted him. And he'd used that trust to his advantage.

A single photo hung from the sliver of wall to her right. Recognition flared. The man from the beach, their witness, Kirk Marshall, stood next to a large houseboat with a fishing pole and his catch of the day. Confirmation this was his cabin. He'd abandoned the vehicle used to take Chloe Francis to the emergency room. Her stomach rocketed into her throat, cutting off her air supply. "Roman, the boat." She nodded toward the photo as the ground dropped out from beneath her feet. "I remember that boat."

He closed in on her. "You're sure it's the same one you saw that night?"

"Yes." The word tore from her throat as images that'd terrorized her every night since jumping overboard crushed the oxygen from her lungs. The icy water, the way her every muscle in her body screamed for release as she'd swam as fast as she could, the dizziness she couldn't get rid of. And the glimpse of the registration number ending in four-five, so clear after all these years. They hadn't been able to build a profile on their killer with so much conflicting evidence. Difference in age between victims over the years, the necklaces recovered at the last four scenes, blue fibers discovered from Ashlee Carr's wrists and ankles. None of it had matched up with her recollection of the abduction or any other missing persons cases involving young children in the state. But... "I was on that boat."

She was sure of it.

A hardness set into his expression, and suddenly Roman seemed so much...bigger than he had a moment ago. More dangerous. "If he brought you and Jessica to that vessel, there's a good chance—"

"That's where he took the others." Her heart rate kicked up a notch. And the only way to hide the evidence of over a dozen kidnappings and murders...was to wash it away. Literally. "Haynes needs to get USERT out here to search that lake."

Roman palmed his phone. "No signal."

"Damn it." She'd forgotten. Drops of water fell from her clothing and hair as she shifted her attention to the hallway at her right. Something pulled deep within her, urged her to search the rest of the basement level, as though she stood on the edge of a cliff and had looked down. Had he come into their rooms at night as he had all those years ago? Shoved that needle in their necks to keep them from fighting back? Brought them to his boat in the middle of the lake to never be seen again? A shiver chased across her shoulders. Brie tightened her hand around the grip of her firearm. The creak of floorboards overhead shut the door to the past as she forced one foot in front of the other to the end of the hallway. The Dream Catcher had already ruined her life. She wouldn't let him ruin another. She lowered her voice, turning her back on the sick display of shelves. "As far as we know, he's still here. We need to clear the rest of the basement."

"On your six." Roman's body heat fought back the chill settling in her bones, but it wasn't enough. Seventeen years' worth of ice had built beneath her skin. It'd take a lot more than a brush of her partner's arm against hers to thaw it. Not when she was so close to finding her sister.

"He's upstairs." Dust fell from the ceiling as the killer moved above them again, and Brie slowed before she met a sharp corner that led upstairs to the main level. He was taunting them. Giving away his position. Serial abductors were careful, patient. Not willing to die for their cause. Which meant the Dream Catcher had most likely installed a security system, surveillance, and countermeasures to avoid capture. Or to fend off anyone who'd uncovered his secret. He knew they were there. She faced Roman, closed the distance between them so he could hear her at a whisper, but the pull to the other end of the house hadn't lessened. The onslaught of his earthy scent dove deep into her lungs, keeping her focused, grounded. Enough that she noticed the large padlock on the only other door in the basement. "Kirk Marshall manipulated officers into believing he was the witness who'd discovered Ashlee Carr's body at the beach, and he's manipulating us now. He's giving away his position to make us think we have the element of surprise."

His dark brown eyes narrowed at the edges. "So we'll walk right into his ambush."

She nodded, twisting her chin to one shoulder. There was only one other room on this level. Their unsub wanted them to take the stairs, but her gut said it was an ambush. Locking her gaze on Roman's, she tried to force her body to relax. She'd been trained for situations exactly like this. They both had, only now, there was a very real chance they wouldn't make it out of this house alive and Jessica would be left with nobody to fight for her. Forgotten. Her nerves buzzed, her heart pounding hard under her ribcage. "He has the advantage here. He could run and easily gain a head start or disappear in those woods altogether, but instead he's baiting us. Because I think there's something in that room he doesn't want us to see."

Or someone.

Roman's attention rose over her head. "He's been a step ahead of us at every turn. Whatever's behind that door could just be another part of his plan to manipulate us."

"That means he'd had to have known we'd recover his vehicle on that road and the exact moment when, that we'd follow his tracks to this place, and break in through that window." There were too many variables to plan something so elaborate, and they were running out of time. Their killer wouldn't wait around for them to come up with a plan. They had to move. Now. Jessica's life depended on it. She curled her fingernails into her palms and squeezed. Brie needed her partner at her side, needed him to trust her. "You think that's a possibility?"

"I was trained to think of every possibility." Water dripped down from the hair around his temples, disappearing into his beard. His dark eyes glittered with challenge, and his shoulders widened as though he was prepared to take out any threat that came their direction alone. "But the only reason to install a padlock on the outside of a door like that is to keep whatever you have behind it inside. So I trust you."

Her mouth flooded with saliva, but she didn't dare swallow as awareness of that admission pressurized the air in her lungs. He'd spoken so confidently, something pinged inside her chest. When was the last time he'd let himself trust anyone after what'd happened with his last partner? Brie gave a single nod. She wouldn't let him down. Lightning and thunder snapped through the sky and shook the house, rain pelting against the windows in rhythm to her racing heartbeat.

This was it. This was what she'd been waiting for. No mistakes. One way or another, she'd end this tonight. For Jessica. For every victim on those shelves. For herself. "The moment we're in that room, he'll have us pinned. One of us should go in alone, and the other should watch the stairs. Stall him until we've had a chance to uncover whatever he's hiding. We might be able to use it to neutralize any leverage he thinks he has."

"Now you're thinking like an operator." Pride resonated in his voice. Roman kept his voice low as he wiped a trail of water from her chin, his touch light. An electric zing pooled in her stomach at the contact, goosebumps rinsing on her arms. He manually racked the slide on his weapon to chamber a round. "I've got your back."

"I know you do." And she had his. Because death wasn't in her game plan. She straightened a bit taller, grip tight around her weapon, and pressed her back against the corner giving way to the thinly carpeted stairs. No door at the top of the stairs. Nothing to keep their killer from putting a bullet in her head at the exact moment she made her play for the padlocked door. Shadows angled across the opposite wall as cloud cover shifted out through the windows. Brie pumped her legs hard, colliding with the door, and raised her weapon. She set her finger over the trigger but hesitated. The padlock hadn't been locked. Desperation clawed up her throat as she tugged the lock free. With one last glance at her partner, she took a deep breath, flicking on the light as she stepped across the threshold.

Stale air dove into her lungs, a mixture of body odor and something salty pulling her deeper into the room. Her ears rang, but not enough to block the lack of sound from upstairs. She maneuvered past another built-in book case, this one filled with actual books, but it was the mattress and dark, loose sheets and a pillow in the center of the room that pulled her further inside. Crumbs peppered the carpet, crunching beneath her boots. No windows. No closet. No escape.

No victim.

"Clear." Dread coiled. There was no one here. No sign of her sister. Nothing to suggest—apart from the mattress and bedding and a few crumbs—that anyone had ever been in this room. And all of those could've been planted to make her believe the narrative. Brie backed toward the door. Roman was right. It'd all been part of the—

The corner of a folded piece of paper caught her eye from beneath the pillow on the mattress. She lowered her weapon a fraction of an inch and, for a split second, couldn't believe what she was seeing. She crouched at the edge of the makeshift bed and reached for the evidence with one gloved hand. She and Jessica used to pass notes to each other every day by leaving them under their pillows when they were kids. Jessica had been here. She had proof. Holstering her weapon, Brie unfolding the note as fast as she could. Then froze. Confusion squeezed a tight fist around her heart as she read the note again. "Go home."

A soft electrical hiss reached her ears a split second before the explosion threw her back into the bookcase. Pain radiated out from her spine and into her skull. Unbearable heat singed over the exposed skin along her neck and face as she hit the floor. She used every ounce of strength to bring her head up, blackness closing in around the edges of her vision. Roman. Where was Roman? The entire room had caught fire, flames consuming everything in its path. Her neck strained to hold her head up as a wave of dizziness dragged her under. Conscious. She had to stay conscious. Had to find her partner… "Roman."

Darkness closed in.

CHAPTER EIGHTEEN

Son of a bitch. His lungs suctioned a combination of smoke and oxygen. The blast had shot him into the opposite wall and deposited him face-first on the floor. A crack of fire burst through his system as he pulled his hands center mass, grip still around his weapon. Heat licked at the back of his neck. Roman forced himself to straighten, a growl vibrating through him. His vision cleared in small increments, but he couldn't wait for his head to catch up. A controlled explosion had ripped through the southern wall of the cabin, but the fire spreading inward wouldn't stop until it'd consumed everything in its path. He'd been right. The killer had rigged the place, and he and Brie had walked right into the trap.

A head of dusty short brown hair stood out from the mess of debris inside what used to be the padlocked room. Shit. She'd been directly in the blast's path. Panic consumed him as he shoved away from the wall and lunged toward her. Rolling Brie onto her back, he set his ear against her mouth. Barely breathing. "Hold on, baby."

Scooping her into his arms, Roman hiked her close to his chest to protect her from the tendrils of fire climbing the walls. The explosion had blown a hole in the outside wall of the cabin, but the addition of oxygen only fed the flames more. He'd have to get her out another way.

Broken glass, hunks of wood, and pain all along the right side of his body where he'd slammed into the wall threatened to bring him down, but he wouldn't stop. Not until he got Brie to safety. Sweat dripped into his eyes as bubbles of flames rolled across the ceiling of the hallway above him. The room of trophies had been destroyed, nothing but a wall of orange and yellow filling its place. A wooden beam dislodged from the ceiling, and Roman pulled back to avoid the flecks of fiery ash spewing into the air. Damn it. Every wall, every window, every chance of escape had been demolished in the explosion and resulting fire. Turning back the way they'd come, Roman ignored the exhausted burn in his muscles from Brie's added weight. And froze as he caught sight of the stairs.

There was only one way out of the basement.

He shifted Brie into a fireman's hold over his right shoulder, his body screaming for release, and latched onto the unfinished handrail bolted into the wall. One wrong step. One wrong decision. That was all it would take, and he'd lose her forever.

Not going to happen.

Brie's pain-filled moan barely registered over the crackling and pop of flames closing in faster than he thought possible. No telling if the explosion had damaged the structural integrity of the stairs, but he had to move. Now. "Stay with me, Brie. We're almost there."

He tested the first step, then the next. He moved in a steady rhythm, his lungs struggling for oxygen as black smoke bellowed at the top of the stairway. He'd get her out of the house. There were no other options. Not for him. Not for the innocent women whose lives were destroyed by the Dream Catcher. Coughs wracked through his chest as he attempted to filter thick air by tugging his shirt collar over his mouth and nose. He'd already lost one partner. Roman wasn't about to lose another.

A deep groan reverberated through the walls, and the hairs on the back of his neck stood on end. There'd been too many missions in HRT where he hadn't listened to his instincts. This wouldn't be one of those times. Not with Brie's life at risk. Slowing his pace, he struggled to catch his breath. The fire had reached the bottom of the stairs. There was no going back.

A second explosion rocked him off balance, his shoulder slamming into the opposite wall. Roman's grip on Brie faltered, and she slid out of his grasp. The stairs buckled right from under him. His stomach shot into his throat as they fell deeper into the inferno, and he hit the ground hard. The impact shuddered through him. Dust clogged his airway, flames already spreading at the base of the stairs above as he rolled onto his back. Shit. Pain ricocheted through the base of his school as he army-crawled toward his partner. Light filtered through the hole above, highlighting the smoke-smudged angles of her face. He smoothed her hair back from her face. "Brie."

No answer.

Using every last bit of strength he had left, Roman shoved off the floor, stretching out of one hand, but the hole they'd fallen through was still too high. Damn it. They were trapped. He shrugged out of his damp suit jacket and used it to cover Brie's mouth as smoke slid through the cracks in the stairs. No telling how many more explosions the Dream Catcher had rigged, or if it was even the killer who'd lured them into this hellhole, but he wasn't going to let Brie die here. Not today. They'd landed on a concrete pad, which wouldn't catch fire by itself without an accelerant, but the stairs had already started burning to ash less than three feet away. The entire house could collapse on them at any moment. His head throbbed like a jackhammer, his balance still unsteady, but he'd get them out of here. Even if he had to sacrifice himself to do it.

"Roman?" Her voice washed through him a before wide eyes settled on him, an angel staring hell in the face. She rolled onto her side as he closed in, a set of dry coughs arcing her back off the cement. She tugged his jacket off her face. "The list of people I want to punch in the face is getting way too long."

"Remind me never to get on your bad side." He slid one hand beneath her shoulders to help her sit up. Dried blood pooled around the stitches at her temple, kicking his blood pressure into dangerous territory. Knocked unconscious, nearly blown to pieces, trapped beneath the stairs of a murderer's hideout. How was it possible the woman was still making jokes? Roman swiped the blood from her temple with the pad of his thumb. Hell, he loved that about her.

"I'm not ready to die here." Her fingertips dug into his forearm as he got her to her feet. Brie craned her neck up, studying the hole in the stairs above. Orange pulses of light reflected in her gaze as she maneuvered to the opposite side of the small space. She brushed her palms over the foundation wall. Flames licked at the opening in the stairs, specs of ember drifting down around them. Another groan echoed through the walls. The support beams were starting to buckle. Another minute—maybe two—and the entire house would crumble on top of them. Her outline disappeared in a wall of shadow. "Over here."

His heart pounded hard behind his ears. "What do you have?"

"Part of the foundation was weakened by the blast. There's a chunk missing from the wall." A hand wrapped around his, tugging him into the darkness. He couldn't see worth a damn, both of their flashlights lost to the fire, but with her fingers intertwined with his, he didn't have to. His other senses engaged as she spread her palm over the back of his hand and pressed it to cold cement. The battle between changing temperatures and her touch wound his insides tight, but he couldn't focus on that right now. She smoothed his hand over a large crack in the wall, and a rush of cool air and the barest hint of rain filled his lungs. The foundations on houses like this were at least a foot and a half deep, but if the structure had been damaged bad enough, they had a chance.

"I need something to break down the concrete. Anything sturdy enough." Wood creaked as fire engulfed the stairs over their heads then crashed to the floor. Roman hunched to avoid the embers kicking up around them. The fire was closing in, and there was nothing he could do to stop it. Roman positioned himself between Brie and the flames as she searched the small space.

A metallic tang echoed off cement, loud in his ears, and a moment later she placed something heavy in his grip. "Will this work? I unscrewed it from the plumbing over there."

"It's perfect." Roman smoothed his hands over the length copper pipe. "Stand back. I'm getting us the hell out of here."

He swung the pipe as hard and as fast as he could at the weakened foundation. Chucks of cement crumbled to the floor, but the heat intensifying at his back said he had to work faster. Sweat dripped into his eyes, the ricochet of metal on concrete vibrating down into bone. His fingers slipped against metal, aching, but he couldn't stop because he was tired. Their lives depended on it. More than a dozen hits to the crack in the wall opened an escape from the west side of the house, and he picked up the pace. The muscles in his arms and back screamed for relief, but faster than he thought possible, a rush of cold, wet air rushed against his overheated skin.

"Roman, hurry." Fear tainted his name on her lips.

Another beam slammed into the floor less than two feet away from his feet, then pain splintered at one ankle. Roman tossed the pipe to the ground, stamping out the flames climbing up his slacks, and reached for his partner. He pushed her through the opening. "Go!"

Brie's outline disappeared into clouded shadow as she tumbled forward.

The fire had spread too fast. He had to go now. Squeezing inside the hole he'd created, he ignored the sensation of chunks of gravel digging into his palms and knees. Pain ripped through his side as a piece of twisted rebar tore through his shirt and caught skin. The smell of atmosphere intensified, drowning the overwhelming nausea of smoke, as rain pelted his face and neck. Heat bled from his muscles as he hit the muddy ground, but there wasn't time to rest.

Familiar hands helped him to his feet, pushing him forward. Brie.

Positioning one arm at her lower back, he shouldered her weight and pumped his legs as hard as he could. They ran together, each holding the other upright. His lungs burned, his head throbbed, and spiderwebs of black had started ringing his vision, but they couldn't stop. Not until they were clear of—

A third explosion discharged from behind. The shockwave blasted them forward, and they went down hard. Shit. His ears rang, vision blurry. How many bombs had the bastard rigged? Thick mud and loose rocks scraped over the exposed skin on one side of his face, but he only strengthened his hold on Brie as he heaved his upper body off the ground. A cloud of smoke and fire mushroomed above what used to be Kirk Marshall's cabin, chunks of wood, dirt, and water spewing into the tree line.

Her heavy breathing broke through the ringing in his ears as Brie straightened to a sitting position. Wiping a mud, smoke, and blood from her face with the back of her hand, she stared at what was left of the Dream Catcher's hideout. "It's gone. All the evidence... Everything's just...gone."

And their suspect with it.

"If Haynes and the rest of the team didn't know where we were before, they do now." Roman wiped at his face with the back of his forearm, searching the trees around them. Kirk Marshall had lured them into a trap. He'd rigged those explosions to blow most likely with the touch of a button from a safe distance. No telling where he was now. If the son of a bitch was smart, he'd keep running. Trying to take Roman out, that was just survival. But targeting Brie? That was a mistake. He dug his fingernails into the ground to keep the blaze in his veins under control. "CSU will go through whatever's left of the house after they get the fire under control. There might still be a chance something survived the fire."

"This survived." Smudges of smoke and mud intensified the exhaustion in her expression as she pulled a piece of paper from her jacket. "In that padlocked room, there was a mattress in the middle of the floor, like someone had been sleeping there. I found this stuffed under the pillow."

Roman unfolded the note. "'Go home.'"

"She was there, Roman. Jessica was locked in that room, but for some reason, she doesn't want me to be the one to find her." Rain mixed with the blood and dirt caked to her angelic features, forging tracks down her smooth skin. She shifted her attention to the inferno a hundred feet away. "She was trying to warn me, but after what just happened, I'm not ready to back down. Are you?"

Hell, there'd been too many times in the last two hours he could've lost her, and the pressure that'd been building since she'd entered that room finally released from behind his sternum. They'd survived. Together. He wasn't ready to give that up yet. Pushing to his feet, he offered her his hand. Callused fingers slid across her palm as she took it and straightened. "We're just getting started."

Short hair slid over her face as she closed the distance between them. Setting her hand over his heart, she stared up into his eyes. "Thank you. For what you did back—"

The crack of a gunshot echoed off the trees a split second before the bullet ripped through her shoulder. Brie lurched forward.

Then another bullet hit home.

CHAPTER NINETEEN

Brie fell into him, her gasp dying as she fisted Roman's shirt to stay upright, but a second shot brought him down with her. They hit the ground, pain, blood, and adrenaline overwhelming any control she'd regained after escaping from the inferno behind them. The Dream Catcher. He must've been waiting in the tree line to see if they'd escaped the fire then positioned himself to finish the job. She couldn't breathe. Couldn't think. She shook her partner as she scanned the trees. The weight of the killer's crosshairs shooting warning through her system. "Roman, we have to find cover." No answer. She shook him harder. "Roman."

"Get out of here." His voice strangled past his lips, his breathing heavy and unsteady. Blood spread through his fingers pressed against his gut as pelting rain fought to wash it away. He used his free hand to unholster his weapon. "Go. I'll slow him down."

"I'm not leaving you." She clamped her uninjured hand over his. No. No, no, no, no. Damn it. They had to get out of here. Find cover. Wait for backup. Their suspect had most likely mapped and memorized every tree and trail in the area. She took a deep breath, forcing the pain in her shoulder to the back of her mind. But so had she. Brie ground her back teeth, his guttural groan forever imprinted in her brain. "Come on. Get up."

The overpowering bombardment of rain made it impossible to hear if the shooter was closing in, but she wasn't going to wait around to find out and give him the chance to finish what he'd started. She suppressed the scream of agony in her throat as she hauled him to his feet, hand pressing against the gunshot wound above his naval. Blood leaked from between her fingers. The faster they moved, the harder his heart pumped, the faster he'd bleed out, but they didn't have any other choice. He'd saved her life back in that cabin. She wasn't giving up on him now.

"Lean on me." Every shaky inhale in her ears rocketed her heart into her throat. There was a first aid kit in the car. If she could get them to the SUV or the kit to him, she could stop the bleeding until he got the medical help he needed. But they'd need to find cover first. Nearly every cabin around Hamlin Lake had a boat house on the property. If they could get to one of them, Roman might have a chance of surviving the night. Then again, the shooter had already planned every step from the beginning. He might have already anticipated her plan. Brie shook her head, water trailing over her nose and lips as she pushed them deeper into the woods. They had to take the risk.

Roman's feet dragged in the mud as they edged closer to the lake's shore, pulling her down, but she only pushed herself harder. The heat from the fire bled into cold as her body shook from exertion and blood loss. He was barely conscious, and her mouth dried despite the rain trailing across her face and past her lips. If he took them down, she wasn't sure she had the strength to get back up. The lake curved to the southern end, a light blue boathouse shadowed in a thick ring of trees ahead. A burst of relief washed through her, but she wouldn't give into it yet. Not until they were safely locked inside. "Just a little bit farther. Stay with me."

His legs dropped out from under him and wrenched Brie to the ground. She slammed into a nearby tree trying to keep him upright, the breath knocked from her lungs. One second. Two. Air rushed down her throat, but the pressure didn't ebb. Her partner had lost consciousness, leaving her to fight alone. She had to get up. Had to get them to the boathouse. Blood combined with rain down her blazer, and she peeled back the fabric as agony ripped through her shoulder. No time to inspect the wound. Mud and water worked into her shoes, and she kicked them off as she reached for her partner. They'd only slow her down. A branch snapped from somewhere in the tree line, hiking her blood pressure higher. Fisting his shirt in her hands, she used every last ounce of strength she had to pull him into her. "Roman, come on. Wake up." She shoved to her bare feet and dragged him across the ground with everything she had left. Her muscles burned, her head and back ached, her shoulder had a bullet lodged inside of it, and her injured foot itched. But she wouldn't give up. She'd survived a killer on her own once. She'd do it again. "Come on!"

Soft grass and dirt gave way to planks of wood as she hauled Roman across the boathouse dock. His heels caught on the ridges, bouncing with each step they took. Twenty feet. Fifteen. Almost there. Water kicked up alongside the dock with added gusts of wind, her feet slipping on the old wood.

Another gunshot exploded from the trees, whipping past her ear, and she released her partner as she ducked. Fragments of wood and paint burst from the boathouse doorframe. She caught movement from the bushes slightly to the left as she kicked the wooded door open and dragged Roman the rest of the way inside. Relief coursed through her as she paused to catch her breath. Taking a knee beside her partner's head, she unholstered her weapon. And waited, staring at the door. The mad thunder of her heartbeat pulsed behind her ears, every inch of her body bruised and aching. Inhale. Exhale. She tightened her grip around the gun in an attempt to control the shaking wracking through her limbs. Tension and anxiety clawed through her before she had the guts to release the breath she'd been holding for fear of giving away their position. The killer knew she'd found cover in the boathouse. Now it was a matter of waiting until backup arrived. Reaching down, she gauged Roman's pulse at the base of his neck. Steady. For now. "It's going to be okay. The team is on their way."

She unpocketed her phone, wiping mud and water from the screen, but dendric cracks spidered across the glass. Mostly likely from the initial explosion. Damn it. Any chance of Haynes and the rest of the team triangulating their signal had been destroyed with the glass. Brie tossed the device. Wouldn't do them a damn bit of good now. There were no windows in the small empty shack. No way to tell where the threat would come from. Bright red stickers caught her attention against one wall. A first aid kit. Her knees popped as she treaded across the shed as quietly and slowly as possible, her feet on fire from the trek through the woods. Rope, a life preserver, cleaning supplies. No sign of food or fresh water, but the first aid kit would help. Gun in one hand, she lifted the kit from the hook on the wall, eyes on the main door as she maneuvered backwards toward Roman.

A hand clamped over her mouth, and she automatically bent at the knees and twisted her head away, raising the gun. A man stood at the edge of the boat bay, dripping wet, only dark eyes visible from beneath the ski mask. Damn it. He must've swam into the bay. "I've missed you, Briohny."

That voice. *His* voice. Nausea churned in her gut. The Dream Catcher, the man who'd taken her all those years ago had found her. She'd worried she'd never be able to identify the shadow who'd come into her room that night, but she remembered that voice, so clearly, as though her abduction had just happened. And he was standing between her and Roman. "Where is my sister?"

"You stabbed me the night you ran away," he said. "Time to return the favor."

Unfiltered rage exploded throughout her system. Brie pulled the trigger. Once. Twice. Nothing happened. She discarded the first aid kit at her feet and threw the weapon as hard as she could at her attacker. And missed.

He lunged. Her assailant went in low, aiming his shoulder right into her gut and hefted her off the floor. The boathouse blurred in her vision as he slammed her back against one wall, the entire shed creaking with the impact. A hook jabbed below her spine, but she shut down the scream working up her throat as she felt for a weapon she could use. Jamming one elbow into the back of his neck as hard as she could, she slumped to the floor as he fell back. Her fingers slid against the smooth surface of a small, handheld fire extinguisher. She pushed to her feet and swung as hard as she could. "Where is she!"

He blocked the hit with his forearm then ripped the device from her hands. Stinging pain rippled up through her fingers a split second before his backhand connected with the right side of her face.

She hit the ground hard, a wave of dizziness closing in, but she forced herself to breathe through her nose to keep control.

A glint of soft lighting reflected off the gun he pulled from his back waistband. Was it the same gun he'd used to put a bullet in her shoulder? The same one that'd put Roman's life at risk? "I've been waiting a long time for this."

"You failed to kill me then. You won't get the chance to kill me know." Brie rushed forward. She dodged his sweeping attempt to aim, a bullet whizzing centimeters past her face and wrapped her hand around his forearm to gain the upper hand. Shooting her knuckles into his face, she kept hold of him when he stumbled back and went for the gun.

"I don't want to kill you. We have too much catching up to do." Her attacker hauled a knee into her stomach, eliciting a strong gasp from her lungs. He latched onto her blazer, bringing her in close as the barrel of the gun pressed against the bullet wound in her shoulder. Pain lightninged down her arm, but she wouldn't give him the satisfaction of another scream. His mouth moved beneath the black mask as she tried to catch her breath. "But your partner on the other hand, I don't have much use for him."

He pushed her off balance.

She knocked back into the boathouse door, falling through the doorjamb, and smacked her head against the dock. Rain fell into her eyes, blocking her vision, as his outline stalked toward her. Brie exhaled hard through the pain. No. Roman wouldn't be the Dream Catcher's next victim. She wouldn't let him. Rolling onto her stomach, she locked her jaw against the pain in her shoulder and straightened, hands raised for the next fight.

"You always were a fighter. I could tell the moment I saw you.

Can't say the same for Jessica. Do you want to know how many times she begged for you to rescue her?" Droplets of water slipped from the gun tip as he approached, his voice barely registering over the pounding at the base of her skull. "Thousands. She just couldn't understand why you'd left her there to die. To be tortured. To be forgotten by the one person who could've saved her."

He was trying to get into her head, manipulate her. Her attacker raised the gun.

"No." She shot forward again, striking her forearm down on top of his, and threw another punch. Bone met the flesh on the left side of his face, the gun falling to the dock with a sharp thud. Her momentum carried her behind him, but she couldn't turn fast enough to avoid the right hook that connected with her mouth. Her eyes watered, but she somehow managed to keep her balance despite the pain and exhaustion tunneling deep into her bones. She stumbled back, the taste of salt and copper heavy on her tongue as her knees weakened. She'd lost too much blood. Knocked into unconsciousness at the hospital, miraculously survived an explosion, now a gunshot wound. How much was her body expected to endure before it gave up altogether? Her breathing strained. She wavered on her feet, but Brie wouldn't go down. Not without putting an end to the killing. "You abducted all those women, left copies of my sister's necklace at their crime scenes, just to get my attention, to let me know you still had her."

"Took you a while though, didn't it?" No hint of an accent, nothing to confirm Kirk Marshall's identity. The man in the mask shrugged. "I was taking a chance those first few cases would get assigned to another missing persons agent, but I knew the moment you saw one of those necklaces, you'd take the bait. You and I, we'll always be unfinished business."

"Your plan failed. I'm still alive." She had to stall, give the team a chance to locate them. Keep the son of a bitch away from Roman. Her gaze flickered to the boathouse door behind her attacker, and a hint of satisfaction pulled at one corner of her mouth. His plan had failed. "You didn't count on my partner."

"And you didn't count on mine," he said.

Stinging pain pinched at the base of her neck. Brie reached back, her fingers colliding with a thin needle as the world tilted on its axis. She hit the dock, unable to force her body to obey her brain's commands, and rolled onto her back.

"I made you into the woman you are, Briohny." His shadowed outline hovered above her, his eyes crinkling at the edges as though he were smiling beneath that damn mask. "And look at you now."

She blinked to clear her head. Whatever she'd been injected with had already spread. She couldn't move. Couldn't think. Had he been…stalling her…too? "Pheno…pheno…"

"Don't worry. The effects aren't permanent." A second outline slid into her peripheral vision as the Dream Catcher crouched beside her, but the darkness had already started closing in. The…partner. Kirk Marshall tucked a piece of hair behind her ear, but she couldn't pull away. "Then again, maybe you're not the fighter I thought you were after all."

CHAPTER TWENTY

ROMAN WAS A MAN OF HIS WORD. SOMEONE WAS ABOUT TO DIE.

He secured a hand over the bullet wound and shot out of the boathouse onto the dock. The son of a bitch who'd shot him—shot Brie—would pay. Dizziness gripped him hard, and he sank to his knees, pulling in deep breaths to counteract the mess in his head. Rain pelted the surface of the lake and his shoulders as he pushed himself to his feet and chanced a step forward. Then another. "Brie!"

He listened for movement, every cell in his body battle ready as he smoothed his thumb over the weapon in his hand. She wouldn't have left her gun behind. Not voluntarily. He kept the pressure against the hole in his gut as tight as he could. Blood seeped from between his fingers, but not enough to make him think the bullet had nicked an artery. He'd live, which was more than he could say for the bastard who'd taken his partner from him.

The last thing he remembered… She'd hauled him into the tree line.

The boathouse door slammed back against the structure, off one of its hinges, hiking his senses into overdrive. How she'd gotten him here with a bullet in her shoulder, he'd never know. The woman had always kept a controlled strength inside of her but dragging his ass to safety couldn't have been easy. Even if she hadn't been injured. And now she was out there with a killer. Alone. Injured. Roman curled his free hand into a fist. "I'm coming for you, baby."

The rain made it nearly impossible to trace the killer's steps, but nothing would stop him from finding Brie. Two lines of deep tracks had been gouged into the mud at the end of the dock, heading west, back toward the main road. Had they dragged her out of here? He followed the pattern under the canopy of trees until it disappeared in a small clearing. Too many options. One wrong choice could mean he'd only ever see her if the FBI recovered her body. The scent of smoke stained the air, black plumes still rising from the fire to the north. They'd been through hell the last three days, ever since she'd pulled that evidence bag with her sister's necklace from Ashlee Carr's crime scene. He hadn't come this far to lose her now. Not when she'd just started to trust him.

The operator he'd been trained to become in his years with hostage rescue surged to the surface. He had to get control of the bleeding in his side. There'd been a first aid kit back in the boathouse, but he couldn't go back now. Brie didn't have that kind of time. The next best thing would have to do. He aimed her weapon at the ground and compressed the trigger. Nothing happened. The explosion could've damaged or warped the firing pin. Unholstering his, he pulled the trigger, the explosion of gunfire loud in his ears. He had to act fast.

Wrenching his shirt higher up his torso, he knelt beside the discharged bullet then extracted it from the mud as quickly as possible. Pain burned through his fingertips, but the bullet was already cooling. Tendrils of steam rose off the metal before he pressed the steel to the wound. Searing pain rippled through him as the heat cauterized the wound, and he nearly collapsed face first. His lungs heaved to keep up with his racing heart beat as his fight or flight instincts kicked in. He'd done enough emergency field jobs like this to know the patch wouldn't hold permanently. He just needed it to work until he found Brie. The bullet fell from his bloodied fingers, disappearing in dead foliage and puddles of water. He holstered her weapon, keeping his in one hand. Replacing her weapon would only add to Brie's stress after he recovered her. She didn't need that added worry. And he would recover her. There was no other option. Not for him.

"Where are you, you son of a bitch?" The tracks had vanished here in the center of the clearing, but there was no way her attacker would've been able to disappear into the woods without leaving a trace. The gunshot had most likely given away his position, but Roman couldn't focus on that right now. Finding Brie. That was all that mattered. He scanned the ridges and valleys carved into the ground, studied the grouping of bushes at one end of the clearing. There. Two thin branches had snapped near the top of one native plant. Recently, telling from the slight green color of the wood. He caught sight of a splash of watery red on one of the leaves, then another a few feet ahead.

Blood.

Brie's? His gut knotted at the thought. At the rate the storm was going, the trail would be washed away in mere minutes. He had to move. Hints of red and orange sunrise bled through the clouds, lighting the way to the next bloody marker. He pushed himself harder. She was in danger, bleeding, and every agonizing second she wasn't with him tore at the edges of his heart. She'd lost everyone who'd she'd ever cared about. Her sister, her parents. She wasn't going to lose him. He'd find her, or he'd die trying.

Flashlights swept across the trail ahead, and Roman slowed, taking cover behind a large tree, and crouched. Evidence suggested the Dream Catcher had worked with a single partner, but he wasn't about to take any chances. Not with Brie's life at stake. The group of three armed men and one woman scoured the knee-high grass, movements slow to counteract the mud. The operative at the head of the group called back to the others, and Roman lightened his grip around his weapon as recognition flared. Backup had arrived. He stepped out from behind the tree, weapon where they could see it. "Special Agent Bradford coming out!"

Every gun and flashlight trained on his position before Aiden Holloway motioned for the team to lower their weapons. Shoulder-length blond hair had been pulled back in a low ponytail at the former interrogator's skull, rain soaking through the man's long-sleeved T-shirt and jeans. "Tell me you're not the one who blew up that cabin up ahead." Holloway slapped his hand into Roman's. "You are, aren't you?"

"It was him," Roman said. "The Dream Catcher. He rigged the place to blow when we were inside."

Behind Holloway, Special Agent Kinsley Luther maneuvered to Aiden's side as two Ludington PD officers expanded the perimeter at her signal. Dark hair had been pulled back under the thick knit hat that matched brown eyes. Long, lean muscle shifted beneath her wet clothing and a navy-blue FBI windbreaker that hit her mid-thigh, which attested to the countless hours the doc spent in the field with them rather than behind a desk. A combination of Dominican and Puerto Rican heritage added to the sharpness in her cheekbones and wide nose. He didn't know much about the team's psychologist and profiler other than she'd been injured in the line of duty the year before and had only come back to work in the last few months, but he was sure as hell grateful for her help all the same. "Where's Brie?"

"He took her. The son of a bitch took her." A surge of pain exploded through his side. The quick cauterization job wasn't holding, and his insides felt as though they were about to spill out through the wound, but he wouldn't stop. Not until Brie was in his arms again. Air struggled to clear his throat. "She's injured. I was following a trail of blood when I spotted you."

"Damn it. Listen up!" Humor bled from Aiden Holloway's voice as he shouted to the officers. "We're looking for blood, tracks, anything to pinpoint where our killer has taken one of our own. We don't stop looking until we find her. We clear?" Nods and confirmation came from both officers from each end of the perimeter as Holloway gripped a two-way radio. "Boss, we recovered Bradford. Agent McKinney is missing."

The last four words pierced through him, and his lungs spasmed for oxygen. Brie had spent years searching for missing persons, and now she'd become one of them. But the team wouldn't stop until they recovered her, and neither would he.

Static reached through the other side of the radio.

"You're injured." Kinsley nodded toward his gut, the weight of that all-knowing attention silently assessing the damage. Or did she see the desperation clawing through every bone in his body? He'd always kept his control in place. Hostage negotiations, counter terrorism missions, interrogations. But, right now, with Brie out there in the hands of a killer, he was that scared eleven-year-old kid he'd fought like hell to forget. The one who'd realized his mother couldn't protect him from his dad anymore before Roman had taken matters into his own hands. Was that what the doc saw? That he'd do anything to get Brie back? Even if it meant throwing away everything he'd worked so damn hard for? Kinsley reached into her windbreaker and extracted what looked like fresh gauze and a roll of medical tape. "Two minutes. Then you can get back out there and search for your partner."

He didn't have time to stop, but he wouldn't do Brie any good in this shape. He'd already lost too much blood and made too many mistakes. He couldn't risk distracting the search party when he needed everyone focused on finding his partner.

"Two minutes," he said.

The doc kept her word, and within half the time, Roman trudged through mud and grass, gun in hand with Kinsley at his side. The tape she'd circled around his abdominals held the gauze in place but wouldn't last long out here. The rain had lightened up in the last few minutes, but they'd already lost the trail of blood. He was back at square one. "The bastard has at least a fifteen-minute head start. He could've taken her anywhere."

"You know this killer better than anyone else on this team aside from your partner, Roman." Kinsley slowed her pace and reached her hand out, pulling him to a stop. Brown eyes locked on his, and everything inside of him raged. They couldn't stop moving. Couldn't stop searching for Brie. If he lost her… The doc raised her hands, palms facing him in surrender as though she could see the fire burning through his veins. "Slow down. Use your training. This case is personal for you, I get that. I want to find Brie as much as you do, but we can't search this entire park without real intel guiding us to this guy's location. Close your eyes."

What the hell was she talking about? "I told you everything—"

"I vetted your personnel file when your section chief suggested you transfer to missing persons. Every mission you carried out for HRT was a success because you're able to think like your target," she said. "You can get in his head. So think about where he would've taken her, why he's doing this, why he targeted *her*. Now close your damn eyes and tell me what he wants from Brie."

"Aren't you supposed to be the profiler?" Roman did as she asked. His heart pounded loud behind his ears. She was right. This assignment was personal for him, but that didn't change the fact he'd trained for this moment for years. Every mission, every extraction, every bullet he'd fired had prepared him for this. Roman forced himself to take a deep breath, to calm the storm inside. "She was the one who got away. He wants to finish what he started."

"That's a good start. Keep your eyes closed. What else?" Kinsley's practiced voice weaved calm and encouragement through his system.

His pulse slowed, the lack of sensory overload clearing his head for the first time in hours. He was an operator for crying out loud, but when it came to the woman who'd drilled past his defenses over the last few months, he'd lost his tightly held control. He took another cleansing breath, humidity and cold working through him. And he'd never fail Brie again.

"Where is he going, Agent Bradford?" Kinsley asked. "Where does this end for him?"

"His boat on Lake Michigan." His eyes shot open. He could see it so clearly in his mind from the picture framed in the basement before the first explosion. Ludington PD hadn't been able to recover the vessel at any of the marinas since Brie had put out the APB, but that was because the damn thing was probably still out in the middle of the lake. Damn it. He should've seen it before. "That's where this all started. That's where he'll want to finish it."

"Now that wasn't so hard, was it?" Special Agent Luther flashed a brilliant white smile as she unclipped her radio from her waistband and brought it to her mouth. "Haynes, we've got a possible location on Special Agent Brie McKinney. Our suspect is most likely headed for his boat. We need backup at every marina along the shore. *Now.* Agent Bradford and I are already in route."

Roman headed west through the trees at a fast jog. Hell yes, they were. And there was nothing that would stop him from bringing his partner home in time.

CHAPTER TWENTY-ONE

She tasted blood in her mouth.

Gut-wrenching nausea circled through her as the ground seemed to tilt and roll. She cracked her eyes, then slammed them shut at the brightness of a spotlight aimed directly at her seared her vision, her skull seemingly trying to separate from the rest of her body.

Brie pulled at the binds around her wrists at the small of her back and at her ankles. Her shoulders ached from the angle, her glutes numb. How long had she been unconscious? Another aftershock rolled beneath her, and her upper body pitched forward. Whatever Kirk Marshall's partner had injected her with still coursed through her, but, as far as she knew, phenobarbital didn't usually cause this kind of reaction. Had to be something else. Her fingernails scraped against the textured flooring as she battled to keep her balance.

Or she wasn't in the woods anymore.

The smell of gas burned in her nostrils. She forced her eyes open as deep-seated fear took root. Sunlight had started to bleed across the sky, barely visible through the clouds, but enough to outline the general shape of the vessel she'd been anchored to. No. No, no, no, no. Not here. Not the boat.

Movement registered to her left.

"I was worried my partner had given you too high a dose." Kirk Marshall's voice slid through her, raising goosebumps along her arms. Her soaked clothing clung to her as she tugged at the ties again, but the Dream Catcher had ensured Brie wouldn't get away this time. Her abductor wound a length of rope from thumb to elbow slowly, the ski mask still in place. "Did you really think you could hide from me?"

The sound of small waves lapping at the hull of the boat threatened to bring her back to that night. The cold. The fear. The desperation to get away. She sucked the side of her mouth between her teeth and bit down to keep her in the moment, her fingers rolling into fists. Brie wasn't a little girl anymore, and she wasn't helpless this time. Zip ties cut into the thin skin at her wrists. No way she'd be able to snap them using leverage with the bullet in her shoulder. She'd have to improvise, and stall for time. "I haven't been the one hiding."

"You're right." His dark laugh rolled on the air, and a shiver chased down her spine. Setting the newly wound rope on the cracked plastic seat cushion at the back of the boat, Kirk Marshall reached one hand up and pulled the black mask from his face. Gray-white hair surrounded a receding hair line, wrinkles around his eyes and mouth. His white beard glittered with evidence of the storm, although the rain had stopped sometime while she'd been unconscious. The file Roman had pulled from the database put the Dream Catcher in his fifties now, but muscular arms and legs shifted beneath his wet clothing. Not an average veterinarian as he'd forced everyone to believe but a fine-tuned killer. The son of a bitch had at least twenty years' worth of sins to answer for. So many lives. So much death. Distinct lines furrowed across his forehead as he closed the short space between them. Her attacker tossed the mask beside her boots. "I have been hiding, but now you see me for who I really am, Briohny. The man who's going to finish what he started all those years ago." He crouched beside her, elbows resting on his knees, as he studied her from forehead to chin. Reaching out, he skimmed his knuckles down her jawline. "Joining the FBI was supposed to keep you safe, but you just couldn't move on, could you? You're one of very few who've ever gotten away from me, and you wanted to know why you. Why not Jessica or all those other girls I've brought onto this boat? You wanted to know what made you so special."

She set her head back against the side of the boat in an attempt to avoid his touch, but with the open lake surrounding them there was nowhere to go as he clamped his fingers around her chin. A pinch dug into the base of her skull, behind her right ear. One of her bobbi-pins holding back the shorter length of her hair. Brie didn't have an answer for him. She didn't know why she'd escaped and Jessica hadn't other than the drug he'd injected her with hadn't reacted the same way in her veins as it had in her sister's. Didn't know why her parents weren't happy with the fact she'd come home and abandoned her to grow up alone and controlled by the black hole where her heart used to be. But she wasn't alone anymore. The minute Roman had been assigned as her partner, that void had started to hurt less and less. And now he was out there with a bullet in his gut. Because of her. "What did you do with my partner?"

"I'd be more concerned with yourself if I were you." Kirk Marshall lowered his hand and straightened. Turning his back to her, he hefted one of the cushioned seat lids open and extracted a small duffle bag from below. In two breaths, he pulled a blade from the depths, sunrise gleaming off polished steel. "We've got a lot of catching up to do."

No. She needed more time. Brie rubbed the back of her head against the boat, trying to dislodge the bobbi-pin in her hair. It slid against her scalp, but the wax tip caught on a few strands. Damn it. Tugging at the zip ties around her ankles, she tested the strength of the plastic. Too tight. Her awareness of the Dream Catcher rocketed to an all-time high as he pressed the tip of the blade into his fingertip and took a single step toward her. The women he'd killed to get her attention had been tormented with a combination of shallow and deep lacerations all over their bodies. According to the M.E., they'd been tortured with a blade similar to the one in his hand. She'd worked dozens of missing persons cases for the bureau. Investigated a handful of victims who hadn't gotten the chance to come home. Men, women, children of all ages, ethnicities, and locations, but they all had an element in common. The perpetrators. Every single one of them believed themselves to be the hero of their own story. She just had to get Kirk Marshall to tell his. Pressing her head against the boat one last time, she strained to untangle the bobbi-pin from her hair. The small accessory fell to the boat's deck with a soft click, and Brie scooped it into her palm before her abductor noticed. "You killed four women to get my attention. Don't I deserve to know why? Why me? Why Jessica?"

Crouching in front of her once again, he narrowed his eyes on her, and she clenched her fingers around the bobbi-pin. "Did you ever wonder how I was able to stay below your agency's radar? How so many girls went missing all over the state without anyone noticing the pattern?" He leaned into her, setting the blade's edge against her cheek. "I've spent the last twenty years getting to know my enemies. The parents of every girl I took, the officers assigned to various police departments around the state. Even the agents of the FBI's missing persons division. I know you and the way you like to work your cases, Special Agent McKinney. So believe me when I tell you, your stall tactic won't work, but don't worry. We're going to have plenty of time together. At least until I'm finished with you."

Brie fought the urge to close her eyes as cold tunneled into the muscles of her face from the smooth edge of the knife. She pried the wax tip of the bobbi-pin from the main accessory with her thumbnail behind her back then straightened the metal as much as she could with one hand. "You don't know anything about me."

"I made you into the woman you are today, little girl. I made you stronger. None of those other girls had the fight that you do." He trailed the tip of the blade down her throat. "Without me, you'd be nothing, a nobody."

"You took everything from me." Fire simmered beneath her skin, counteracting the cold soaking through her clothing. Brie inserted the exposed tip of the bobbi-pin between the interlocking ratchet and teeth of the zip ties and pulled her wrists apart. Pain bolted down her shoulder and into her hand, but the ties gave way enough to slip her hands free. "And little girls don't stay little forever."

She hiked her knees into her chest and kicked him square in the gut as hard as she could. The zip ties fell from her wrists, and she folded her upper body forward, bobbi-pin in hand. The knife skidded across the boat deck as the Dream Catcher struggled to his feet. She inserted the end of the bobbi-pin into the locking mechanism, but she wasn't quick enough to loosen the ties around her feet. Faster than she thought possible, her attacker wrapped his fingers around the blade's grip and swung. The tip sliced through her clothing as Kirk Marshall lunged at her to gain control, and she collapsed back to the deck.

The accessory fell from her hand, sliding across the wet, textured deck, out of reach. Twisting toward the seat at the back of the boat, she grabbed the rope he'd wound a few minutes before, throwing it at him as hard as she could. He stumbled back against the side of the vessel, and Brie shot her hand out to grab the bobbi-pin. The zip tie loosened with some leverage from her boots, and she pushed to her feet as the killer straightened. She rushed forward, tucking her shoulder into his ribs just as he'd done to her in the boat house, and lifted him off his feet with her momentum. The boat rocked as she slammed him against the side. He recovered quickly, throwing an elbow into the back of her neck. A gasp escaped from between her lips as agony shot down her spine. She barely dodged the swipe of the blade mere centimeters from her face, then took a step forward and applied pressure to his elbow between both of her forearms.

The sickening crunch of bone and his scream echoed off the water around them as she swung him as hard as she could to the opposite side of the vessel. He hit the seat where the rope had been and fell to the deck, blade sliding into the galley below. His heavy breathing registered over the loud pound off her heart in her head. He swung a fist up, aimed directly at her face, but a kick to the back of his knee threw him off balance. She rammed her knee into his kidney, and Kirk Marshall collapsed to the deck, out of breath. Out of fight. Her lungs worked overtime to keep up with the race of her pulse.

"This isn't over, Briohny." His laugh shook through him as he spat a mouthful of blood onto the deck of his prized boat. "The nightmares that have kept you up all those nights? They're just getting started."

"As long as I'm still standing, so are yours." Brie put everything she had into the downward right hook as the man who'd abducted her all those years ago turned his face to smile up at her. The hit reverberated up her arm and into her injured shoulder, and she clamped her throbbing hand to the wound as he collapsed, unconscious, at her feet. Stumbling back, she exhaled as a surge of exhaustion ripped through her. The back of her knees hit one of the boat's cushioned seats, and she fell back. It was over. It was finally over. Kirk Marshall, the Dream Catcher, would never hurt another woman or girl again. Pent up tears burned in her eyes, but she didn't move to wipe them away as the boat swayed from side to side.

Roman. She had to get to Roman. He'd been shot. But she couldn't take the risk of crossing lake. The bullet in her shoulder wouldn't let her swim for it. Crystalized air particles formed in front of her mouth. She didn't have much time. Kirk Marshall wouldn't stay unconscious for long. She swiped the back of her hand beneath her nose and inhaled sharply to regain composure. The boat's radio. Pushing one foot in front of the other, she ignored the sharp jabs of pain lightning up her legs as she scooped the length of rope her attacker had wound earlier from the deck. It'd tangled during the fight but would hold the Dream Catcher until the team arrived.

She pinched the boat's VHF radio in her grip, the rope in her free hand. Hitting the distress button, she cleared the blood from her mouth and compressed the main switch to open the channel. "Mayday, mayday, mayday. This is Special Agent Brie McKinney in need of assist—"

Movement registered in her peripheral vision a split second before her attacker lunged. She spun toward him, dropping the rope and radio, hands out. She hit the deck, the weight of his body on her chest. His hands gripped her throat, cutting off her air supply as her training kicked in. She shot her hand across her body, wrapped her fingers around his wrist, repositioned one foot outside his shin, and bucked her hips upward, but he was too strong, too heavy, and nothing she did made him budge. His growl cut through her struggled gasps.

"It was always going to end like this, Briohny," he said. "You were always mine."

The tip of a blade punctured the Dream Catcher's sternum from behind, blood blooming across his clothing. His mouth dropped open, his grip lightening on her throat. Kirk Marshall rolled to one side, eyes wide, revealing the woman sheltered on the galley staircase.

Brie's breath sawed in and out of her chest as familiar blue eyes stared back at her. Shock flared, and she pushed onto her elbows. "Jessica?"

CHAPTER TWENTY-TWO

Roman pumped his legs as hard as he could as the rescue team pushed the outboard boat to the lake's shore. His feet sank in the sand, but nothing—not even the bullet in his side—would stop him from getting to her. He plunged into icy water in order to help bring the vessel in. And froze.

Oxygen mask over her nose and mouth, Brie locked those mesmerizing blue-green eyes on him. Her hair was slicked back with water, clothing clinging to her small frame, blood spread across her white blouse. A medic was patching the wound in her shoulder as she huddled into the blanket draped over her the other half of her body. She blinked slowly at him, as if she were relieved to see him as much as he was to see her, and his heart kicked into overdrive. But the tension building beneath his sternum wouldn't release until she was in his arms.

Climbing aboard, Roman ignored the ache in his feet and side. One step. Two. Her gaze remained steady on him as he crouched in front of her. The weight of every officer in the boat and agent on their team's attention centered between his shoulder blades, including Special Agent in Charge Haynes's. He couldn't touch her despite the desperate need clawing through him. Couldn't hold her to chase back the newest shadows in her eyes, to make sure she was actually in front of him and this wasn't some horror-filled nightmare he couldn't wake up from. Not without putting both of their careers at risk. Soft exhales fogged the mask over her face, blocking his view of the origin of blood dried on her chin. The muscles in his jaw protested as he ground his back teeth. He lowered his voice. "Tell me you killed the son of a bitch. Tell me he suffered so I don't have to go out to that boat and make him pay for putting his hands on you."

"He's dead. Captain Hobbs is waiting for the medical examiner to take possession of the body." She closed her eyes as the medic secured fresh gauze and tape to her wound, then followed the EMT's movements as he maneuvered toward the back of the boat. Removing the oxygen, she revealed the laceration in her lip. She reached one hand for his, intertwining her fingers in a tight grasp, and every nerve ending in his body fired in response. Mud, ash, and blood crusted along her arms, her touch cold. Her gaze darted down his body, warming a path to his gut. "Roman, you've been shot. We need to get you—"

"Kinsley patched me up in the field. It'll hold until can get you checked out at the hospital. So I'm not going anywhere. I'm exactly where I need to be." He meant it. The pain, the blood, none of it mattered right now. She mattered. "What the hell happened out there?"

"I'll fill you in on all the details after someone gets me a cupcake," she said. "But long story short, we survived."

Her voice graveled, and he noted the slight bruising around the base of her throat. Wasn't enough the bastard had tried to blow her up, put a bullet in her shoulder, and taken her. He had to strangle her, too? His hand tightened around hers. If the son of a bitch wasn't already dead, Roman would've found a way to finish the job himself.

Hell, she was shaking. Screw what their team thought, what the officers and medics around them thought, screw the consequences. This woman had been through unimaginable hell in the last two hours, and he couldn't keep his distance any longer. He wrapped one arm around her, pulling her to the edge of her seat and into his chest. The tremors vibrated down the front of his body, but there was nothing he could do or say to stop them. Shock had to run its course. "Don't hold it in. I've got you, baby."

And there was no way in hell he'd ever let her go. Not this beautiful creature who—in only the span of three short months—had selflessly given him everything he hadn't realized he'd been missing. The support of a partner he could rely on, the trust he'd craved since he was a kid, but more importantly: hope.

"We did it, Roman. We found her." Brie dug chipped, red fingernails into his spine as EMTs shifted the tilt of the vessel. They buzzed around another victim he hadn't noticed until now, his entire focus on no one but his partner. "We found Jessica."

The woman's long, dark hair brushed past her shoulders. Full lips and a long nose gave way to familiar blue eyes and a distinct mole barely visible through the oxygen mask just above her mouth. Years of captivity had obviously weakened Jessica McKinney, the bones in her hands and cheeks more pronounced than a healthy woman of her size. Shades of bruising covered her arms and neck, but it was the darkness in her gaze as she locked on him that prickled his protective instincts. No woman should've had to have gone through what she did to survive. Ever.

He forced himself to relax his hold on Brie. "She's alive."

"She cut herself loose after I knocked the Dream Catcher's knife into the boat's galley. She didn't even recognize me, but I don't blame her. She's been through a lot. Kirk Marshall has kept her hostage for twenty years, tortured her, cut off one of her fingers to send to us." With a nod, Brie twisted her gaze back over her shoulder. Color had drained from her complexion, accentuating the shadows beneath her eyes and in her cheeks, and he wanted nothing more than to take her back to the beach house and help her forget the last three days of their investigation. "She killed him before he could kill me. I owe her my life."

"Then so do I." Jessica McKinney had risked her life to save the one person who'd become the center of his world. He'd find a way to repay her. Roman moved out of the way as EMTs helped Jessica from the boat, but he couldn't drop his hold from his partner. Not after everything they'd been through. Inquiry from his superior be damned. He offered Brie his hand as two ambulances backed toward the shore, the other members of the missing persons division waiting. "Come on. We need to get you checked out at the hospital."

She smoothed her fingertips over his palm, using the remnants of his strength to stand, but didn't release him when he led her to the back of the boat. "Roman, wait. Before we face the rest of the team, I need you to know something."

His heart threatened to beat out of his chest. Mere inches separated their bodies in the small space, waves rolling across the lake's surface rocking her closer. Right where he needed her. He couldn't lose her again. That much was clear from the moment he'd woken in that boathouse with a bullet in his gut and found her missing. He'd never felt more out of control—powerless—than he had searching those woods, being led by a trail of her blood. He'd trained to be in the center of the action, to control it, actively respond to it, but when it came to the woman standing in front of him, all of that had gone out the window. He should've been there, should've protected her better. And if he hadn't gotten to her in time... He'd have spent the rest of his life punishing himself and the bastard who'd taken her from him.

"I don't regret it. Kissing you." Her throat worked to swallow. Her attention cut to something behind him then back, and she released his hand. She hiked the blanket around her, flinching as she rolled her injured shoulder. "When he had me on that boat, and I thought for the second time in my life I was going to die, the only thing that got me through the fear was you. Knowing you were out here, injured, because of me...but it was more than that." Brie pushed a hand through her wet hair. "I was terrified of the idea I'd never get the chance of seeing if whatever this is between us could be something real, something worth fighting for." She took a deep, steadying breath, and focused on him. "But I won't ask you to risk your career—"

"You don't have to ask." He slipped his hands around her upper arms, careful of her injured shoulder. Awareness of her hummed in his veins, chased back the cold setting up permanent residence since they'd been assigned this case, and the possibility of being with her—

in every way—only intensified his desire. Her strength, commitment, loyalty to the victims they were assigned to find, her courage, and willingness to fight for what was right deepened the trust and admiration he held for her. Hell, he'd risk everything for her. "Nobody will take you from me again."

She pressed her hand over his heart, out of the line of sight of the rest of the team, an action he'd come to crave over the last few days. "Then I'll never have to add your name to the list of people I want to punch in the face."

A burst of laughter exploded from his chest. "Let's get that shoulder looked at."

"Do you think the ambulance would stop at the bakery on the way to the hospital?" she asked.

"One thing at a time, cupcake." Helping her down from the boat, he escorted Brie to the back doors of the empty ambulance, the weight of the team's attention on them every step they trudged through the sand. And someone else's. One glance to the other ambulance showed Jessica McKinney being attended to by a team of EMTs, but her gaze had steadied on Brie. Did the woman realize whose life she'd saved? That the sister who'd survived had stopped at nothing to bring the son of a bitch who'd taken them to justice? Pain ebbed at the edges of his wound as Roman helped her step into the ambulance and the rush of adrenaline drained from his system. He'd pushed himself too hard, the gauze and tape Kinsley had applied soaked through.

"Good work, Bradford. You and Agent McKinney saved a lot of lives today." Special Agent in Charge Mitchell Haynes stepped into his peripheral vision and slapped him between the shoulder blades. His boss hiked his suit jacket behind his hips, shoving his hands into his pockets. "Agents Holloway and Luther will keep on top of things here until Ludington PD has cleared the scene. You and McKinney can head back to Washington as soon as you've cleared your physicals." Haynes nodded, the dimple in his chin disappearing. "Well done."

"It's not over, sir." Not even close. "Kirk Marshall was working with a partner. We need to get USERT to scour the bottom of that lake for victims. There could be dozens more victims the bureau doesn't even know about, and any one of them might give us an identity on who he recruited." The assignment wasn't finished, and he wouldn't take the chance of the partner coming after Brie again to finish the job. "We owe it to the families and to any surviving victims who might be targeted."

"Including your partner." SAC Haynes studied Brie in the back of the ambulance as EMTs did their job then faced him again. "Coordinate the search, Agent Bradford, and keep me in the loop if you find anything useful that could give us an ID on the second half of our serial killer team."

Roman straightened, hand pressured against his side. "Yes, sir."

"I'll leave Holloway and Luther for support and send a USERT team as soon as I can." Haynes maneuvered around him toward two waiting black SUV's parked a dozen yards from shore, then slowed. "One more thing, Agent Bradford." He lowered his voice as Roman turned and got in close enough his cologne overwhelmed the smell of smoke, sweat, and dirt. "I'm going to ignore what I saw between you and Agent McKinney on that boat a few minutes ago to show my appreciation for the work you two have done the last few days. But know, once you cross that line, you're not just putting yours and your partner's life at risk, you endanger my entire team and the lives of every person we're searching for. I can't let that happen. Understand?"

Every muscle down his spine tightened, but Roman couldn't defend his actions. There was no defense. He'd forgotten the last decade of his training in an instant when he'd discovered Brie missing, and if it hadn't been for Agent Luther's help, he might never have known where the Dream Catcher had taken her until it was too late. Emotions led to mistakes, mistakes led to consequences. He shifted his gaze to Brie. He'd been willing to risk his career for a shot at filling the hollowness in his gut. But was he willing to risk her life? The team's? A victim's? Roman nodded. "Understood."

"Good." SAC Haynes trailed a path through the sand toward the SUVs, calling back over his shoulder. "Find the partner before anyone else gets hurt."

Roman hauled himself into the back of the ambulance and took a seat beside the stretcher. The weight of Brie's attention settled on his chest, but he couldn't assure her right now. Haynes was right. He'd let his emotions override his training and dictate his actions in the middle of an investigation, putting everyone on his team—including Brie—at risk.

The Dream Catcher's apprentice was still at large.

He leveled his gaze with Brie's. He'd already lost one partner. He wouldn't lose her.

CHAPTER TWENTY-THREE

TWENTY NEW STITCHES IN HER SHOULDER. A SLIGHT CONCUSSION FROM the explosion. Lacerated bottom lip. Over all, surviving the killer who'd abducted her—twice—could've ended far worse. Would have if it weren't for her partner. And her sister. She switched the brown paper bag in her free hand to the one in a sling and pushed her now clean hair out of her face, the fresh change of clothes far better than any cupcake she imagined. Maybe not a peanut butter chocolate cupcake but close. Muscles she hadn't used since Quantico ached, exhaustion slowing her steps, but Roman had messaged her he'd wrapped up with the doctor, and they weren't finished with their conversation.

They'd brought down the Dream Catcher and recovered her sister. Together. What that meant for the future—if they had one—she didn't know, but she had a sense of closure now and that had opened her eyes to the possibility. She'd guarded herself against emotional attachment for so long, but Roman had broken through her armor. They'd risked their lives for one another, trusted one another. Knowing he'd been out there, bleeding out from his injuries—alone—had driven her to the point she'd overpowered a killer with eighty pounds and six inches on her. Roman mattered to her. That had to count for something.

The hospital's halls buzzed with nurses, doctors, patients, and overhead pages as Brie counted off room numbers. She stopped in front of 201, lifting her uninjured arm to knock, but doubt crept from the back of her mind. Why hadn't he looked at her during the ambulance ride from the scene? What had Haynes and him been talking about while the EMTs rushed to evaluate her? Her hand wavered as two familiar voices reached her ears.

One glance across the hall—into her sister's hospital room—was all it took, and she just...froze.

Air struggled up her throat as the older couple standing at the foot of Jessica McKinney's bed hugged one another. Tears trailed down the woman's face, but she wiped them away quickly before shooting across the room to hug the daughter she hadn't seen in twenty years. The man kept his hand at his wife's back in support, in disbelief, before wrapping everybody in his massive arms. Brie had witnessed dozens of scenes exactly like this, played them over and over in her head, imagined what this day would be like so many times. It was supposed to be a joyous occasion, proof the missing were never really forgotten, but watching Ted and Glenda McKinney welcome their oldest daughter back from the dead widened the chasm that'd been cut through her heart.

"Didn't you say something about cupcakes?" he asked.

His voice slid through her, reaching past the hurt, the pain, the betrayal, and wrapped her in a secure bubble as though he'd pulled her to his chest. In six words, he'd replaced the despair with reassurance and a smile at one corner of her mouth. She hadn't realized he'd opened the door and turned to face him, trying to bury the slip into vulnerability. The bullet in his gut had been removed less than twelve hours ago, but her partner moved as though the injury hadn't even affected him. Dressed in a dark fitting Henley shirt and jeans, he was the epitome of tall, dark, and handsome in that moment, and her mouth watered in response. "It's Sunday. Nothing in this town is open on Sunday, including the bakery, so we'll have to make do with hospital cafeteria pudding." She lifted the brown paper bag between them then maneuvered her way inside the private room, shutting the door behind them. The sound of joyful crying only echoed in the back of her mind now. "The lady downstairs told me butterscotch is the best flavor…as she was eating chocolate, so I got both."

She unpacked the pudding cups and spoons from the bag, twisting to offer him one, and was suddenly pinned between the hard plastic railing of the bed and his body.

Roman set his index finger beneath her chin, skimming the pad of his thumb across her bottom lip, careful of the split, and her entire body heated. It was more than the physical attraction that drew her in. It was his strength, the way he spoke to her, each and every gesture that underscored the man beneath the hardness, the care he took when he touched her. Bandaging her foot after the chase on the cliffs, trying to get her out of the cabin when flames threatened to consume them both, the way he'd pushed himself to his physical limits despite the bullet wound in his side to find her. All of it had bulldozed through the wall she'd built to protect herself, but right now, she couldn't remember why she'd tried so hard to keep control when it came to him. Not when he looked at her as though she were the only woman in the entire world. *His* woman. "You okay?"

She battled the shiver climbing her spine at his touch, a habit designed to deny herself any kind of reaction that would lead to an emotional connection. But she couldn't deny whatever this was between them anymore. Not after everything they'd suffered together. "I am now."

And it was the truth. Having him close—alive—released an imaginative breath she hadn't realized she'd been holding all these years. Agents Holloway and Luther were still wrapping up the scene on the boat as far as she'd been informed, and SAC Haynes had flown back to Washington as soon as Kirk Marshall's body had been claimed by the medical examiner. There was no one here to stop her from closing the short distance between them. Nobody but them. She flicked one spoon upright in her hand between them. "Butterscotch or choc—"

He crushed his mouth to hers in a punishing, desperate kiss. Her bottom lip screamed in agony. She didn't care, dropping the pudding cups and spoons as he wrapped his arms at the small of her back and hauled her against his body. How he had the strength to stand let alone pull her into him after an injury like his, she had no idea. And it didn't matter. She fisted his shirt in her uninjured hand to keep in him place. The pain her shoulder ebbed, the rush of adrenaline from his kiss addictive. Her pulse rocketed into dangerous territory as he tugged her hips into his and lifted her onto the tip of her toes. Her fingers tingled to slide her hands up his shirt, to feel the ridges and valleys of muscle built into his abdominals. The longer he held her, the quicker the last twenty-four hours bled from her memory. When was the last time she'd let go of her legendary control and just felt?

Desire replaced pain, need replaced fear, until there was only Roman. Her Roman. They'd always had a connection, from the moment they'd been assigned their first case, there'd always been something about the shadows in his eyes. Like recognizing like, but this…this was different. In the span of three days, he'd somehow reached past her inner most insecurities and reminded her of a strength she'd forgotten existed. And she wanted more. Her entire body had caught fire with every stroke of his tongue in her mouth, hints of peppermint cooling her senses, but all too soon he pulled away, setting her flat on her feet.

His fingers dug through her slacks and into sore muscle. "I've wanted to do that since I saw you on that boat, but Haynes and the team—"

"I know. Me, too." She traced the edge of his mouth with her fingertip. Her nerve endings buzzed, every inch of her body finely tuned to his. Her breathing matched his in pace as though their bodies had been waiting for this exact moment. She smoothed her good hand over his shirt to counter the wrinkles her grip had ironed into the fabric, attention on the small broken thread above his heart. "The only thing I remember thinking out there was that I don't want to lose you. I'm standing here because you had my back when so many others have turned theirs on me, and there's nothing I could do or say to even the score. But I'm willing to try to hide whatever this is between us from brass. If you are."

"Brie..." He lightened his hold on her hips. He increased the space between them, taking any passion he'd generated inside her, and an immediate sense of withdrawal exploded through her system. Warning flared in her gut as an internal battle played across his features. He ran one hand through his dark hair. "When I discovered you'd gone missing, I went insane searching those woods. Everything I've trained for, every logical thought disappeared the second I'd realized the Dream Catcher had taken you." He lowered his hands to his sides, defeat plain in the shadows of his expression. "I put the entire operation and our team at risk because my feelings for you got in the way of the job. I failed you. I let my emotions get the better of me, and I'm sorry."

Ice worked through her. Her mouth dried as the gravity of his admission set in, and her stomach soured. She'd given him a piece of herself, something she hadn't dared share with anyone, and he was sorry? Her body grew heavy, her feet cemented to the bright linoleum floor as she fought to regain composure. A slight ringing echoed in her ears. "What are you saying?"

"I'm saying I'm never going to let that happen again. I can't. There are too many lives at risk. I made a mistake, but I will never fail you or the team again." Roman stepped into her, sliding his fingers up her arms and over the sling. He stared down at her, a new level of desire swirling in his dark gaze, and her invisible guard crumbled. "And I needed to know you wouldn't write this off as mistake an hour from now, a day from now, a year from now. I want you, but let me make one thing clear: you are more to me than just my partner."

A swirl of emotion exploded from behind her sternum. He wanted her? After everything she'd put him through? Brie swallowed the tightness in her throat.

"Then let me make one thing clear: you didn't fail me. I wouldn't be standing here if it weren't for you. You got us out of that cabin. You took a bullet so Kirk Marshall's second shot wouldn't hit me. My sister is across the hall—alive—because you pinpointed where the Dream Catcher was hiding." She parted a path through his beard with her chipped fingernails, and the breath rushed out of her as realization hit. "You're more to me than my partner, too, but brass will tear us apart if they find out. The bureau could transfer you again, fire one or both of us altogether," she said. "Are you sure I'm worth it?"

One breath. Two. Pressure built behind her ears as he stared down at her.

"Baby, you're more than worth it. You're everything." Roman trailed a scorching path down her arm through her blazer, leaning down to claim her mouth once again, this time more careful of the cut in her bottom lip. His clean, woodsy scent wrapped around her as he pressed her the back of her thighs against the end of the hospital bed. He growled into her mouth, the vibration burrowing deep into her core, and she couldn't suppress the laugh bubbling up her throat. It seemed he was the only one who could make her laugh like that. Rocking her off balance, he maneuvered them around the foot of the bed toward the mattress, but never let her out of his hold. He lifted his shirt over his head as she bounced onto the edge of the bed and revealed the fresh gauze taped over his wound. He closed his eyes as she rippled her fingers over his abdominals, her fingers dipping and rising with hard, lean muscle. "Hell, you feel so damn good." He caught her wrist in a gentle grip and slid the pad of this thumb over the thin skin. "Now tell me how to get this sling off your arm before I tear through it with my teeth."

"That's something I'd like to see, but I've ripped enough stitches open for one lifetime." Tugging her hand from his grasp, she slowly arced the sling's strap over her head, her gaze locked on his every moment of agony they were separated. Pain flared in her shoulder, but not enough to make her want to stop the burn happening between them. She parted her knees, slipping her fingers between his jeans and hot skin, and pulled him closer. She'd never crossed this line with her previous partners, never stepped out of line in all her time with the FBI. Never considered the intense attraction breaking the rules might have on her. But none of those partners had been Roman. None of them had made her feel like this. "Although I'm a little offended you forgot about the pudding I went all the way downstairs for and bought for you."

His gut-wrenching smile fluttered butterflies in her stomach as the mattress dipped under the weight of his knee. He lowered her onto her back, so slowly she feared she'd explode if he didn't touch her soon. Keeping his weight off of her, Roman kissed a path of chaste kisses along her jaw and down the column of her throat. "Who says I forgot about the pudding?"

CHAPTER TWENTY-FOUR

HE COULDN'T FALL INTO SLEEP WITH HER, EVEN AFTER THEY'D BEEN discharged from the hospital and had returned to the beach house. Not when Kirk Marshall's partner was still out there, possibly hunting her. Brie's soft, steady breathing said she was asleep, her body pressed to his, but they couldn't pretend reality didn't exist anymore. They had a killer to find.

Roman slid his arm from beneath her head and set his bare feet on the hardwood floor, her sultry scent clinging to his skin. He slipped from the bed and dressed quickly. Closing the bedroom door behind him, he checked his phone and found a handful of messages from Aiden Holloway. The USERT team from Washington had arrived on the scene less than thirty minutes ago. If The Dream Catcher had disposed of his victims' bodies as Brie had theorized before they'd nearly been burned alive in that damn cabin, the Underwater Search and Evidence Recovery Team would find the evidence.

Another message pinged through as he headed into the living room for his laptop, only his screen lighting the way. Confirmation from the bureau's IT department. The video sent to Chloe Francis's boyfriend's phone of a victim and the killer traced back to Kirk Marshall. Same with the detonation cord used to destroy the collection of trophies and any other evidence they might have found in the Dream Catcher's hideout. He scanned the report forwarded by SAC Haynes from Ludington's fire chief, clicking through the scene photos one by one.

Charred siding, roof collapse, broken windows, smoldering remains, and peeling paint. Phantom heat seared under his skin as flashes of the fire played across his memory, and he tightened his grip around the phone to keep himself in the moment. He and Brie had been lucky to make it out of the inferno alive. He glanced toward the hallway, the stitches in his side stretching with the movement as he listened for sign he'd woken her. And Kirk Marshall was lucky he was already dead.

He forced himself to breathe evenly, to focus, and clicked through the rest of the scene photos. The trophies, the det cord, the cabin's title. Even the blue fibers found on Ashlee Carr's body, and the phenobarbital purchases. Every single piece of evidence in this case had connected to Kirk Marshall once they'd identified him as a suspect. Roman sat back on the couch, the glow of the laptop screen bright. A humorless laugh escaped his chest. Almost as though... "Your partner wanted it that way. He wanted you to take the fall for all of it. He was manipulating you the whole time."

"Which means it's going to be hell to prove he had a partner at all." Her voice carried across the scarcely furnished room before the pad of bare feet registered in his ears. She smoothed her hand across his back, leveraging her hip against the edge of the couch, and he couldn't help but drink in the sight of her. Tussled bed hair, swollen lips from his kisses, a brightness in her gaze that hadn't been there a few days ago. And the fact she'd taken to wearing nothing but his crisp white button-down shirt and panties only rocketed his blood pressure higher. She threaded her fingers through his hair, nails scraping his scalp, and his body immediately hardened. Hell, it was as though she was a living angel sent to earth strictly to tempt him. "And we're back at square one."

"We're going to find him." He set the laptop onto the small circular coffee table in front of him, sliding his hand across her low back before pulling her into his lap. Her thighs pressed against his as she wrapped her uninjured arm about his neck, and he breathed her in deeper than ever before. Committing her to memory. Every touch, every inhale, every kiss. Until she'd become part of him. The bruise at her neck from where she'd been drugged had darkened since their release from the hospital twelve hours ago, and he brushed his thumb over the contusion. "He's never going to lay a hand on you again. I'll do whatever it takes to keep you safe."

"You already have." Brie trailed her fingers along his jaw, eliciting new sensations with each stroke. The low light of the laptop highlighted the stitches at her temple as she faced the screen. "But he's still out there. He's hunting for his next victim, and if Kirk Marshall's partner used him to carry out his kills and take the fall, we're dealing with someone even more dangerous than we originally believed." She settled her gaze on his, her hand fisted a bit tighter in his shirt. "We haven't been able to find a connection between any of the victims, which could mean he doesn't have a specific type, or he's chosen them for exactly the right purpose, and we haven't caught on yet. Either way, he's breaking typical serial behavior. He's not driven by the urge to kill. He's careful, patient, intelligent. And he's waiting for the perfect moment to strike."

"You said Kirk Marshall admitted to killing all four women to get your attention, that he wanted to finish what he started with you all those years ago." Pressure built behind his sternum, and Roman smoothed his hand down her shin, the silkiness of her skin catching on rough calluses in his palm. Hell, the woman did hazardous things to his body. "But now you think the partner chose Ashlee Carr, Chloe Francis, and those other two women and let Kirk Marshall take the credit. Why?"

"I don't know." She shook her head, short loose curls bouncing below her ears. A solemnity tinted her words as she studied the crime scene photos splayed across the laptop screen, and the brightness in her eyes he'd noted before vanished. "All I can tell you is every trophy we saw on those bookcase shelves before the fire didn't belong to adult women, Roman. They came from the Dream Catcher's victims."

"So our new theory is Kirk Marshall was a puppet." He ran a hand down his beard, the bristling vibrated up his jaw and into his ears. "And now we're looking for the puppeteer."

Brie slid from his lap, her bare feet softly padding across the hardwood floor to the kitchen. Waning moonlight shot through the window over the kitchen sink, caressed her arms and neck as she got a mug from one of the cabinets. Lean muscle flexed at the back of her thighs. She reached for the coffee pot and filled the mug.

Heat raced through his body, but he forced himself to drop his gaze to the fresh bandage on the sole of her foot. No matter how many times he'd tried pushing the events of the last few days out of his mind, it wasn't possible. He'd lost control. In the field. In her. They'd both gone through hell and back when they were focused on one serial killer. Now there were two, but this time, he wouldn't make the same mistake. He wouldn't lose her.

Turning toward him, she wedged her low back against the granite countertop, and spread her fingers along the ceramic mug between her hands. "Kirk Marshall was a seasoned serial killer who operated under the bureau's radar for years. It took us three days and two bodies to narrow our suspect pool to him." She brought the mug to her lips. "Kind of hard to imagine what kind of person could manipulate a killer like that."

"One who lost a major piece of his plan." Roman shoved to his feet, his wound screaming for relief, but he didn't trust his reaction time on the pain meds the doctor had prescribed. The only painkiller he needed took another sip of her coffee. Closing the distance between them, he set his hands on the counter on either side of her hips, and forced her to look up at him. "He can't hide behind the Dream Catcher anymore, which means he's having to re-evaluate. And so do we."

"He was the one who drugged me." Her voice barely rose above a whisper, fingers stroking along the bruise at her neck, gaze distant. "I was so focused on the threat in front of me, I didn't hear him coming from behind. I knew Kirk Marshall had a partner, but he said he was going to kill you." She looked up at him. "I couldn't let that happen."

"Then let me be the first to thank you for saving my life." Roman wrapped his hand around her coffee mug and set it on the counter behind her. Pinning her against the granite, he explored the curve of her ribcage over his button-down shirt, traced the path of her collar bones exposed at the neckline. Her breath quickened, and a part of him reveled in his ability to crack through that legendary control she'd held onto for so long. He'd done that to her. She'd let him in, this beautiful creature who'd seemingly been made just for him. Every bruise, every cut, every stitch added to the strength she was so damn determined to prove to others but spoke of survival. He couldn't keep himself from wanting to taste her over and over, until she'd become a permanent part of him. He swept his tongue past the seam of her lips, lost in her all over again, but forced himself to pull away. Just enough to reach the refrigerator door. Light from inside spilled across the kitchen tile as he grabbed the small, plain cardboard box from the top shelf and handed it to her. "Thank you."

"You know, the last time I held a package like this, it had a body part inside." Taking the box, she smiled up at him before sliding her fingers along the edge. Excitement and curiosity deepened the lines between her eyebrows. Then pure surprise as she got the package open, and every piece of him vibrated with the joy in her expression. Blue-green eyes shot to his, then the contents. "This is so much better than a significant piece of evidence. It's perfect. Exactly what I needed."

"You deserve every bite." Roman stepped into her as she pulled the devil's food chocolate cupcake free of the box. She flashed that gut-wrenching smile up at him, spreading satisfaction from the crown of his head to the soles of his feet, and something released inside of him. He'd been walking around a mere ghost of himself since that night at his former partner's cabin, but now, standing barefoot in this kitchen, celebrating the fact he and Brie survived one of the most treacherous cases they'd been assigned, he was…happy. For the first time in a long time—maybe ever—he was happy. Because of her. "But I'm not finished thanking you."

"You thanked me so well at the hospital, and with three separate instances in the bedroom, I'm not sure my shoulder could take another round. Don't forget you were pretty great yourself out there. We never would've survived that fire if it weren't for you." Her eyes glittered up at him with the help from the refrigerator light, a trace of chocolate cupcake at the corner of her mouth. "What more could you possibly have to thank me for?"

"Everything." He swiped the frosting from her lips with the pad of his thumb, careful of the cut in her bottom lip. He'd never hurt her. "I told you I lived and bled with my HRT team for years, that we were brothers, that we trusted each other without hesitation. But after what happened with my partner, I wasn't only transferred to missing persons, I was excommunicated from the rest of my team."

Her eyes widened. "They cut you out?"

He'd never admitted the fact he'd lost everything with the single pull of the trigger to anyone before, not even his old section chief, but trusting her with his inner most weakness felt right. Felt…liberating. "I was worried I'd never be able to trust anyone after what happened. I came into missing persons dreading the day Haynes took me off probation and assigned me to a partner because I knew I'd never be able to rely on anyone but myself in the field, that I'd never really have backup again. But then I met you, Special Agent Briohny McKinney." Her exhale brushed along his neck, raising his awareness of the small bubble of safety they'd built separate from the rest of the world. "You had my back from the beginning while simultaneously ensuring the job got done. You gave me a reason to believe in this division, to trust them. You gave me something I wasn't sure I'd ever have again." He brushed a strand of hair behind her ear. "A team. And I'll never be able to thank you for that enough."

"That's what partners are for. I'll always have your back, and if you keep bringing me cupcakes, I may even help you hide a body or two. I know all the good spots." She lifted onto her toes and pressed a quick kiss to his mouth. Chocolate exploded across his tongue as she lowered herself back onto her feet. The mere taste of her rocketed another rush of desire through him. "But I'm not sharing this one with you."

Realization hit. "What'd you just say?"

"That I'm not sharing my cupcake with you," she said.

"No. Before that, you said you know all the good spots to hide a body." Air rushed from his lungs. Roman pushed off from the counter, straightening. "In order for Kirk Marshall to abduct and kill his victims for so long without raising the bureau's suspicions—or any law enforcement agency's for that matter—he had to have extensive understanding of forensics and police procedure, but IT hasn't recovered any record of that. No library loans, no college courses other than veterinary school, no searches on his computer, no ties to the police department." There was only one other source where a killer could get access to information like that. "He wasn't the one with the education."

"The partner is." Brie wiped her mouth with the back of her hand, her cupcake seemingly forgotten. "We're looking for a killer in law enforcement."

CHAPTER TWENTY-FIVE

"Are you sure you don't want me to go in with you?" he asked.

"No. Thank you. This is something I have to do on my own." The house was exactly has she remembered. Dark tan siding, white trim under an avant-garde pointed roof, a splash of green around the front door and windows that had been built on the side of the home rather than the front. Twelve concrete steps had iced over leading down a sharp incline to where Roman had parked the SUV at the curb. She'd broken her arm running up those steps on a winter day almost exactly like this one, the memory so clear as she stared out the passenger side window. It was almost fortuitous she'd climb those same steps with her arm in a sling all these years later, but she wasn't a little girl anymore. Today, she was the investigating agent in Jessica McKinney's abduction case. And Brie couldn't avoid her sister anymore. "You should check in with Aiden and Kinsley and Captain Hobbs at the lake. See if USERT has recovered anything we can use to ID the partner."

"Call me when you're done." He slid his hand into hers and squeezed. "I'll get to you as soon as I can."

The past four days had ripped her world apart, but not because the killer who'd abducted her had finally met the end he'd deserved. For the past twenty years, she'd ensured she'd never had to rely on another living soul, not for food, clothing, money, shelter. Love. She'd done a damn good job keeping emotional distance and rejecting others before they could reject her. Needing someone made her vulnerable, gave another person power—control—to use against her. But with Roman... none of that mattered. She needed him to fight back the nightmares, to surprise her with cupcakes, to bandage her wounds, and to watch cheesy romantic comedies with her on the couch. She needed his clean, masculine scent on her clothing, his touch on her skin, her name on his lips, and his hands threaded in her hair. She needed him—her partner— more than anything, and in that moment, she didn't care if that made her weak. Because Roman would never use that power against her. She trusted him, and he trusted her.

"I will." Nodding, she untangled her fingers from his and pushed her way out of the SUV before her confidence waned. They'd worked this case together from the start, but she had to interview this witness on her own. For her own sake. She shut the door, shoving her hands in her coat pockets as the engine growled to life, and her partner pulled away. Snowflakes fell in silent waves as she turned to face the house then carefully dredged up the stairs. Tension thickened the tendons between her neck and shoulder with each step, her injury pulsing in rhythm to her heart rate. Nervous energy shot down into her fingers and toes, but she couldn't turn back now. There was a killer still out there, one who might want to finish the job Kirk Marshall started, and both she and Jessica could still be targets. Stepping onto the wrap-around porch, she almost smiled at the initials carved into the front door's frame as she raised her hand to knock. Glass vibrated under her knuckles, and Brie forced herself to take a deep, steadying breath as a shadow centered itself on the other side of the door.

Hinges protested as the door swung inward.

High cheekbones, graying shoulder-length hair, and beautiful blue-green eyes—same color as hers—filled the doorway. Dr. Glenda McKinney OB/GYN wiped her hands with a dish towel, her five-foot-five frame smaller than Brie remembered the last time they'd been in the same room together. A tentative smile stretched across her mother's lips, and a blossom of hope surged through Brie. "May I help you?"

Her stomach shot into her throat as though she'd been punched in the gut. No hint of recognition. Air stalled in her chest. One second. Two. How could she have been so stupid? Of course her mother didn't recognize her. Her parents probably hadn't thought about her since the moment they'd left her in Captain Hobbs's custody on their way out of the hospital that night. They hadn't checked in on her, followed her career, looked up a recent photo. Every muscle in her body battled to suffocate the burn in her eyes, and Brie cleared her throat.

"Yes, hi. I'm the FBI's investigating agent assigned to Jessica McKinney's case." Pulling her credentials from her coat pocket, she flashed them quickly. "I'd like to ask her a few questions if she's up for it. I understand she's been through a lot, but any information she's able to give us on her abductor would be helpful."

"Been through a lot?" Glenda McKinney pulled back her shoulder, the dish towel gripped hard in her hand. "You have no idea what that girl has been though, agent. She's already given her statement about what happened to the police and to two other people dressed just like you, and I'm not about to submit her to anymore questions that make her relive it over and over—"

"Mom, it's okay." Another woman appeared at the door, sliding her hand around Glenda's arm. Her sister. A few inches taller than Brie, Jessica McKinney had embodied the younger version of their mother almost identically when she was younger, but now... Twenty years of captivity and torture had changed her. She was still the beautiful sister Brie had looked up to her entire life, but different. Aged. Weathered. Sad. Long honey brown hair, now washed and dried since the last time Brie had seen her, thick dark eyebrows, full lips. Bruises marred creamy tan-prone skin along her neck and too stark collarbones, but everything about her, down to the beauty mark above Jessica's mouth matched the thirteen-year-old girl in Brie's memory. "This is the agent who saved my life. She fought off Kirk Marshall until I could get free."

Sky blue eyes—the color of the lake—pinned her in place. After everything she'd been through the last twenty years, did her sister recognize her? Did she realize why Brie had been on that boat in the first place? The note she'd recovered from the padlocked room in Kirk

Marshall's basement before the first explosion demanded attention from her coat pocket, and Brie clenched her fingers around it the longer her sister studied her. Jessica knew. But would she tell their mother?

"Oh, my." Glenda covered her mouth with her free hand then wrapped it around Brie's wrist. Discomfort surged through her at her mother's touch, and she politely pulled back in an attempt to keep her guard in place. "I'm so sorry. I had no idea. Please,"—Glenda swept her arm inside—"come in, please."

Ringing echoed in her ears, gravity pulling at her until she felt the blood drain from her upper body. She forced one foot in front of the other until a wave of warmth rolled over the exposed skin of her neck and face. The smell of freshly baked bread with a hint of sugary cinnamon filled her lungs, and her stomach churned at the all too familiar scent. Under the weight of Jessica's stare, she couldn't remember the last time their mother had made her famous sticky treat. Brie slid her coat from her shoulder carefully, gathering it in her uninjured hand. "You must be baking cinnamon rolls."

"I am. Would you like one? It's the least I can do for the agent who rescued my daughter." Always the perfect hostess, the perfect wife, the perfect mother on the outside. What a perfect illusion.

"No, thank you." She shook her head, catching sight of the collection of family photos gathered on the mantel above the fireplace to her right. Her fingers curled into the center of her palms. Every photo she'd been featured in had been altered. Crude score marks spread across her face of the photo of her and Jessica on Easter morning in their backyard, colorful baskets stark against pretty pale dresses. Scissor cuts surrounded a picture of Brie on Christmas morning in another, but her head had somehow been taped back together, and her heart squeezed in her chest. They'd cut her out of their lives, out of their memories, then attempted to fix the damage, but nothing could repair that thread. Clearing her throat, Brie shifted her gaze to her sister's watchful study. "If you don't mind, Mrs. McKinney, I'd like to speak to Jessica alone. I just have a few follow up questions. Won't take more than a few minutes of your time."

"Of course. I'll be in the other room with Dad if you need me, honey. The rolls should be done soon." In her next breath, Glenda slipped her hand into Jessica's with a nod then disappeared below the arch leading into the kitchen, towel in hand.

"You're not going to tell them." Jessica maneuvered to the nearest chair in the front room, sunlight highlighting the sharpness in her cheekbones. The oversized black blouse and cropped pants her sister wore hid most of the bruising and cuts Brie remembered from the boat, but some lacerations tunneled further than skin deep.

"It wouldn't change anything. They made their decision a long time ago, and I've moved on." Brie gripped her coat tighter, her fingers aching. Sitting on the edge of what used to be her favorite reading chair, she focused on the fraying edges of the deep red area rug at her feet. It was amazing. Nothing about this house had changed in twenty years, but she hadn't come to fix things with her parents. Hers and her sister's entire lives had been torn apart, but she wasn't the victim here. She'd gotten to live her life, move on, graduate college, make a career for herself so she could help those in the same situation as her sister. Jessica had never had that chance, but she could save lives now. "I wasn't lying when I said I've been assigned to investigate your disappearance. My partner and I believe Kirk Marshall had an accomplice, someone who was helping him stay off law enforcement's radar all these years. Was there anyone else there when you were being held?"

"Your partner. He's the agent from the boat, right? The one who couldn't keep his hands off you?" Pulling her legs into her chest, Jessica wrapped her arms around herself, coiled as though she was still being held captive. As though she didn't feel safe. How many times had she slipped into this same defensive posture when confronted by her abductor? The bandage around her hand emphasized the missing index finger on her left hand. "He cares about you."

"Special Agent Bradford is my partner. We have each other's backs when we're out in the field. That's in the job description. Same with the rest of my team." Heat worked into her neck and face, the gunshot wound in her shoulder suddenly screaming for attention. Her mouth dried, and she shot her tongue across her lips.

"It's more than that. You weren't relieved to see the rest of your team. You were relieved to see him. Happy, even. You care for him, too, but I get the feeling you don't want anyone to know." Jessica's voice dropped as she lowered from knees away from her face but still kept her feet off the floor. "You know I thought about you. Every day. I wondered if you'd survived, if you'd made it to shore after you jumped overboard, if you were getting help to come back and look for me." Sunlight glistened off the tears in her sister's lower lash line as Jessica raised those familiar eyes to hers, and a hardness set in as she gritted her teeth. "But day after day, year after year went by, and I was still in that hell with him, constantly moving from one location to another, being forced to listen to the screams of his other victims night after night, and I realized no one was coming to save me."

"Jessica, I—" She what? Always knew her sister had been out there, alive? Had never given up hope? Stiffness strained down her spine. Neither of those things had been true. "I'm sorry." Nothing could make the situation less black and white. Jessica had been out there—alone—tortured, beaten, more, and Brie had…run. "Nothing I say is going to change what I did. I was a scared ten-year-old girl, the police had stopped looking for you, and after our parents decided they wanted nothing to do with me, I made the selfish choice. I did everything I could to forget what happened and I left, but it was a mistake. I'd started hunting him a few years ago, but I'd given up hope of finding you. And I'm sorry. When I found the note you left in Kirk Marshall's basement, I knew I had to find you. Even though you told me to go home."

Jessica flinched, but quickly recovered as she swiped her face with the sleeve of her blouse. She diverted her gaze to the photos above the fireplace. Rolling her lips between her teeth, her sister broke the silence with a soft sniffle. "I don't blame you, Briohny. I know you're not the one who lied on the original incident report. You're not the one who called off the search teams after only two weeks after I disappeared."

No, she wasn't.

"When he wasn't holding me on the boat or in his veterinary office,

Kirk Marshall kept me locked away in a room in his basement. Occasionally, I'd hear voices, but they were mostly cries or screams from the other girls he'd taken. Nothing to make me think he was working with someone else." She unraveled her legs. "I lost count of how many there were." Jessica rose to her feet, closing the short distance between them. Her sister reached out and traced her fingers down the strap of Brie's sling. "My little sister, the FBI agent." A smile cracked through the anguish etched into Jessica's features. "I'm happy for you, Brie. Really. You got to live your life. Now it's my turn."

CHAPTER TWENTY-SIX

FRIGID TEMPERATURES AND AN UNRELENTING BREEZE DROVE ROMAN deeper into his coat. A thin layer of snow crumbled beneath his boots as he headed for Agent Holloway at the impromptu command center on the scene. Kirk Marshall's boat had been tugged back to shore, a separate crime scene unit collecting and photographing evidence a dozen yards away. Ice chunks bobbed at the shoreline. How the hell the USERT team dared to dive in these waters, he had no idea, and they'd been at it for close to two hours now.

He checked his phone. No word from Brie, but it wasn't hard to imagine her going dark after confronting the sister she believed she'd never see again. Every part of him wanted to track her down and take that guilt and pain away, but as she'd said, this was something Brie had to face on her own. Roman stepped under the portable umbrella shed blocking the bureau's equipment from sun damage and snow, three rows of bright blue tarps lined on the beach demanding pulling at him. And he had a killer to find. "How many have they recovered?"

"Fourteen. So far." Aiden Holloway kept his focus on the laptop screen in front of him, shoulder-length blonde hair secured back in his signature low ponytail against the wind. Dark ink slipped out from beneath the former interrogator's shirt seam at his collar. *Death before dishonor*. Holloway would've made one hell of an HRT operative. "Kinsley's on mental health standby for any of the officers who might need it, the medical examiner is having a hard time keeping up with the bodies dropping in this case, and your friend Captain Hobbs has his guys processing the scene on the boat." Holloway rounded the folding table, reaching for a stack of plastic bags and a sharpie. "With as many bodies USERT says are still down there, it's hard to see why nobody picked up on this guy for over twenty years."

Maybe they had, only Kirk Marshall had had someone on the inside to help him get away with murder. Roman lowered his voice, stepped in close so as not to gain the attention of the Ludington PD officers around them. "Brie and I have reason to believe the Dream Catcher's partner is law enforcement."

"Well, shit." Holloway's shoulders deflated as he shifted his weight between both feet. Piercing blue eyes scanned the beach as a low drone of a boat engine echoed in Roman's ears. They both saw the incoming USERT team about one hundred yards out. How many more victims were still out there? "This case just keeps getting better and better."

"I'll fill Haynes in, but this stays with the team, got it? We can't risk our suspicions getting back to the department." The moment they approached the Chief of Police, the team would lose access and manpower to hunt the second killer down. Roman caught movement in his peripheral vision from Kirk Marshall's boat. Captain Hobbs and his team were in the process of searching every inch of the deck and collecting and bagging evidence. Whoever'd covered up the Dream Catcher's abductions had been doing it for a while, possibly years. Roman pegged most of the officers in the Ludington Police Department around forty, maybe as young as thirty-five. It was possible one of them had played a hand in the cover up, but there was only a handful of reasons a law enforcement officer offered those kinds of services: to advance up the ranks. "Especially Captain Hobbs."

"You got it," Holloway said. "What's our next move?"

"We process the bodies for now. We need IDs on as many as we can manage to construct a pattern to how Kirk Marshall chose his victims. Maybe if we have the Dream Catcher's pattern, we'll get an idea of how long his accomplice has been covering up the abductions and nail the bastard." The high-pitched shrill of a cell phone echoed in his ears, pulling Roman's focus to Captain Hobbs. In a matter of seconds, the captain headed for his cruiser, and every instinct Roman owned hiked into suspicion. Hobbs had been the lead detective on the Jessica McKinney case, a case that had garnered him a rise up the ranks once the investigation had been closed. According to Brie, he'd lied on the original police report to protect her, but what if it'd been more than that? What if Greg Hobbs had falsified the information in that file because he knew who'd taken Jessica and her sister in the first place? Roman gripped the edge of the table. There was only one way to find out. "Get Kinsley, and grab a box of gloves. Treat every victim as a separate case. No cross contamination, and nobody else touches these remains until they've been processed. We've got work to do."

Within two hours, they'd processed six of eighteen bodies, but while the USERT team was forced to break from diving for another few hours, they'd hadn't come close to pulling all of the evidence from the lake. Roman changed out his gloves for a fresh set as he crouched in front of the next tarp in a long line of victims. Six bodies and nothing that could lead them to an ID for the Dream Catcher's partner. The medical examiner would have to perform the autopsies on each victim, but Dr. Allie Meyer was already trying to play catch up in this case. It'd be a matter of months—maybe a full year—before the bureau had official cause of deaths on these bodies. How many more would surface between now and then? How many more victims would be taken?

The growl of a car engine announced Captain Hobbs's return before the man himself stepped out onto snow and sand, with Brie climbing from the passenger side of the cruiser. Every nerve ending Roman owned focused on her as he straightened and dove into his pocket for his phone. No alerts. No missed calls. No messages. Captain Hobbs headed straight for the boat his guys were still processing as Brie forged a path around four rows of flapping tarps, brilliant blue eyes on him.

"You didn't call me," he said. "Everything okay?"

Her attention darted to Agent Holloway and Luther's positions as she slid her fingers in her pockets and buried her neck in the collar of her coat. "Yeah, fine. I had to talk to Hobbs about something, and I knew you were busy with the recovery efforts. I didn't want to pull you away." What little color had returned in her face over the last twenty-four hours drained as she scanned the beach. "Is this…is this all of them?"

"No." His mouth dried. She'd had to talk to Hobbs about something? Something she couldn't tell him, or was it the fact Holloway and Luther were within hearing distance? "USERT estimates at least a dozen more from what they showed us on the radar before pulling out, all decaying at different rates. They should be able to bring the rest up tomorrow after the divers have had a chance to decompress."

"There's so many. I didn't know…" Swiping her hand beneath her nose, she smeared deep red lipstick at one corner of her mouth, and it took every ounce of control he had left not to reach for her. Not here. Not now. But when he got her alone again, they wouldn't have to be careful. She pulled a pair of evidence gloves from her pocket and slid them over her hands. "Where do you want me to start?"

Roman stepped into her, his heart rate automatically spiking as her perfume filled his lungs. They'd only been separated two hours, yet his body was as hard as ever as though it'd been a lifetime. Every muscle, every nerve ending, every cell in his body acutely attuned and addicted to her. "You don't have to do this."

"I want to help, Roman." She raised watery blue eyes to his, and his gut clenched. Brie wasn't the kind of woman to express how deep their cases cut, especially not in front of the rest of the team. Even after she'd been rescued from the Dream Catcher's boat, she'd kept her control in place until they'd been gotten back to the beach house. Something had happened during the interview. Something she wasn't telling him. "I need to do this. I need to find him. So tell me which victims you want me to process."

"You can help me with this one." If she needed this, he wasn't going to be the one to stop her, but he wasn't letting her out of his sight either. Nodding, he maneuvered out of her way and crouched at the tarp at his feet. The wind picked up a corner, driving her scent from his system, and replaced it with nothing but the smell of soaked decomposition and carnage. Roman pulled back the plastic, noting the size and shape of the preserved remains. Cold temperatures had inhibited bacteria production, the body forming a wax-like substance instead of breaking down immediately. Probably the only thing that kept the victim from becoming a buffet to the lake's residents. No way to tell how long the body had been submerged without the medical examiner's help, but there was one thing that stood out from than any of the other victims they'd processed so far. "This is an adult."

"Female from the curve of the pubic bone." Brie leaned in closer, her hair blocking the mole on the left side of her face. "I'd guess around thirty years old, maybe thirty-five. Fits the age range of the last four victims."

The skin had formed a tight vacuum against the muscles and skeleton, sharpening the victim's cheekbones, collarbones, and ribcage, and showed off the wide laceration at the throat. Bruising darkened the remains at the wrists and ankles. Whoever the victim had been, she hadn't gone in to the lake voluntarily, but to be in the same general area as the Dream Catcher's dump site was too much of a coincidence. "The remains aren't that old. Less than a year. Could be another one of Kirk Marshall's latest."

"The first three women were placed and positioned at their crime scenes. Chloe Francis was suffocated in her hospital bed after Kirk Marshall knocked me unconscious. He accounted for all of them." Rolling back onto her heels, Brie balanced her forearms on her knees. "If this is another one of his victims, there's only one reason she's here with the rest." Eyes the color of the lake behind her met his, and everyone and everything around them disappeared. Leaving only her. "She could be his first adult."

"It's possible." He scanned the body for any other evidence that might lead them to an ID of the victim, but even with as much as had been preserved by cold temperatures, there were no tattoos, piercings, or scars from what he could tell. The hands had decomposed so brutally, he couldn't see whether the victim wore a wedding ring or had any other identifying features. "Kirk Marshall had already made a habit of dumping his victims here. He could've been treating her like any of his other kills."

"Exactly." She slid her gloved hand beneath the victim's, curling the victim's fist back toward her face then set it carefully back in place. For always having that invisible guard up around the living, it shouldn't surprise him to see Brie taking such care with the dead. Not because of the risk of losing evidence but because she truly cared about what'd happened to them, internalized it, made it her mission to get them the justice they deserved. That was only one of the reasons he'd started falling in love with her. "This woman's throat was cut. The Dream Catcher liked to suffocate his victims, but he wasn't used to preying on a fully-matured victim. If his partner was the one calling the shots, maybe Kirk Marshall was nervous, maybe he made a mistake, or maybe he wasn't the one who killed her at all."

"I'll have Dr. Meyer make identifying these remains a priority. The autopsy results could give us an identity on our killer." Roman stood, pressure building behind his sternum. Adrenaline buzzed down to his toes and out to his fingers. They were making progress, closing in on the son of a bitch who'd plunged that needle into Brie's neck, but even with this step in the right direction, they wouldn't have answers until the medical examiner took a look at the body. They'd have to focus on other aspects of the investigation until then. "How did it go with your sister?"

"She's angry." Brie straightened and discarded her used gloves into the hazardous material bin nearby. "She knows Hobbs lied on the original police report, and she knows he's the one who called off the search teams after two weeks." She ran her uninjured hand through her hair. "I understand why he did it at the time, but having to explain that to a woman who's been held captive by her abductor, a killer who put her through God knows what... I called the captain to pick me up because I wanted to warn him." Her gaze shifted to the rows of tarps around them, distant. "There was just something about the way she said it was her turn to have a life now that makes me think she'll try to hurt him."

Blue eyes settled on him. "And I can't let that happen. He was the only one there for me after my parents left. I'm not going to lose him, too."

Hell. He wasn't going to let her know about his suspicions until he had proof, now... Roman pulled back his shoulders, the stitches in his side stretching with the movement. He took a step toward her. "Brie, that is exactly why I believe Captain Hobbs is the Dream Catcher's partner."

CHAPTER TWENTY-SEVEN

HER EARS RANG, THE BEACH ONE GIANT WAVE OF BLURRINESS. NO. IT wasn't possible. Greg Hobbs had saved her that night, had stayed at her hospital bed side when her parents decided they couldn't look at her anymore, had helped her through school, paid her college tuition and for her books. He'd given her a recommendation when she'd applied to FBI. He was the closest thing she had to a father. And Roman wanted her to believe he was a killer?

Her heart thundered in her chest, stomach solid as a rock. Brie shook her head, but it only added to the dizziness. Roman wouldn't lie to her. Not about this. He had nothing to gain, nothing to prove in the investigation or to her. Hobbs had told her he'd falsified the police report that night because her parents asked him to, but what if... She forced herself to swallow the bile working up her throat. No. "You're wrong. Hobbs isn't a killer."

"Look around you, Brie. We've got eighteen bodies on this beach, and more still out there. Kirk Marshall's partner had to have been in law enforcement to hide this many abductions for this long. The bureau has analysts to spot these kinds of things, but only if the information they're given by law enforcement is accurate." Roman's clean, woodsy scent fought off the sickening smell of wet sand and decomp as it had that first morning they'd arrived in Ludington but failed to clear it from her system. Her insides rolled. "You said it yourself. He lied on the police report that night, he called off the search teams looking for Jessica after only two weeks." Her partner moved in closer, invading her personal space when it took everything she had to focus on getting through the next breath. "He knew exactly what he was doing. Jessica's case—your case—made his career, but you have to consider the possibility that Hobbs took you under his wing to keep you close, to make sure you wouldn't identify him as your abductor's partner."

Her voice barely registered above a whisper. "I didn't see anyone else that night."

"But he doesn't know that. He could've been there. How else would he have found you so fast when you got to shore?" Roman lowered his voice, pushing more care into it than he had a few moments ago. "We need to bring him in for questioning. You know that."

She did know that, and she trusted he was telling her the truth. What reason would he have to lie to her?

"He told me he'd been responding to a vandalism call that night. There should be a report filed. Easy to prove why he was there. And if he lied about that, too..." She'd never had any reason to dig up that old file. She'd taken Hobbs at his word. She couldn't think. Couldn't breathe. The ringing in her ears grew louder, every sense she owned scattered. Her head pounded in rhythm to her racing heartbeat. Roman was right. It all added up but knowing the man she'd considered a surrogate father for most of her life might be a killer didn't ease the crushing sensation in her chest. "Excuse me."

"Brie, wait." Roman's voice drowned in the sea of darkness working in at the edges of her vision.

She didn't stop. Everything about this town, about the people she'd been told she could count on—the people who were supposed to protect her—it'd all been a lie. A manipulation. The shore blurred in her peripheral vision as she closed in on the captain. Hobbs was crouched over the boxes of evidence already collected from Kirk Marshall's boat, and she raged hotter. "You knew, didn't you? You knew exactly where to find me on this damn beach once your partner told you I'd escaped. You knew because you were in on it the whole time."

Greg Hobbs straightened, the lines at the edges of his eyes deepening. He studied the officers around them. "Special Agent McKinney, I don't know what you're talking—"

"I deserve to know the truth, Hobbs. This is *my* life. He ruined my life, and you were there. There was no vandalism call, was there? He told you I'd escaped, and he still had Jessica." She planted her uninjured hand on Hobbs's chest and shoved as hard as she could, but it wasn't good enough. She'd only managed to throw him off balance, and in a split second, two officers rushed forward to contain her.

"Touch her and you'll never use your hands again." Roman's body heat tunneled into her from behind, his voice dropping into dangerous territory, and a shudder quaked down her spine. Was he the only one she could trust now?

Captain Hobbs ran his hands down his shirt. Eyes wide, he nodded at his officers to back off. "Brie, what exactly are you accusing me of?"

"You're the Dream Catcher's partner." Wrenching free from both officers, she pushed her hair out of her face. The weight of Ludington PD's and her team's attention rocketed her heart into her throat, but for the first time since waking up on Kirk Marshall's boat, she could finally think clearly. Roman had been right. Reaching to her low back, beneath her coat, Brie pulled her handcuffs free. Hobbs's eyes locked onto them instantly, and she stepped forward. "And now everybody knows it. Greg Hobbs, you are under arrest for conspiracy to commit murder."

Reading him the rest of his Miranda Rights, she passed Hobbs off to Agents Holloway and Luther before climbing behind the wheel of hers and Roman's rental SUV. The fuel of her rage drained, taking her strength with it as she sagged into the driver's seat. She spread her uninjured hand in front of her, but she couldn't control the shaking. The last few days had left her raw, vulnerable, reckless. She needed the numbness she'd mastered as a kid, the ability to shut down when she got too close to a case. She didn't know how else to compartmentalize what'd just happened. Was it even possible to detach herself from this investigation now? The sun had starting setting at the lake's horizon, reds and oranges bleeding across the sky. She'd arrested the Dream Catcher's partner. So why wouldn't the knot in her stomach release? At the push of a button, the vehicle's engine growled to life, but the passenger door opening prevented Brie from escaping the scene.

Roman settled into his seat and slammed the door closed. And waited.

Through the windshield, she watched the rest of her team load Greg Hobbs into the back of their SUV. "I should've confirmed the vandalism report before arresting him."

"You followed your gut. That's all you can do on a case as personal as this one," he said. "You okay?"

"No, so don't be surprised if I make you watch another movie with me tonight." They pulled onto the main road, the pressure beneath her sternum easing as the tree line thinned. Tires against asphalt sent a low vibration through her, and she was finally able to loosen her grip on the wheel. Within thirty minutes, they'd pulled into the beach house's driveway, neither of them having said a word. Gravel crunched beneath her boots as she stepped from the SUV and headed inside. Pending Dr. Meyer's autopsy reports on the dozens of bodies USERT recovered today, hers and Roman's assignment in Ludington was officially over. By this time tomorrow, they'd have their next case in another city, and she'd move on with her life. There was nothing more to keep her here. She fought gravity with every step toward the bedroom. The investigation was over. Wasn't she supposed to be happy—relieved—they'd closed the case?

"You haven't said a word since we left the scene. Tell me what's going through your head." His voice slid through her, reaching past her guard, her doubt and fears, and held her upright. Footsteps registered from behind as he closed the distance between them. "Please."

She didn't need to know how close he'd gotten. She could feel him in every part of her, under her skin, a part of her nervous system, as though he were a piece of herself she never knew had been missing.

Was that even possible? Brie faced him, exhaustion urging her to collapse, to sink into the floor. But Roman would catch her, and something in the way he looked at her now said he always would. "I'm supposed to feel something now that the case is over. Relief or closure, but there's nothing." She shrugged, biting back the pain in her shoulder. "I don't feel anything."

"You don't have to feel a damn thing. Not tonight." One step. Two. His fingers trailed a heated path along her forearm and ignited her nerve endings into overreaction. She notched her chin higher, unstable on her feet, but he quickly righted her before she fell forward. She didn't have the energy to fight as Roman swept her off her feet. "For once, let someone take care of you, Brie. Let me. You've been through enough."

The beach house's light gray walls past in a rush as he carried her down the hall. In less than two breaths, he'd settled her on her bed and started unlacing her boots. Gravity pulled her deeper into the luxurious bedding and mattress, but she forced herself to stay awake. He slid her slacks down her legs, helped her remove the sling from her arm. Tugging her into his chest, he carefully maneuvered her arms out of her blouse, and it crumpled onto the floor, but he didn't move onto the bed with her. Instead, he disappeared into the attached bathroom, the sound of water beating against porcelain too loud in her ears. Steam billowed around him as he stalked toward her, and something inside of her broke, spilling out at the care and concern etched into his expression, into the way he handled her so delicately.

She'd relied on her hardened exterior to get her through the last few years, was comfortable with the invisible distance her coworkers and the few friends she had kept, but with Roman, she wanted more. She wanted him to see through her defenses, beneath her hot-headed temper when things got confrontational, past the trauma of her childhood to the woman underneath. Because she couldn't it fight anymore. She'd fallen for him.

Her partner. Her protector. Her everything.

"Come here." He slipped his hands into hers and tugged her off the bed. Leading her into the bathroom, toward the tub now filled with steaming hot water, he stripped her out of her bra and panties then helped her step over the edge.

Her skin prickled at the heat enveloping her as she sank lower into the lavender-scented bubbles he'd added. The cold that'd set up residence in her muscles since the moment she'd set foot back in Ludington drained from her body. She closed her eyes, the soft click of a lighter echoing off the walls as he lit the tall, white candles strategically placed around the small bathroom. When was the last time someone had shown her such care? "Thank you."

"We're just getting started." Diving one hand below the surface, bubbles popping at the intrusion, he slid his fingers around her ankle and pulled it from the water. Goosebumps prickled where he massaged deep into the aching muscles of her calf, and she couldn't hold back the soft moan escaping past her lips. He worked his way up to her knee.

She jerked in automatic reaction. "That tickles."

"Duly noted." That gut-wrenching smile flashed wide, her stomach summersaulting at the sight. Doing the same the other calf, he released the stress she hadn't realized she'd been holding then made his way back down to her feet. He reached behind him to the counter, wrapping that magic grip of his around a small bottle she hadn't noticed until now. Nail polish? "Give me your toes."

A wave of heat that had nothing to do with the temperature of the bath water simmered beneath her skin, but she did as he asked. "HRT operator, special agent, and pedicurist. I'd hate to think of the reasons you're single."

"I used to help my mom with her nail polish after her first stroke. She never went anywhere in Los Angeles without having a fresh coat of paint." A hint of that smile stretched his mouth at the corners as though he were right back in one of those memories. Roman unscrewed the lid to the bottle, swiping the brush against the glass edge. Carefully, he set the tip of the brush at the base of her toenails and swiped to the edges. Like a professional. "It got harder after the second stroke, to the point she couldn't leave the house." His movements slowed then stopped altogether, her injured heel in his palm.

"She died the week after I joined the military. She'd formed clots in her brain as a result of years of head injuries from my father beating on her. It was a miracle she'd managed to protect me and live as long as she did, but towards the end, I think she just got lonely."

"I'm sorry. It sounded like you two were close." The respect in his voice cut straight through her, and Brie straightened, compelled to have him closer. She slid her hand over his, hoping to give some kind of comfort to the partner who'd put so many others' needs before his own. His mother, his former team, her. What she wouldn't give to take the pain in his gaze away. She took the bottle of nail polish from him and set it on the edge of the tub, confusion etched in his expression. Fisting her hands in his button-down shirt, she pulled him on top of her. Water sloshed over the edges of the tub, but she didn't give a damn about the floors or the mess they'd have to clean up later. There was only him, and the fact they'd barely made it off this case alive. Crushing her mouth to his, she slid lower in the tub to accommodate his size. She might've run from Ludington, chased the missing across the country, and tried to hide from the past, but this was where she belonged. With him.

CHAPTER TWENTY-EIGHT

To need her this much was a very dangerous thing.

Their plane would be leaving in a few hours, but Roman didn't dare move. Not with the length of her body pressed against his. Her heart pulsed in perfect rhythm with the thud of his in his chest. That perfume of hers teased his senses and invigorated every nerve ending he owned, urging him to memorize her all over again, but he'd let her sleep. She deserved it. She deserved any ounce of peace he could give her. Now. Forever. Not wanting to wake her, he slowly stretched his hand toward the nightstand and gripped his phone. The lit screen highlighted inches of flawless skin tucked beneath the sheets, and he couldn't help but trace the fresh gauze and tape at her shoulder. The nightmare of that memory—of her being shot right in front of him—would stay with him for the rest of his life, but he'd spend the rest of his life making it up to her. If she let him.

Tapping the internet browser app on his phone, Roman logged into the FBI's database with one hand. Greg Hobbs had claimed he'd been on the beach that night after Brie and her sister's abduction because a group of teenagers had been spray-painting graffiti onto the Big Sable Point Lighthouse. Easy enough to confirm if the captain hadn't falsified that report, too. He narrowed the search to Ludington, MI, the complaint, and the year of the incident, and hit search. No matter how perfect their theory of Hobbs conspiring with the Dream Catcher fit, they didn't have shit without evidence. And he couldn't let Brie wonder if she'd done the right thing for the rest of her life.

The page loaded. Three reports concerning vandalism had been filed that year, two of which pegged Detective Greg Hobbs as the primary. But nothing that involved Big Sable Point Lighthouse or the area near the lake's shore. The captain hadn't been there as he'd claimed the night of Brie's abduction, had lied on an official police report, and had opportunity and motive to cover Kirk Marshall's crimes. His thumb hovered over the screen. Still, Roman couldn't purge the restlessness from his system. The Dream Catcher had taken credit for the latest four missing victims' deaths, including Ashlee Carr and Chloe Francis, so why wasn't the captain working to cover those up murders now?

"I can see the wheels turning in your head." The sound of Brie's sleep-adled voice raised the hairs on the back of his neck. Trailing her middle finger between his eyebrows, she stared up at him with that stormy gaze in the light of his phone's screen. The split in her lip was already looking better despite the hours of his mouth on hers, and his body hardened instantly as she swiped her tongue over the injury. They'd spent more than half the night consuming one another, eating and sleeping until they had the strength to go for another round, but, still, he hadn't had enough of her. He had the feeling he never would. "Tell me."

"I can't find a police report filed by Hobbs concerning vandalism that night. Or any other night." He lifted her chin higher as that beautiful gaze lowered to his chest. With her hand splayed over his heart, Roman hurt knowing the pain ripping her apart inside, but she wouldn't spend the rest of her life wondering if the man who'd raised her was innocent. If she'd made a mistake. The Dream Catcher's partner had taken her under his wing, convinced Brie to trust him, for one reason: to ensure his identity was never compromised. And Hobbs would regret it for the rest of his life. Roman would make sure of it. He threaded his fingers into her short hair, reveling in the feel of the soft curls against the inner side of his wrist. "You did the right thing, and now he can't hurt anyone else. It's over."

"No. It's not." She shook her head, leveraging her elbows into the mattress. "It'll never be over. Not for families of the victims the search team pulled from that lake or Chloe Francis's boyfriend. Not for me. Not for Jessica and any other victims Kirk Marshall got his hands on. Having Hobbs arrested might give us closure, but these memories and the scars... They'll always be part of us."

"You're a survivor. You always have been, only now it's written all over your body." He stroked the back of his hand down her cheek, giving his system another boost of the dopamine he'd craved since setting sights on her all those months ago. But he'd never be able to satisfy that dark hunger. He'd never be able to let her go. His mouth followed suit. He kissed the dark bruising around her throat from where the Dream Catcher had tried to strangle her. Her pulse skyrocketed at the base of her throat. "But you are still the most beautiful woman I have ever seen."

Her breathing smoothed. "He didn't break me, Roman. Most people don't survive their kidnapping." Her words vibrated through him as Brie drew patterns into his skin with the tips of her fingers. "Jessica and I were lucky enough to escape. In my case, more than once, but I've been through this before. I'll do it again. Maybe I can help others who've been through something similar. Start a support group—"

"Others." Air caught in his chest, and he pushed to a sitting position, the headboard at his back. Of course. There could be others out there, girls—women—who'd escaped the Dream Catcher as Brie had. All this time they'd been digging deeper into their victims' lives. Maybe they needed to take a look at the survivors. "What if you two weren't the Dream Catcher's only survivors?"

"You think there are more of us out there?" The lightness in her eyes burned bright as she repositioned herself on the bed, sheets clutched her to chest.

"The dive team pulled more than two dozen bodies out of that lake yesterday," he said. "Kirk Marshall was good at what he did, but there's a chance there's a witness out there we haven't found. Someone else who might've gotten off that boat. Maybe more than one."

"How would we even know where to look?" she asked. "Those bodies we recovered span twenty years of abductions all along Lake Michigan. We don't know age, location, we won't have any of their names to link related cases to until the medical examiner files her reports. And that could take years to get through them all."

"Hobbs couldn't have covered them all up. People would've started noticing, especially desperate families looking for their loved ones. He'd have to have let some slip through." His instincts had already told him the answer, and the knot in his gut loosened. "The first woman who was recovered with a duplicate of Jessica's necklace, the one we connected to the investigation after Chloe Francis's disappearance."

"Kara Holmes." Brie leaned in as he typed the name into the FBI's database. "Why her? Her body was recovered by the Frankfort PD. She's not a survivor. She's—"

"One of the Dream Catcher's earliest victims." Roman turned the screen toward her. She was right. Kara Holmes wasn't one of Kirk Marshall's survivors. This time. The statements Frankfort PD had taken told the entire story. There was no file directly created for the victim, or if there had been Roman was sure Hobbs had most likely gone back and destroyed it, but there were statements from a captain of a fishing crew who recovered a twelve-year-old Kara Holmes in the middle of the lake the night she'd been abducted. According to the crew, the victim had told them she'd been taken from her bed, stabbed with a needle, and had woken up on a boat not far from shore. She'd managed to escape by jumping overboard but didn't make it far before they'd pulled her from the water. "You know as well as I do serial killers narrow in on a specific type of prey when they're on the hunt. It didn't make sense Kirk Marshall had changed his MO to older women after years of successful abductions and killings. So there had to be a connection between the women." He typed in the second woman's name linked to their current case. Lisa Knowles. Then Ashlee Carr's and Chloe Francis's. Every one of them telling the same story. Girls who'd been abducted, drugged, and had miraculously escaped a serial killer. All of them. "Now we have it. Hobbs must've destroyed the main case files on the victims, but these statements weren't linked to the originals when departments starting scanning their documents into the database. They were nomads. That's why we didn't see the connection until now. We didn't have all the information."

"They're all former victims of the Dream Catcher. Like me." Her eyes widened, that perfect mouth of hers parting. "They were targeted and killed because they managed to get away the first time. But why would Hobbs leave behind random statements with no attached case in the federal database?"

His phone chimed with an incoming message before three hard bangs on the front door hiked his blood pressure higher. Nobody but Aiden Holloway and Kinsley Luther knew they were staying here, and both agents had been assigned protection duty for Jessica McKinney until the case was officially closed. Brie slid from the bed as he set down his phone and reached for his weapon on the nightstand. His feet hit the floor as he unholstered it and checked the magazine. The only reports they were waiting on were the medical examiner's IDs of the bodies recovered from the lake, but Dr. Meyer wouldn't deliver them in person. "Expecting someone?"

"The reservations are paid for through tomorrow." Brie dressed as fast as she could with a bullet hole in her shoulder, shoving her legs inside a pair of form-fitting jeans. She tied her hair back and wrapped her grip around her own weapon. Disheveled, with swollen lips from his mouth on hers, a dreamy satisfaction in her eyes, she was the most beautiful creature he'd ever seen. He'd done that to her. He'd broken through that armor and memorized the sound of her calling his name over and over. She was his. And there was no going back. For either of them. "Nobody but Haynes is supposed to know we're here."

He tugged a T-shirt over his head, gun in one hand, teeth locked against the pain in his side, and his phone chimed again. Another message from Holloway. Picking it up off the nightstand, he exhaled hard. "Hobbs was released from custody an hour ago."

She dropped the magazine from her weapon, quickly counted the rounds, and shoved it back in place before loading a round into the chamber. And hell, if that wasn't the sexiest thing he'd ever seen. Blue-green eyes shifted to the bedroom door, the muscles in her jaw flexing. "Then let's go see what he wants."

"Damn, I love you." Everything inside him froze at the admission.

One second passed. Two. Or was it a full minute? He had no idea, but he'd needed to say the words. Needed her to hear them and know everyone might have failed her in the end, but he wouldn't. Ever.

"You love me?" Her fingers regripped the weapon at her side as she shifted her weight between both feet. Another round of banging from the front of the house echoed down the hall, but he couldn't move. Not until she responded. Not until she confirmed whatever the hell this was between them, what it could be.

"Since the moment we were partnered together," he said. "It's always been you."

"What do you mean? We've only known each other for three months." Her voice remained steady, detached. How did she always stain in such perfect control? Expression guarded, she dropped her shoulders away from her ears, but he wouldn't let the fact she hadn't responded in kind break him.

"I mean exactly what I said." He pulled back his shoulders enough to stretch the stitches holding his wound together then maneuvered around the end of the bed, toward her. "I don't care how long we've known each other, or if you think whatever this is between us is only happening because of the case or adrenaline or some shit. I love you, and I needed you to know."

"Roman, I…" She swiped her tongue across her lips. "I'm not ready to get hurt again."

"I keep my promises, cupcake." He feathered his fingers over her hip and lowered his mouth over hers. "I will never hurt you, and I will kill anyone who tries." The hollowness that'd taken residence inside released, and for the first time in years, he could breathe fully. He might've broken through her armor, but his partner had filled the hole inside of him with her strength, her vulnerability, her ability to tear him down to nothing and help him be rebuilt. Stronger, faster, reborn into the man he'd always wanted to be. Because of her. "And I'm not ready to give up on us. Now answer the door so we can get the hell out of this city and move on with our lives."

She smoothed her hand down one side of his face. "I'm not ready to give up either." Brie headed for the front of the house, unlocking the main door. A clean breeze rushed into the house around her as he closed in from behind. "Hobbs. What the hell are you doing here?"

"I did not kill those girls, Briohny. I never laid a hand on any of them." Hobbs moved to step inside the house, but Roman cut him off. No way in hell. He slipped his finger over the trigger. One move against Brie. That was all it would take, and Roman would shoot. Hobbs stepped back. Tears filled the captain's dark eyes. "Everything else you said...it's true. I covered up Kirk Marshall's crimes. For twenty years, I deleted police reports, altered witness statements, and lied to families."

Tension pulled back Brie's shoulders, a physical thing overwhelming her tightly held control. Roman pressed his arm into her side. No matter what happened next, he'd have her back. "Why?"

"That night I found you on the shore." The captain—former captain now that charges would be brought against him—swept his hand toward Brie. "I took you home after the doctors cleared you to leave the hospital, after your parents..." He shook his head. "You didn't have anyone else, and I thought you'd be safe with me, but you weren't. I couldn't protect you from him."

"What are you talking about?" she asked.

"I've always been a light sleeper, ever since I became a cop." Hobbs hiked one hand to his hip, the other running over his bald head. "But you were having nightmares, so I decided I'd sleep in the recliner I pushed into your room in case you needed me, and I didn't hear him break in until it was too late." Hobbs dropped his hand, sagging in on himself. "He threatened to take you away from me. Kirk Marshall told me if I didn't help him, he was going to come back for you. He was going to finish the job he started, but I swear I never hurt those girls."

Her soft exhale reached Roman's ears, but he only tightened his trigger finger. "You could've moved. You could've gotten her someplace safe. Instead, you chose to keep her in harm's way."

"You have no idea what she'd been through, Agent Bradford." Hobbs pointed a finger at him. "Her parents walked out on her. I was the only one she had left, the only one who gave a damn about what happened to her. I wasn't going to take away her friends, her school, or the rest of her life."

"Bullshit. None of that mattered. Not when her life was at stake, when all those girls' lives were at stake." Fire burned behind his sternum, and Roman took a step forward. Seagulls called in the distance, the only interruption to the silence that'd settled between them.

"Enough." Her voice broke on that single word. "I don't want to hear anymore."

"I've made mistakes." Hobbs shifted his focus to Brie. "And I'm prepared to pay for every single one, but I needed you to know. I'm not the murderer you accused me of being yesterday."

"Twenty-six victims, Hobbs. That's how many bodies USERT pulled from the lake yesterday." Brie took a single step toward the man who'd taken position at the head of the long line of people who'd betrayed her, and Roman tensed. "You might not have killed them, but as far as I'm concerned, every single drop of their blood is on your hands."

"I couldn't lose you, Briohny," Hobbs said.

"You're not my father, remember?" She turned away from him, calling over her shoulder as she headed deeper into the house. "I was never yours to lose."

CHAPTER TWENTY-NINE

Sometimes you couldn't see the monsters right in front of you.

Hundreds of twinkling lights lit the back patio of the beach house as Brie pulled her legs into herself on the hard, plastic beach chair. Half an acre of grass stretched out to the edge of the cliffs in front of her, not another house for quarter of a mile. Isolated. Quiet. Dark. But she wasn't alone.

"Dinner is served." Roman slid the porch door closed behind him, a large platter in one hand. The scent of tomato, basil, and oregano cleared the beach smell from her system as he headed for the large patio table on the other side of the deck, but she wouldn't be able to escape Ludington anytime soon.

Hobbs had admitted to helping the Dream Catcher cover up his crimes, which the prosecution could easily prove as long as he cooperated at trial, but she believed him when he'd said he hadn't killed those women. Which meant there was still a killer out there. Hunting down the handful of Kirk Marshall's victims lucky enough—strong enough—to escape him.

Including her.

Pushing off the chair, she padded barefoot to the table with six other chairs surrounding it. Fresh bread and melted cheese pulled her closer, and her stomach growled. "Is that chicken parmesan?" Shock pushed through her. Pointing at the baking dish with crusted shredded cheese around the edges as he lit the two candles in the center of the table, she slid one chair out to take a seat. "So when I was showing you how to cut onions and peppers for the fajitas a few nights ago, you already knew how to cook, didn't you?"

"I never said I couldn't cook." He filled up her wine glass with a water pitcher from the fridge. No alcohol on the job. Not when they'd both been pushed so very close to the edge. Any mistakes now could cost them the investigation. Or their lives. "That was one of the things my mother insisted I learn before I headed off to basic training. She didn't trust I'd be able to fend for myself."

"I see. So, really, you just wanted to get into my pants." She couldn't hold back the laugh bubbling up her throat and took a sip of water. She couldn't remember the last time someone had cooked for her. Other than Hobbs's attempt at adding vegetables to ramen noodles and burning hamburger-added boxed meals. It was a wonder he'd managed to fend for himself for so many years before she'd come along. Nothing like Glenda McKinney's southern style cooking, but she'd realized even then Greg Hobbs done his best with what he'd had. For an established Ludington PD officer suddenly left with a ten-year-old girl who'd been through the worst kind of trauma, he'd kept her fed, provided shelter, and security. He'd done what a parent was supposed to do. And now... No. Brie closed her eyes, forced herself to stay in the moment. Roman cooking for her was unexpected. Nice.

"Can you blame me?" Setting down the water pitcher, Roman settled one hand on the back of her chair and leaned in. His mouth brushed against hers but only gave her a tease of what they'd shared over the last few days. "Everything in your pants comes with a treat at the end."

The promise of pleasure swirled in his eyes, but he pulled away, taking his own seat across the table from her. Her body tingled in all the right ways at the memories they'd created under the sheets. But no matter how much they wanted to pretend the investigation was closed, take the next few days to themselves, and only surface for food, rest, and the occasional shower, the unspoken truth between them couldn't be ignored forever. As one of the Dream Catcher's former victims, she was still in danger.

Brie scanned the tree line around the back of the property. Kirk Marshall hadn't broken into the beach house and left her that message. His partner had. Someone who knew the layout of the area, who was faster, stronger, and more intelligent than the Dream Catcher himself. Were they out there right now? Watching her? Hunting her? The clatter of Roman cutting a piece of chicken for her pulled her back into reality. Her shoulder ached as she clutched the knife off to the left of her plate, mouth dry. Could she protect him when—not if—the threat struck?

"Brie." That dark gaze locked on her and the fear snaking up her spine slithered out of her mind. For years, she'd fought to prove she was the strongest, that nothing and no one could shake her, that she had control of her life and didn't need anyone. She'd survived a serial killer, damn it, but now Roman's life had been put at risk. Because of her. His rich scent intensified as he stood, rounding the table to her side. He wrapped his hand around hers that gripped the knife and settled it in her lap. "We're in this together. Partners. You're not doing this alone."

"You can cook and read minds." She forced herself to nod. The wind picked up, carrying a hint of sand and water on the air, and her stomach pitched. Where was her legendary control now? Where were the sociopathic tendencies her coworkers accused her of having? Why couldn't she keep it together? "Tell me again why you've been single all these years."

"Because I was waiting for you." He pried the knife from her hand and set it on the table. Sliding his fingers into the hair at the nap of her neck, he tugged her forehead to rest against his. "All my life, I didn't know what I was missing. Until I was assigned as your partner, and there's nothing you can do to get rid of me now. Got it?"

Because he loved her. A weak smile pulled at her lips. "Got it."

Her phone rang from the other chair where she'd left it, and she brushed at her face to regain any semblance of the woman she'd once been. In vain. She wasn't that woman anymore. She couldn't keep her emotional distance. Not from him. Not when she was fairly certain she loved him, too. Brie crossed the deck and picked up the phone, swiping her thumb across the glass as Special Agent Kinsley Luther's name flashed across the screen. "Hey, what's going—"

"Brie, Jessica's gone. We can't find her trail anywhere." Distress tinted the profiler's voice. Heavy breathing crossed the line as though Kinsley was running, muffled shouting in the background. Was that Aiden? "We're searching the property now, but there's no sign of her."

"What do you mean she's gone?" Brie spun toward Roman, warning firing in her gut. Someone was out there hunting the Dream Catcher's former victims. That included her sister. She dropped her head in her hand then scored her fingernails over her scalp. No. No, no, no, no. She'd just gotten Jessica back. This wasn't happening. Not again. She tapped the button for the speaker phone so Roman could listen in on the conversation.

"Everything was fine when I checked in with her an hour ago. We searched the house, cleared every room, including the basement. Aiden and I were right across the street, and we had a patrol car stationed on the other side of the house. Nobody came out or went into that house." Kinsley was out of breath. "There's no forced entry on the doors or windows either. It's like she just disappeared."

Disappeared. Like the night she'd been abducted. Brie stilled as Roman trailed his hand along her arm. Locking her attention onto him, she followed the instinct churning nausea in her gut. She closed her eyes as defeat clawed through her and readjusted her grip on the phone. "Kinsley, did my sister know Hobbs was released from custody earlier today?"

"Yes." The line suddenly went quiet. No hard breathing. No static. And anxiety hardened the muscles along Brie's spine. "We explained we were assigned to watch her and the house as long as Greg Hobbs was free."

"Oh, no." Brie pumped her legs hard, ripping open the house's back sliding door, and ran through the darkness for her bureau-issued radio. She twisted the tuner to Ludington PD's channel and compressed the button, every lungful of air clawing up her throat. Her eyes fought to counter the dark as white clouds edged in around her vision, but she only searched for her weapon harder. "All units, backup requested to Greg Hobbs's house at two-seven-six-eight Tamarac Drive for a possible homicide. Suspect is female with long brown hair, five-foot-six, armed and dangerous."

"I've got the keys. Let's go." Roman tossed her coat at her and wrenched the front door open. They flew out into the night. Gravel gave way to asphalt as confirmation from officers all over the city came through. In seconds, she dropped into the passenger side seat of their SUV. The engine growled to life at the touch of a button, and Roman propelled them down the hill.

Her heart pounded in her chest. City lights spread for miles west of the lake. Postcard perfection trying to convince those who visited that Ludington was a nice place to live, that they could be happy here. That they were safe. But Brie knew the truth. No one was ever safe. Not here. She tried to swallow back the tightness in her throat. Hobbs had known that truth, had tried to protect her from the ugly realities of the world when her parents decided it wasn't their job anymore. She battled to keep her balance as Roman wrenched the wheel to take a sharp right turn. Two blocks out. No sign of patrol lights or the echo of sirens. Damn it. She unholstered her weapon as the SUV's tires screeched to a stop and shouldered her way out of the SUV. "Backup isn't here yet."

"I've got the back." Roman forged a path alongside the large, wooden cascading deck at the front of the house toward the back yard and disappeared into the trees.

The double bay window at the front of the house was dark. A false portico over the front door demanded attention as she heel-toed beneath the vinyl, one slow step at a time. The deck creaked under her weight on approach to the front door, weapon drawn. And she froze. A sliver of black outlined the frame. A Ludington PD captain never would've left the front door unlocked, let alone ajar. Panic threatened to tear into her, but Brie forced one foot in front of the other. She templed her fingers against the door and pushed. And met nothing but darkness. "FBI! Is anybody here?" No answer. "Hobbs, answer me!"

She instinctively reached for the light switch to her right as she had hundreds of times before with her opposite hand, trigger finger in place. The light seared her vision for a split second before— Blood. Everywhere. The living room had been drenched in it, and there, in the middle of the floor Hobbs jerked with his hands at his throat. Brie lunged, setting her weapon beside her as she collapsed next to him. His clothing had been soaked. How long had he been bleeding to death? A minute? More? His throat had been cut. There was no way she'd be able to stop the bleeding on her own. "Roman!"

Hobbs's eyes were wide, pleading for help, but only a gut-clenching gurgle whispered past his lips.

"It's okay. It's okay." She scrambled for something to stop the bleeding—anything. Ripping a small flannel blanket at one corner, she barely heard the hard thump of footsteps over the material's protest. Brie threaded one end of the fabric behind Hobbs's neck and secured it as much as she dared, but it wouldn't be enough. Sirens pierced through the ringing in her ears. "We need an ambulance!"

"Apply pressure to the wound." Roman took position on the other side of Hobbs. "We've got to slow down the bleeding. EMTs are two minutes out. Hobbs, you've got to stay still."

"Who did this?" The blood soaked her hands. He was losing too much, too fast, and she was losing *him*. He jerked again under her grip, but the more he moved, the quicker he'd bleed out. And she couldn't let that happen. "Hobbs, who did this to you? Was it Jessica?"

"Not…her." Hobbs's eyes blinked closed, then struggled to reopen.

"Hobbs, you have to stay with me. Stay awake. Come on, listen to my voice. Hang on." Brie glanced over her shoulder as Aiden Holloway and Kinsley Luther barged through the front door, weapons drawn. Tears filled her eyes, but she wouldn't give up. She couldn't. He was the only one who'd been there for her when everyone else had turned their backs. He got her the therapy she'd needed after the abduction, gave her a roof over her head, fed her, clothed her. Cared for her. Protected her. "Where is my damn ambulance!"

"I...did..." The former captain battled to raise his hand toward her face, and Brie leaned in. She didn't care about the blood on his fingers or the coldness settling in at his touch. "...for...you."

"I know you did, but you're not going anywhere. Who's going to force me to eat my vegetables with crappy ramen noodles if you die?" A humorless laugh escaped. Roman repositioned the soaked fabric at Hobbs's throat, but the captain wasn't struggling for breath anymore. Wasn't moving anymore. He'd gone completely still. Brie shook his shoulders, those trusting dark eyes distant. "Hobbs, look at me." She shifted her weight over him as terror and loss and rage took control. He wasn't dead. He wasn't going to leave her here like this. The tears fell to his blood-soaked under shirt. She raised her voice, while still trying to control the hysteria exploding through her. "Dad, look at me."

He was gone.

"Brie, I'm sorry." Roman released his hold on the fabric she'd wrapped around the captain's neck and lowered onto his heels. In her mind, she knew he'd stood, threaded his hands between her arms and ribcage, and pulled her to her feet as first responders arrived on scene, but the only thing she could focus on was the man on the floor. Her dad lying in a pool of his own blood. "He's gone."

And suddenly, the entire world was different.

CHAPTER THIRTY

SHE WAS FURY AND FIRE, JUSTICE BRIGHT IN HER EYES AS SHE FLED from the scene.

"Brie." Roman followed on her heels. Red and blue patrol lights lit up the scene, but it'd been too late. They'd all been too late. Greg Hobbs was dead. Blood crusted his hands and shirt, but he didn't give a damn about any of that. His partner had lost her only parent, and the person responsible was about to find out just what kind of war he'd only sensed in her these past few months. "Brie, wait."

"The killer couldn't have gotten far." She ran past the officers and emergency personnel headed inside the house, down the extended deck toward the SUV. Wrenching open the door before she got behind the wheel, she pegged him with that blazing gaze. "Don't you dare try to stop me."

He rounded to the passenger side of the vehicle and threw open the door, settling inside. The overhead light faded after a few seconds. Her shallow breaths reached his ears inside the darkened interior of the SUV. "We agreed we're in this together, remember? You can't get rid of me now."

"I warned him." Brie wrapped the underside of her grip around the stick shift near the steering wheel. Her words barely rose above a whisper. "I told him she blamed him for her being stuck with that monster, but he didn't listen." Her hands fell to her side, her expression hidden in shadow. "Why didn't he listen?"

He didn't have an answer. Not right away.

"After what happened with my partner in hostage rescue, I wasn't surprised when my section chief suggested I transfer. For a while there, I believed it was the least I deserved after what I'd done to his family, what I'd done to our team." And it'd eaten at him for months. Until he'd met her. Now he had a new team, a new partner, and he'd do whatever it took to keep them alive. No hesitation this time. "Maybe Hobbs thought he deserved whatever was coming at him. Maybe he'd accepted the consequences of his sins."

"The only difference is you didn't hide twenty years' worth of abductions for a serial killer." Brie shoved the SUV into drive and let her foot off the brake. They maneuvered around the half dozen patrol vehicles and headed east. "And you didn't leave anyone behind."

"Not anyone as close as you and Hobbs, no." Only the support system he'd spent years building when his team had turned their backs on him. Roman waited for the resentment to spiral through him, as it always did when he thought back to his former unit. But it never came. Because now, he had Brie. And there was nothing—and no one—that would get in his way when it came to protecting her. Including a killer with a grudge. "I'm sorry about Greg."

She slipped her hand into his, balanced precariously on his thigh. "Me, too."

Scanning every street, every sidewalk, every house as they drove through Ludington, Roman searched for movement, runners, anything suspicious that might tie back to the scene at Hobbs's house. "The medical examiner's office is notifying families of the victims they've been able to identify this far. Every one of them has motive to make Hobbs pay for his part in the Dream Catcher's sick game. We're searching for a needle in a haystack here."

"I'm not interested in the victims' families for Hobbs's murder." Brie pulled the SUV to the side of the road. Staring through his passenger side window, she nodded toward the all-too-familiar house on the hill. Her childhood home. She pushed out of the vehicle, and Roman hit the sidewalk. "It's too much of a coincidence Jessica slipped her protective detail at the same time Hobbs was bleeding out five minutes away. She could've walked to his house, killed him, and run back by the time anybody knew he'd been attacked." Her coat bounced around her thighs as they jogged up the twelve steps leading to the front door. Rain collected on the frayed wool but fell as she pounded her fist against the door. Lights flickered on inside, and she pulled her shoulders back as if ready for battle, one hand on her weapon. "Something about this—about *her*—isn't right. And I'm going to find out why."

Hobbs had said it wasn't Jessica who'd attacked him, but the captain had been losing a lot of blood at the time. He could've gotten confused. And Roman couldn't ignore the fact Brie's sister had motive, means, and opportunity to do the deed. Hobbs had falsified not only years' worth of police reports regarding the Dream Catcher's abductions but had called off the search team for Jessica after only two weeks. He moved his suit jacket out of the way of his holster. There were far lesser reasons to exact revenge. And the fact five other victims over the course of this investigation had been killed in the same way as the former captain didn't escape him. "I've got your back, partner."

Always.

The door swung inward, outlining a taller man with white hair, circular rimmed glasses, and deep lines running down his jaw. Ted McKinney. Brie's father.

"Mr. McKinney, we're looking for Jessica." Brie pushed past the homeowner, stepping over the threshold. "Do you have any idea where she is?"

Surprise contorted the man's expression. "Like I told the other two agents, Jessica's not here. We haven't been able to find her all night. The last time we saw her was at dinner. She said she wasn't feeling well and went up to her room. Then she was just…gone." Ted McKinney glanced at Roman then stepped aside to let him in. "Did something happen? What's going on?"

"Greg Hobbs has been murdered." Roman scanned the front room of the house, noted the family pictures across the mantel above the fireplace. Pictures where a young Brie's face had obviously been defaced. A surge of rage bubbled to the surface. His partner had come into this house, interviewed her long-lost sister possibly right in this very room, and been confronted with the reality of her parents' decision all over again. How she could stand to even be in the same room as these people, focused on the case, only hiked his protective instincts into overdrive. Nobody would never hurt Brie like that again. He'd make sure of it. "Someone cut his throat."

"And you think our daughter is responsible?" Glenda McKinney tucked her robe around her as she stepped into the front room from the kitchen. Thin fingers spread across her loose-skinned neck, voice hardening with every word out of her mouth. "Greg Hobbs betrayed Jessica. He lied when he filed her police report so detectives didn't have all the information they needed to find her. He might not have taken her from this house, but that man got everything he deserved."

"No, he didn't." Brie physically stiffened, and the muscles down his spine tensed right along with her. Her expression hardened, darkening the stain of dried blood on her cheek. Hobbs's blood. She hadn't stopped long enough to clean herself up after leaving the scene. "That man you're talking about saved lives every day protecting this city from monsters like the Dream Catcher. Including mine."

"Jessica saved your life, too, agent." Glenda turned her attention to his partner, her daughter. "How can you come in here accusing that girl of anything other than surviving? You have no idea what Jessica has been though. To think she's capable of something like that after everything she was forced to endure—"

"There's a panic room upstairs in the master bedroom." Brie curved around the wall leading into what Roman assumed was the kitchen as leftover aromas of dinner trailed around his partner, the tension evaporating from her shoulders. Ted and Glenda McKinney weren't going to give them anything, even if they knew where their daughter had gone. They'd gotten one daughter back, and they were prepared to ensure they'd never lose her again. "Inside, a set of stairs leads to a hidden opening in the corner of the garage. Jessica used to play in it as a kid, and she probably still remembers the code. She most likely got out of the house that way."

Ted McKinney homed his gaze on Brie. "How do you know that?"

Brie froze. He knew she hadn't revealed her true identity, and from the state of the family photos behind him, with good reason. The McKinney's certainly played the part of doting parents with their eldest daughter, but Roman knew the truth.

"Because you had to file permits with the city to have it installed by the contractor you hired." Roman lowered his hand to his side. Their suspect wasn't here, and they were wasting time. "We're going to run a final search of the house, and we'll be on our way. We'll leave the patrol stationed outside until the investigation is closed for your protection."

"Find her." Glenda reached out, curling those long fingers around Roman's forearm as he passed. "But please don't take her away from me again. I don't think I could survive losing another daughter."

"Guess you shouldn't have abandoned the other one then." Her grip slid away, confusion and shock in her eyes—the same color as Brie's—and he kept moving. No, he wasn't going to apologize for that. Taking position behind Brie, they headed up the stairs, the subfloor creaking under his weight. More family photos, none recent, had been positioned along the walls, but from what he could tell, she was going out of her way to avoid looking at them. They passed by the first room on the right, a home gym, and a half bathroom across the hall. He followed Brie through the door at the end of the hall. The master bedroom. In two breaths, she'd slid back the false wall at one side of the room and revealed the thick steel door and the keypad behind it.

"Six-one-seven-one-nine-eight-six." She typed in the numbers, a soft beep accompanying each digit, then stood back to wrench the door open. Overhead lighting flickered to life from above, highlighting shelves of canned goods, survival gear, and a handful of weapons and ammunition. "Code hasn't changed."

Jessica's birthday. He recognized it from the woman's file but confirming it would only deepen the wounds already evident in Brie's eyes. Stepping into her, Roman framed one side of her face with his hand. He swiped at the patch of blood blemishing her cheek, but his attempt only smeared the mess further. Every single person charged with protecting her, caring for her, loving her had all turned their backs on her, and she hadn't deserved any of it. Hadn't deserved to be abducted by the Dream Catcher, to be abandoned by her parents, or betrayed by the man she'd viewed as a father at the end. But Roman would spend the rest of his life making up for their mistakes. He'd show her exactly how a woman of her caliber deserved to be treated. "Do you remember what I said to you after the rescuers brought you to shore three days ago?"

"You wanted to confirm Kirk Marshall was dead so you didn't have to go out to the boat and do it yourself." She nodded, her perfect, creamy skin catching on the calluses in this palm. A humorless laugh burst from her mouth as though if she didn't have this small release, she'd shatter right in front of him.

But he'd catch her. Every damn time. He'd be the one person in this world she'd never have to doubt. He'd hold her up, put her first, and love her until the end. "I wasn't going to let him get away with what he'd done to you. I protect what's mine. For the rest of our lives, I choose you, and I will never give you any reason to believe otherwise. Understand?"

She rolled her lips between her teeth. "It's a good thing I like you then."

Roman's phone rang with an incoming call from the medical examiner's office. He'd asked Dr. Meyer to prioritize the female remains USERT had recovered yesterday from the lake as the rest of her team worked tirelessly to identify all the other victims. He dropped his hold on Brie as she put space between them. Swiping his thumb across the screen, he answered and tapped the button for speaker phone to bring his partner into the conversation. "Bradford."

"Agent Bradford, it's Dr. Meyer. I'm calling about the remains you asked me to prioritize." A slight echo reached though the line. Allie Meyer was most likely standing in the morgue with their victim, their conversation bouncing off the hollow openness of the room. "I confirmed the victim is female, approximately five-foot-five based on the length of the femur, and between thirty-one and thirty-three years old. Cause of death was massive blood loss from the laceration across the carotid arteries with a very narrow blade. The murder weapon wouldn't have been very long either, maybe twelve to seventeen centimeters. Like a boning knife, slightly curved at one end."

"Kirk Marshall used his fishing boat to contain his victims." He raised his gaze to Brie as she turned toward him. The partner had most likely been on the vessel, but there was no way they'd be able to prove it now. Any evidence collected from that scene wouldn't hold up in court. Not when Captain Hobbs's credibility had gone out the window with his arrest. "The knife could've come from there."

"A knife like that would fit the size of the wound. Given the slight upward angle of the cut, looks like your killer attacked from behind. They would be only a fraction taller than the victim and right handed since the blade was swept from left to right."

"Thanks, doc." Brie swept her attention across the small panic room, heading toward the set of stairs at the back. "We'll be on the lookout for a weapon that matches that description."

"There's more." Dr. Meyer's voice pierced through the haze on theories running through his head. "I ran dental records, DNA, hair, all of it, then ran them again to make sure I hadn't made a mistake. The results are still the same."

"You got an ID on the body." Roman grabbed for the pencil and paper left on the small desk to his left. One more piece of the puzzle. Maybe this one would lead to the Dream Catcher's partner. "Who's our victim?"

Dr. Meyer cleared her throat. "It's Jessica McKinney."

CHAPTER THIRTY-ONE

HER SISTER WAS DEAD. HOW WAS THAT POSSIBLE? HOW HADN'T SHE known the woman posing as Jessica wasn't the sister she'd left on that boat twenty years ago? They'd had the same color hair, same build, same eye color. Same finger missing from the left hand. Gravity sucked her body toward the earth with greater force, or maybe the sinking feeling was only in her head. Didn't matter.

Brie forced herself to breathe evenly. The seconds ticked off on Roman's phone, silence on the other line, then suddenly sped up as she grabbed for the phone. "Dr. Meyer, I need you to compare the lacerations from Jessica's body against the other four women we've connected to this case. I want to know if the same murder weapon was used on all of them. Contact Special Agent in Charge Mitchell Hayes to get a judge to exhume the bodies if you have to."

"You got it." The line went dead.

"She's the partner, and she's been in front of us this entire time." She handed Roman back the phone and maneuvered past him back into the master bedroom. His clean, masculine scent followed her into the hallway. They had six bodies on their hands, including Greg Hobbs's, and there was only one way this was going to end. Rounding into the hallway, she bolted for the room at the other end of the house. The light pink color on the walls hadn't changed, every single piece of furniture in exactly the same spot as she remembered. Posters of long forgotten boy bands, polaroids of friends, hair elastics. It all looked the same. A shrine to the daughter Ted and Glenda McKinney had lost. Brie gloved up then pulled back the sheets on the bed, threw the pillow to the other side of the room. Movement registered in her peripheral vision, but she didn't have to turn to know Roman had followed her. There had to be something—anything—here that would give them an idea of who'd taken Jessica's place, an idea of who'd killed so many women who'd spent the last years of their lives battling for a second chance. "She played the perfect victim, even cut off her own damn finger to make us believe she was the one who'd been held by Kirk Marshall."

She should've seen it.

"Do you smell that?" The light hint of bleach burned her nostrils, but it was Roman who held up the wastepaper basket full of cleaning wipes, and her stomach shot into her throat. He skimmed his gloved finger across the small desk pressed up against the only window in the room. "No dust. Looks like she wiped everything down. How much do you want to bet we aren't going to be able to pull a clean print from anything she touched in this room."

"She couldn't have gotten everything. Call Ludington PD. We need to get a crime scene unit in here as soon as possible." Short of burning the house down, it wasn't impossible to clean every molecule of evidence from a scene. Didn't matter how intelligent, manipulative, or charming the woman had been, there were some things suspects couldn't hide. Brie skimmed her fingers across the bedpost. The room had obviously been cleaned, but Jessica—the woman pretending to be Jessica—couldn't have accounted for them discovering her secret so quickly. She'd killed Hobbs in a rush. To tie up loose ends? His death wasn't like the other victims where she'd taken her time, experimented with pain tolerance and how her victims would bleed out before cutting their throats. Hobbs didn't have her signature. Killing him hadn't given her the feeling of completion—satisfaction—because she'd been in a hurry. Because they'd pulled the real Jessica McKinney from the lake.

And like most serial killers, their suspect needed that internal pleasure from the kill. "She's going after another victim."

Roman slowed his search. "We know her secret. We uncovered she's not your sister and can safely assume that's why she ran. What makes you so sure she's not getting the hell out of the city?"

"All of her victims were tortured. The way she kills says she hates them, wants to punish them. So she takes pleasure in their screams and suffering. She takes her time because she wants that feeling to last as long as possible, but she didn't take that time with Hobbs. He'd been working with Kirk Marshall, might have even been able to identify her. He was just a loose end that needed tying." Brie shook her head. "Are there any other witness statements we might've missed when you were searching the database? Any missing victims who fit Kirk Marshall's profile and have floating documents that aren't attached to a case? If there are more of the Dream Catcher's survivors out there, we need to find them. Before the killer does."

Roman had already extracted his phone and started the search. The line between his eyebrows deepened as he scrolled his thumb down the screen. Every killer had a weakness. And they'd finally uncovered their unsub's. If they could find the next victim, they might make it in time to save her. "Got something."

"A name?" She moved in close and read the short witness statement from a next-door neighbor of a girl who'd been taken when she was only nine. "A neighbor claims someone hopped the fence to the backyard of Emma King's residence the night before her parents reported her missing. According to this, the girl was found the next morning walking through town by herself by an early-morning jogger." A quick entry of the victim's name into the FBI's database brought up the woman's current address. In Ludington. Air caught in her throat, and she handed Roman's phone back at him. "She could be the next victim on our killer's list. We have to move."

The light gray walls and family photos blurred in her vision as they barged into the hallway and down the stairs. Fresh January air hit her hard, and she pumped her legs hard. The killer already had a two-hour head start, and she could've taken her latest victim anywhere by now.

"Crime scene unit is on its way." Roman shouted to the two uniformed officers across the street as he pounded down the steps to the street and rounded to the driver's side of the SUV. "No one goes in or leaves this house!"

"Yes, sir," both said in unison.

Brie ripped open the passenger side door and climbed inside, ice working through her. "She won't kill Emma in her home. She's too smart for that. She'll take her prey somewhere no one will interrupt." She had to think. Back to their conversation after they'd been rescued from the boat. What had the killer said about where she and the other victims had been kept? She rubbed at her temples, sweat building against her overheated skin. *When he wasn't holding me on the boat or in his veterinary office, Kirk Marshall kept me locked away in a room in his basement.* Both the boat and the padlocked room in the cabin's basement had been declared active crime scenes. No. The vet clinic. Ludington PD had searched it when Kirk Marshall initially became a suspect, but they'd never had reason to station officers on location after the Dream Catcher had been killed. "My gut says she went straight for Emma after killing Hobbs and took her to Kirk Marshall's veterinary office. It's closed this time of night, anyone passing by wouldn't think much of barking animals, and vets keep phenobarbital and surgical supplies on hand."

"Then that's where we're headed." Roman spun the vehicle around and floored the accelerator. Momentum pushed Brie back in her seat as rubber and asphalt screamed in her ears. They didn't have much time. Every second they were left playing catch up was another opportunity for their killer to add to the list of mounting bodies in this case. And Brie couldn't shoulder anymore. "There's a first aid kit with extra water and towels under your seat."

That deep, soothing voice pulled her back from the edge, kept her in the moment. "What?"

"For your hands." He nodded toward her lap. "You still have Hobbs's blood on your hands."

She hadn't noticed. Hadn't really had time to think about what'd happened since she'd flipped on the light in Hobbs's living room. Only time to react. Spreading her fingers wide in front of her, she studied the splotched stains clinging to her skin. But she wouldn't let the dam of emotion building inside break. Not now. Not when they were so close to finding the killer. Brie searched beneath the seat until her fingers brushed the hard case and extracted a bottle of water and a small, thin package of wet wipes. But no matter how hard she scrubbed at the skin, the feeling of Hobbs's blood washing over her hand had been burned into her memory. "Thanks."

"We're going to catch her. She's going to pay for what she's done." The weight of his gaze pressed the air from her lungs. So much of their job involved working in darkness, yet Roman promised her a glimpse of the sun. He'd gotten to her. Slipped under her skin, broken through the ice she'd built to protect herself, and showed her it was okay to feel again. To trust. To love. For her, there wasn't a difference. She loved him because she trusted him. His attention seemed to burn through the shadows inside the vehicle. After years of looking over her shoulder, wondering when the past would catch up to her, Roman made her feel safe. Separately, they were damn fine agents, but together, they were unstoppable. "We're here."

Brie unholstered her weapon, hit the magazine release, and reloaded. The first waves of adrenaline spiked in her veins as he pulled into the clinic's parking lot. No other vehicles in the lot. No way to know if their killer was already inside without going in. Aiden Holloway and Kinsley Luther as well as the entire Ludington PD were tied up at Hobbs's scene. For now, she and Roman were on their own. She reached for the door handle, but a strong grip pulled her back in her seat. The building's exterior lighting highlighted the warning etched into his expression, and she nodded in silent agreement. Sliding her hand over his, she gave into her body's craving for his touch. Just for a moment. "We do this together."

"Together." His hand fell from her arm, and he pushed from the vehicle.

Brie followed suit, both hands gripped around her weapon as she lightly jogged to the clinic's glass front door. Keeping to one side, she waited until Roman had taken position across from her, each out of sight from anyone looking toward the parking lot from inside. Slowly, she tested the handle. Locked. Which meant in order for the killer to bring her latest victim here, there had to be another way inside the building. She kept her back pressed against the plastic siding and half rock walls, moving alongside the perimeter of the clinic to the east side. Parking lot lighting reflected off three more windows and a second glass door. She tested that one, too, this time finding it unlocked. No way into the building without announcing their presence. But maybe that was what their killer had been counting on all along. The echo of a single barking dog from inside tensed the muscles down her spine, and she turned back to Roman. "We go in on three."

"One." Her partner circled around to her back, gun in hand as she slid her hand over the cold metal handle of the door. "Two. Three."

Lifting her flashlight to meet her weapon, she breached first, Roman close on her heels. Silence. Only the sound of her breath sawing in and out of her lungs registered in the dark reception area of the office. And the smell of blood. Her stomach revolted at the rush, but there was no sign of their victim in the reception area. The odor was coming from the back of the clinic. One step. Two. They moved past the long desk at the front in tandem, through the door leading into the rest of the clinic. She tested the light switch off to the left of the door, but nothing happened. No lights came on, which meant the power had been cut. The hairs on the back of her neck rose on end. She shortened her inhales to combat the coppery stench. The further they headed into the clinic, the stronger the smell. Were they too late? Had their suspect already killed her next victim?

The industrial carpet gave way to stained white linoleum, her shoes squeaking on the fake tile. Rows of metal cages lined the walls. Luminescent eyes stared back as she swept her flashlight over the hospital-like space. Her shoulder brushed one of the cages, and a full-grown German Shepard—possibly the same Kirk Marshall had used to contaminate Ashlee Carr's crime scene—called out with an ear-bursting protest. She backed away, heart in her throat. Roman's hand on her aching shoulder loosened her grip on the trigger, but she couldn't let her guard down yet.

She pressed forward, instincts running on high, every sense she owned tuned to any change in environment. This was what she'd been trained for. This was what she was good at: bringing home the missing. A set of thick double doors at the back of the room swayed on their hinges as the heat kicked on overhead. The surgical suite. The smell of blood was strongest there. Two windows into the suite had been blocked by some kind of black paper or poster board, making it hard to confirm if their victim was here without going straight into the other room. Most likely into a trap. But they couldn't turn back now. Not with Emma King's life at stake.

Brie paused outside of the double doors, locking her gaze on her partner. This was it. This was the moment. She exhaled softly. Then gave the signal. They burst through the double doors, immediately assaulted by the stench of blood. They swept their flashlights over the room, both landing on the same shape in the center. Emma King—bloodied, gagged, and jerking for freedom—tied to a surgical table. Brie took a single step toward the victim. "Emma, it's going to be all right. We're here to help."

The woman screamed from beneath the duct tape against her mouth, shook her head.

"I was hoping you'd get here in time," a voice from the shadows said. "I've been waiting for you."

CHAPTER THIRTY-TWO

Roman swept his flashlight across the room. Where the hell was she? Too many spots to hide. Too many places where the killer could strike. More cages and medical equipment took up most of the room. No windows. A single door to the left. They didn't have time for this. Their victim was bleeding out on the table, Emma's jerks lessening now. They had to get an ambulance here. He reached for his radio.

"You don't want to do that, Agent Bradford." The killer's voice slithered through the room, raising goosebumps along his forearms, and Roman spun toward where he thought she'd taken cover. She could see them, enough for her to notice his movements. "One wrong move and you could make Emma's next breath her last. I'm not sure you could handle the responsibility of another life of your shoulders. Not after what happened with your last partner."

Groaning escaped from behind the duct tape across their victim's mouth.

"Nobody else has to die today." His fingers brushed the radio's antenna. "We know you're not Jessica McKinney, that you killed Greg Hobbs and at least five other women. There's no way out. It's over."

"Over? No." A singsong laugh filled the room. The sound came from his left, opposite from where he'd aimed a few seconds ago. How the hell was she everywhere at once? Killers went out of their way to ensure they're never apprehended, but the imposter had stayed. She had a plan. "We haven't even gotten started."

Nausea rolled through him.

"Who the hell are you?" Brie shifted her weight between both feet beside him, her arm brushing his as she scanned the darkness. This was all a sick game, the kind designed to run out the clock while their victim bled out on the table. Only he and Brie had no intention of losing. Gurgling reached his ears. Shit. Emma wasn't moving anymore. "What do you want?"

"Tick tock, tick tock... Emma's not screaming anymore." An attempt at concern cut through the melodic drone of the woman's voice, but Roman knew she didn't have an ounce of empathy in her body. Sociopaths didn't work like that. They were good at mimicking emotions but nothing more. "You can save her, agents, but you're running out of time. Some of those cuts are a lot deeper than they look." Hell, had the bitch cut one of Emma's arteries? "It'll take two of you to try to stop all that bleeding or..." Light spilled across the floor as door to the left crashed against the outside of the building. The outline of a woman centered in the door frame, her head cocked to one side. "You can finally catch your killer. Which is it going to be?"

The floor vibrated under him as the door slammed shut.

"Son of a bitch." Roman holstered his weapon and lunged toward their victim, heart in his throat. Biting down on the end of his flashlight, he clamped his hands over what he thought was the worst of the victim's lacerations, but without power to the building and a clear visual, he had no way of knowing. They were working blind. He applied pressure, but there was so much blood. It'd soaked through Emma's clothing, spread across the cold metal table beneath her. "Stay with us, Emma."

Static reached his ears a split second before Brie's voice chased back the panic climbing up his spine.

"This is Special Agent Brie McKinney requesting an ambulance to two-for-three North Jebavy. Victim is a Caucasian female with multiple lacerations and stab wounds identified as Emma King." Brie replaced her radio with the flashlight from between his teeth and set two fingers against Emma's throat. "Pulse is weak. We're losing her." She maneuvered down the victim's body. "Roman."

Her simple use of his name pulled his focus from the pools of blood growing around their victim. He noted the damage to Emma's thighs and legs as Brie held the flashlight over their victim. Hell. The killer had sliced nearly every inch of this poor woman, and he automatically increased the pressure on the wounds he had access to. Their suspect was right. Stopping the bleeding would take two people, but he couldn't stand the thought of the imposter—whoever she was—getting her hands on her next victim. It was a miracle this one survived long enough for them to get to her. The next one might not be so lucky. He shook his head. "You have to go after her."

Those mesmerizing blue-green eyes snapped to his, her lips parting. "We have to stop the bleeding. If I leave—"

"The ambulance is already on its way. I can control the pressure until they arrive. This place has medical supplies. It'll be rudimentary at best, but I can do the job." Locking one hand around a pulsing wound in the victim's arm, Roman reached for the medical cart off to the side of the table. Bloody tools and an empty syringe rolled across the surface as he brought it closer. Sweat dripped into his vision. The killer had been right before. He couldn't shoulder another death. Couldn't live with the fact he'd just helped a killer escape. It wasn't in his nature. "We can't let her do this to someone else, Brie. We can't let her get away. Go."

Brie rounded the table, and the muscles down his spine pulled a bit straighter. Framing his face, she planted a soft kiss against his mouth. Her light perfume battled the coppery undertones of the blood on his hands. That legendary control slipped over her expression, and a rush of confidence settled over him. This wasn't the woman who'd asked him to stay on the couch with her when she couldn't sleep, the woman who'd smiled when he'd brought her, her favorite flavor of cupcake, or who'd woken from nightmares screaming in her room. In that moment, she wasn't Brie any longer. At least, not the one he'd come to know over the last five days. She was the agent who'd never turned away from a challenge, who carried the entire team with her strength. The agent who'd kept distance from everyone else in her life to survive. In an instant, she'd become exactly who their colleagues feared. A sociopath. "Do whatever you have to, to save her. And stay safe."

"Stay alive." His jaw warmed with her touch, but then she was gone, running toward the door the killer had disappeared through less than two minutes ago. The woman had a spine of steel under skin of silk. No matter how much he wanted to be there at her side, to help her fight the monster hiding behind the mask of her past, Emma King wasn't going to make it out of this room without his help.

Setting his flashlight on the cart at an angle, he tore pieces of gauze with his teeth into long strips and wrapped them above the deepest wound in the victim's arm. The fast pump of blood slowed when he released the pressure, but not enough. Their victim had already lost too much blood. And heaven only knew how many more arteries her torturer had cut. He had to move fast. Tying tight strips above each fatal wound, he fought to control the adrenaline spike flowing through him.

Clamps. Vets had to use clamps during surgery on the animals. He kicked at the cart, using his shoe to open drawer after drawer as he kept pressure on the worst of Emma's wounds. His vision had started adjusting to the darkness, but the flashlight only provided so much light to ascertain the damage to the victim's entire body. Tools hit the linoleum floor. Every second he scrambled was another second Emma's chances plummeted. Where the hell was that damn ambulance? "Come on."

He pulled the third drawer down. Bingo. Threading his fingers through the first set of handles, he studied the victim's face in as much light as the flashlight allowed. Her skin had paled, gone waxy, but she was alive. He still had a chance to save her. Still had a chance to make up for the blood on his hands. "Sorry, Emma. This is going to hurt like a bitch." He clamped the artery in her arm as best as he could, holding her down as she arched away from the table, her scream piercing through him. By the third clamp, she'd sunken into unconsciousness, but he'd stopped most of the bleeding.

"FBI!" Footsteps combined with voices echoed through the outer door of the surgical suite. Overhead lights flickered to life, and he closed his eyes against the burn of the sudden onslaught.

"In here!" Roman exhaled hard, folding his hand in Emma's as EMTs rushed through the double doors. Agents Aiden Holloway and Kinsley Luther followed close behind, both slowing at the sight on the table. "Victim's pulse is weak. I clamped the cut arteries I could find, but there are a dozen more or so lacerations I wasn't able to see. She needs a transfusion. Fast."

"Holy shit." Holloway buried his nose and mouth in the crook of his arm. Both agents kept their distance as Roman slipped his hand out of Emma's and took a step back to give the EMTs room to do their job. Medics shouted orders to each other. A stretcher arrived to move the victim from the scene, and Roman hoped like hell he'd done enough.

"Did you see who did this?" Kinsley asked.

"Yes. Grab your gear. You two are with me." He wiped his hands on a nearby towel, his cuffs soaked and crusted at the same time. Rolling up his sleeves, he cleaned up as best as he could then followed the EMTs out the side door their killer had used to escape. Dropping temperatures bit into his exposed skin along his forearms and neck. And Brie… She was out there alone. It was all too easy imagining her body spread out on that table after what he'd just seen, but Roman wasn't going to let that happen. Not her. Not like that. Morning light had started to break through low cloud cover. Soon, sunrise would chase back the shadows of the small ring of trees surrounding the vet clinic, but he couldn't wait that long. His partner was in danger, and this time, he wouldn't fail her. "Get me a layout of what's on the other side of these trees. We're going hunting."

Within minutes, strapped with FBI-issued Kevlar and extra ammunition, Roman picked up two separate trails in the thawing mud, both heading straight for the patch of woods. One of them their killer's, the other Brie's. His partner had moved fast, almost in line with the second set of prints. Puffs of air crystalized in front of his mouth as they jogged alongside the tracks, Roman in the lead. Branches and dead foliage cast shadows across the forest floor, every brush of breeze freezing another layer of his body. Their killer was on the run, but there was only one place she'd want this to end. And according to the map Holloway had uploaded on his phone, they were a quarter of a mile from where this had all started. He picked up the pace. Brie had at least a five-minute head start on the team. The imposter even more. His legs screamed for release, the stitches in his side chafing against the gauze, but he wouldn't stop. Not until they'd brought down the killer, and not until Brie was safe in his arms.

Luther and Holloway kept on his heels as mud gave way to thick, wet sand and the trees thinned. A different kind of crispness in the air coated the back of his throat. They were closing in. Two sets of heavy breathing reached his ears. "Hope you know where you're going," Holloway said.

"We're already here." Clear tracks transformed to thousands of wells in the sand, and Roman slowed his pace. They couldn't track Brie's footprints in one of the most tourist-centric locations in the state, but he didn't have to. The outline of Big Sable Point Lighthouse lay dead ahead. He scanned the landscape, searched for movement. Tall grass swayed on a gust of wind as reds and orange painted the sky. He crouched below the first set of small dunes and faced the rest of the team.

"The killer is the woman posing as Brie's sister. Jessica McKinney. She was the Dream Catcher's partner. She's the one who's been experimenting on and killing our victims." Weapons drawn, Holloway and Luther nodded in confirmation, and in that moment, he was an HRT operator again, leading the next mission. Warmth chased back the permanent ice that'd settled in his muscles since he'd been reassigned to the bureau's missing persons division. He'd lost the support of his team the moment he'd been forced to put down one of their own and had no reason to believe he'd find it again. But Holloway, Luther, Brie, even SAC Haynes, had supported him on this case, trusted him to get the job done. He tightened his fingers around the grip of his weapon. And he trusted them. He had a new team now, one he'd risk his life to protect. Just as they'd risk theirs. Hell, if that didn't feel good. Roman locked onto the boat docked a few hundred feet from the black and white lighthouse ahead. The crime scene unit had already processed the scene, but there was a chance the killer had gone back to familiar ground. "We'll clear the boat first. Stay alert. She knows we're onto her, and she'll kill anyone who gets in her way."

CHAPTER THIRTY-THREE

BRIE KICKED IN THE DOOR OF THE RED-ROOFED GIFT SHOP ATTACHED TO the lighthouse, gun aimed high. She'd tracked the killer through the trees and across the beach. To the spot where she'd been given a second chance, a new life, a new purpose. Big Sable Point Lighthouse. Darkness deepened as she stepped inside, every cell in her body on fire as warning surged through her. The killer wasn't going to escape this time. Time to end this. "I know you're here. Come out, hands up, unarmed, and nobody else has to die today."

Her heart thudded hard in her chest. Had Roman been able to stop Emma King's bleeding, or would they have to add her name to the long list of lives lost during this investigation? Her stomach soured at the idea. Six women—including the real Jessica McKinney—had been abducted, tortured, and punished for surviving their killer as children. Too many.

To the right, carousels of souvenirs, treats, T-shirts, and small stuffed animals gave ample cover to anyone not wanting to be found. She moved slowly, heel-toeing it across the narrow spaces between glass cases showing off all manner of lightning glass and jewelry. No movement. Only silence. Brie turned back the way she'd come, attention on the partially-open door leading to the lighthouse itself. She swiped her tongue across her lips to counter the sudden dryness, but there was no turning back now. No escape from the past she'd battled to bury for the last twenty years. Metal protested on old hinges as she swung open the door, a cold draft of wind surging downward through the tower.

"You should've left well enough alone, Briohny." That voice. Her voice. "You should've left Jessica where I put her, and none of this would've had to happen. The captain might still be alive, you would've gone on thinking I was your sister, not having to deal with that crushing guilt you carry anymore. At least, until I came for you myself."

"I think we're past the point of lying to each other. You would've killed Hobbs whether Jessica had been recovered or not. He knew, didn't he? That's what he was trying to tell me as he was bleeding out in my arms. Not that Jessica hadn't killed him, but that the person who'd cut his throat wasn't Jessica at all." Brie forced the sob in her throat down, searching the stairs leading up to the lighthouse's light, but only noted shadows. "You're not my sister. So who the hell are you?"

"Seeing as how you won't make it out of here alive, I guess there's no harm in giving you my name." Goosebumps prickled along Brie's arms and neck despite the warmth of her coat and the sweat beading at her lower back. "My name is Tabitha Gray."

The helix of stairs hugged the wall to her right, and at the top, the light that'd led so many sailors through the darkness. Just as it'd led her the night she'd escaped her killer. "You must've been a teenager when Kirk Marshall abducted you, Tabitha."

The anger, the punishment, the revenge. It all added up. So many victims had escaped the Dream Catcher, but Jessica hadn't. And neither had her killer. Her voice carried up through the tower, toward the breaking dawn. Brie cleared the main level, sidestepping her way to the stairs. She had the disadvantage. No matter how careful she was, no matter how well she followed her training, Tabitha had the upper hand. The killer would see her coming. Metal stairs vibrated beneath her with every step she took. She slid her gaze upward, but it was still too dark to make out anything solid. Too dark to get a visual on the killer's position. "I can't imagine how hard it must've been for you to watch all those girls escape, move on with their lives, be happy. All the while you were trapped with him. Alone, scared for your life. Desperate for someone to save you."

"I wasn't alone." The voice echoed down the bricks from above, and Brie slowed her ascent up the metal stairs. Caution slid through her, air caught in her throat, but she wouldn't stop. Couldn't. There were too many lives at stake. "He drugged us, took us from our beds in the middle of the night. I woke up first on that damn boat same as you. He'd tied our hands behind our backs so we couldn't swim if we jumped overboard." A humorless laugh pierced through her. "An extra precaution, I learned, after he told me one of his latest victims had gotten away."

Brie.

"Us?" Bricks caught on the wool of her coat as Brie took another step up. She'd reached the first platform scaling up the belly of the tower, but still couldn't pinpoint Tabitha's location.

"Me and my sister." Sadness tainted the killer's words, a distance that hadn't been there before. "She was only seven when he kidnapped us. She'd just barely learned how to ride the bike I'd gotten too big for. She'd wake me up early every morning, begging me to take her out to practice. Charlotte loved that bike."

Dread pooled at the base of her spine as Brie aimed her weapon high and advanced toward the next platform. Two pairs of sisters, both taken by the Dream Catcher, two families destroyed. Two very different outcomes. The muscles in her throat ached as she scanned the stairs above. Shadows shifted along the tower's walls with the rising sun. There was nowhere to hide. "You stayed with the Dream Catcher to protect her."

"I had to! She was innocent." Rage and hatred embedded each word, twisting the guilt inside Brie tighter. "She didn't deserve what that bastard had planned for her. So, yes, I stayed. I did what you never had the courage to do, but none of it mattered." Tabitha's voice grew louder. Closer? But that wasn't possible. There were no alcoves or doors leading off the tower. Only the platform at the top. The woman posing as Jessica had been manipulating them all this time. This was just another mind game. "He killed her right in front of me anyway."

"And now you're punishing all those girls who escaped. Because if you can't be happy, if your sister didn't get a chance to live the rest of her life, neither can they, right?" Brie strengthened her grip around the gun and slowed as warning fisted inside. Pressing her back into the bricks, she stared straight into the wall of shadows straight ahead. Her adrenaline spiked, pulse beating wildly as though her heart was looking for an escape out of her chest. The space below her earlobes heated, skin prickling, and she was suddenly too hot despite the freezing temperature of the wall behind her. She fought to keep the tremor in her hands out of her voice. "You killed Jessica. Why? She was a victim, same as you."

"Jessica, Jessica, Jessica…" A lightness cut through the rage echoing around them. "Yes, well, I wasn't the only one Kirk Marshall decided to keep as a pet." Shuffling sounded from what she thought was above, but Brie couldn't pinpoint the origin with the tower echoing the killer's every word. "It was only the two of us left. For years, it was us against him. Like sisters. We survived together, protected each other, even convinced Kirk that we could help him find more victims until one day, he might believe we were really on his side. That we weren't his victims anymore. We were his partners. I trusted her." Venom coated Tabitha's voice. "Until she betrayed me trying to escape, trying to leave me behind. Just as you did to her."

A flash of movement was all Brie registered before the pain exploded throughout her middle. Her back hit the wall, her weapon falling to the floor, as she followed the hand around the blade in her gut up to the hard expression of the killer. Pinned against the bricks, she struggled for her next breath as she wrapped her fingers around Tabitha's wrist. Blood bloomed around the slim but powerful boning knife, possibly the same blade used on all the other victims.

"You're right about all those women who escaped, the ones I'm hunting. They don't get to be happy, to have families, to move on with their lives, and neither do you." Tabitha got close, close enough her exhales feathered across the underside of Brie's jaw. Stepping back, she pulled the knife free. "I'm not going to stop until I find every single one of them and take back that time they stole. I'm going to make them pay, make them hurt, and put their families through the same pain Kirk Marshall forced on me when he killed my sister. And there's nothing you or your partner can do to stop me."

Roman. He was still out there, still a target as long as Tabitha was free. He wouldn't stop hunting this killer. Air crushed from her lungs. Brie's knees threatened to collapse out from under her without the added support. She pressed her hand over the wound in an attempt to staunch the bleeding, but she couldn't slow her racing heartbeat. She had to get control, ignore the pain. What she wouldn't give for one of Roman's patch jobs right now. She forced herself away from the wall, nearly doubled over, but stood solid. "You're not going anywhere."

Brie launched her fist into Tabitha's face, the sound of flesh meeting bone loud in her ears. The momentum knocked the killer back on her heels, and she followed it up with another hit from her injured arm. Pain lightninged down through her fingers then bounced into her chest cavity, but she held back the scream as Tabitha lashed out with the boning knife. Throwing herself back into the wall, Brie barely managed to dodge the blade from cutting into her cheek, then lunged.

Her attacker slipped out of the way, and Brie slammed into the stairway railing. Fire burned as the boning knife sliced a trail down her spine. Metal vibrated beneath the sound of her scream. She hauled her elbow back as hard as she could, connecting with the killer's face. The killer hit the platform, metal on metal reverberating through the tower. Tabitha had lost the knife. Sunlight skimmed across the wall to her left, giving enough light for Brie to see the stained blade balanced precariously a few stairs down.

She raced forward at the same time Tabitha rolled toward the stairs, too late. The killer wrapped her hand around the blade and swiped up. Brie threw her hands out to keep her balance, but it wasn't enough. She fell backward, and faster than she thought possible, the killer attacked. She caught her attacker's wrists mere inches before the boning knife's tip punctured her throat. Her muscles burned, her body screaming for release as the woman she'd believed to be her sister pushed the tip of the blade ever closer. The stitches in her shoulder burst, and she gritted her teeth against the groan building in her chest.

Sweat slid down Tabitha's cheekbones to her chin. "You look like her, you know. Jessica." The tendons between the killer's neck and shoulders stretched as Brie pushed back with everything she had left. "I told her what I'd planned to do once we got rid of Kirk Marshall, how I intended to make every single one of those girls who'd escaped pay for leaving us behind, and do you know what she said to me? What her last words were?"

The tip of the blade scraped against the over sensitized skin of Brie's neck, drawing blood. She felt it trickle down her neck as she battled for her life. She was losing too much blood. Her body would start shutting down organ by organ if she didn't get help soon, but she couldn't let go. Couldn't give up. She couldn't let Roman's name come next on the killer's list. Not him.

"Jessica promised I'd never get to you," Tabitha said. "Guess she was wrong."

Silence buzzed in Brie's mind. Her sister had protected her until the end, sacrificed herself for the slightest chance of keeping Brie safe, even after she'd abandoned her sister that night. She constricted her grip around Tabitha's wrist. That sacrifice wouldn't go to waste. Brie would make sure of it. She tucked her left foot on the outside of the killer's shin and planted her other foot between Tabitha's legs. Pulling her attacker closer, within centimeters of the blade's tip, she hiked her hips higher and threw the Tabitha as hard as she could. The knife disappeared over the side of the platform, steel on cement echoing up to their position at least two stories above. Brie darted for the gun and wrapped her grip tight, before swinging around to take aim.

"You agents are all the same. You just can't resist being the hero. That's what makes you so vulnerable. And predictable." Tabitha stood at the edge of the platform, something that resembled a small detonator in one hand, her thumb positioned above the red button. The killer's chest heaved as she struggled for audible breath, a trail of blood sliding over her eyelashes. It was only in that moment, as Tabitha blinked to clear her vision, that Brie realized the brown in her eyes had moved. Color contacts. She should've spotted that before now. "Your forensics units didn't get the chance to search the entire boat before they were called away to Captain Hobbs's murder scene. I made sure of that. Otherwise they would've known the Dream Catcher didn't just set up the cabin to explode. He wired all of his hideouts in case law enforcement caught onto his operation and had to destroy the evidence." Tabitha took a single step forward. "Do you want to guess where your partner and the two other members of your team are right now, Special Agent McKinney?" One breath. Two. "If you shoot me, I'll kill them all and still get away with it. Right after I finish with you."

There were no windows in the tower apart from the opening at the top, no way to confirm Roman's—or the rest of the team's—position. No way to tell if Tabitha was telling the truth. The killer had been one step ahead of them the entire investigation, manipulated one of the most deadly serial killers into doing her dirty work, and posed as a victim when there was only a monster behind that smile. Killers would do and say anything to prevent themselves from getting caught, and there wasn't a single word out of her mouth Brie was ready to accept as truth. But if there was a chance her team was in danger—

"Time's up." Tabitha compressed the button, and the entire tower rumbled around them. Dust dislodged from crevices, catching the orange glow rising well above the lighthouse. "You should've stayed with your partner, Briohny."

"No!" Brie pulled the trigger.

CHAPTER THIRTY-FOUR

Roman had heard the soft beeping coming from beneath the stained mattress a split second before he'd run for the galley stairs. Holloway and Luther. He had to get them off the deck. "Move, move, move! The boat is rigged—"

The blast propelled him over the back of the boat, a burst of orange and yellow the only thing he saw before he hit the water. Ice worked under his skin, dove deep into larger muscles that controlled his movements. Paralysis set in as the weight of his gear dragged him into the depths of the lake. Blackness was closing in, but he couldn't tell if he was from losing consciousness or if he'd been pulled deep enough morning rays of sunrise couldn't break past the surface. Didn't matter. The boat. Holloway and Luther were on the boat at his order. And Brie... Where the hell was Brie? Had she been caught in the blast? Did the killer have her?

The fog clung tight to his brain, but he had feeling in his fingers now. Stretching them wide, he went for the Velcro on his Kevlar and ripped it from his chest. The vest floated past his feet then disappeared toward the bottom of the lake. He kicked for the surface, water already in his shoes. Bubbles rushed over the burned skin along his neck and arms then raced ahead of him as he clawed his way toward the surface.

His head broke water, and he gulped air as fast as his lungs allowed. Fire licked at debris scattered across the lake, dock, and beach, but there was no sign of the rest of his team. Chunks of ice and remnants of the boat scratched exposed skin as he swam for shore. Hell, he'd been thrown at least fifty feet. The lake wrestled to pull him back under as he waded into knee-deep water. He scanned the beach, lungs heaving against the cold. "Holloway! Luther!"

The familiar sound of gunfire exploded from inside the lighthouse, and every nerve in his body caught fire. The breath rushed out of him as realization hit. Brie hadn't been near the blast. He caught sight of the gift shop's front door, partially open, and Roman's gut clenched into a hardened fist. She'd followed the killer into the tower. He headed for the lighthouse. "Brie—"

A groan registered over the pop and burn of the flames surrounding the boat, and he froze. The sound had come from the left. The gunshot had come from the lighthouse tower to his right. And he was the only member of their team still standing. He dashed around to the other side of the boat. Sand kicked up behind him, threatened to trip him as he homed in on a soaking wet Kinsley Luther clawing her way up the shore. He pumped his legs hard when he spotted the large gash at her hairline. Sliding his hands around her vest, he helped her climb higher up the beach and turned her face up. "Luther, where's Holloway? Did you see where he was thrown?"

Her head fell back on her shoulders, eyes closed, the agent's body limp in his arms. No response. All three of them had been on the boat. Holloway couldn't have been thrown far. But whether he'd hit the beach or the water, Roman had no idea. He set Luther into the sand, wiping the trail of blood from her forehead with his shirt before he checked her pulse. Steady. She'd live.

A flash of black dragged his attention back out into the water—Kevlar—but was gone in the next instant. Damn it. He rocketed down the beach and lunged back into the lake, swinging his arms as fast as his body would allow. Freezing temperatures slowed him down, but he kept pushing. The object he'd spotted might just be another piece of debris from the boat. Or it could've been Holloway. Muscles down his back and across his shoulders burned as he kicked with everything he had left, but exhaustion caught up with him fast. He treaded water, waiting for something—anything—to give him an idea of where the missing agent had gone under. He had no other option. He'd have to dive.

"People need to stop trying to blow me up." He exhaled hard, clearing his lungs, then took a full breath before he plunged into the icy depths. Pressure built in his chest the deeper he swam. He hadn't trained for underwater rescue, but that wouldn't stop him from finding his teammate. Because every single person in the missing persons division would do exactly the same thing for him. Seconds ticked by, his heart pounding hard in his skull. He fanned his arms wide, but he only managed to skim a few pieces of debris. He'd had to ditch his Kevlar to keep from being pulled toward the bottom of the lake. There was a chance Holloway had been knocked unconscious and couldn't get the vest off in time, dragging him down. Roman swam deeper, his body using what little precious oxygen he had left. He'd have to surface soon, but he'd never left a man behind. And he wasn't about to start now.

The dark outline roughly the same size of a human male materialized through the blue water. Roman swam harder, faster, ignoring the pain in his side and the ache in his legs. Reaching out, he brushed his hand over cold skin and wrapped his hand around the agent's arm. His stitches strained as he tugged the one-hundred-and-eighty-pound interrogator toward the surface. Then ripped. The bolt of agony pushed air from his lungs, huge bubbles of oxygen rising to meet the surface of the lake. He sank deeper, Holloway's weight tugging him down. They were running out of time. Brie was running out of time. He couldn't fail her again.

He had to risk it.

Giving into the agent's weight, Roman let Holloway's unconscious body pull him further from the surface. Further from Brie. He hauled his team member face-to-face and went for the Velcro on his teammate's vest. Precious seconds slipped by as he maneuvered the agent's arms out of the armor and let it disappear toward the bottom of the lake. The team had been ripped apart. Unconscious. Left for dead. They had no hope of bringing down the killer who'd been two steps ahead of them at any given time in this investigation. Not without a miracle. But he couldn't give up. He couldn't let the Dream Catcher's partner win. He'd fight until the end. For the families, for the victims. For Brie.

He hauled Holloway into his chest, his entire body straining toward the surface. The last of his oxygen supply slipped from his mouth as a groan rumbled through his chest. Five feet. Three. They were almost there. Almost at the surface. Sunlight pierced through the water, beckoning him upward. Using every last bit of his strength, he shoved Holloway ahead of him. The agent crashed to the surface, far from shallow water, but with better chances than if he'd been left to die.

Cold temperatures slowed Roman's movements, increased the pressure in his chest. He reached for the rippling water above, but gravity had taken his last reserves of strength. He was sinking again. Strains of red colored the water mere inches from his face. Blood slipped through his fingers as he tested the bullet wound in his side. Holloway's shadow cast him into darkness from above. Or was his vision going dark? Didn't matter. He hadn't mistaken the gunshot from the tower before. Brie needed his help. She needed her team. One way or another, he'd get to her.

Because he loved her, damn it.

Loved the way she fit against him, loved the fire in her eyes when she got angry, loved the mole on her left cheek and the way it shifted when she released the smile he couldn't get out of his mind. She wore darkness and strength equally well and held others up with that strength. He'd chosen her. His Brie. And there was no way in hell he'd lose her now.

Roman kicked with everything he had left, which wasn't much, managing to gain a few more inches. A scream built in his throat, but he clung to every last molecule of oxygen to keep himself conscious. Another kick. Another few inches. Within seconds, his hand broke through crystal clear water, and he pushed his head above the surface. Gasping for air, he locked onto a still unconscious Holloway with one hand and a floating piece of debris with the other. He squinted against the brightness as tendrils of blackness bled from his vision and rested his head back on his shoulders. He had to get to Brie. "Move, damn it."

He spotted Kinsley Luther on the beach and gritted through the next few strokes of agony. She waded knee deep to meet him, hands outstretched to help bring her partner in. How long had Holloway been under the water? Two minutes? Three? The chances the interrogator had survived the explosion in addition to nearly drowning went down every second he struggled to make it to shore. He hauled Holloway onto the beach, dropping him to the sand fast. Smoke filled his lungs, heat from the fire thawing his fingers fast. Roman doubled over to catch his breath, his strength making a comeback with each inhale. "He's not breathing. Pulse is weak."

"If you think Aiden would let an explosion and a little bit of water kill him, you don't know him well at all. Back up is on the way. Take care of yourself before you bleed out." Nodding toward Roman's midsection, Special Agent Luther counted off a rhythm of chest compressions. She pressed her ear against Holloway's lips and covered his mouth with hers. One breath in, two. Holloway's chest rose with the added air, but no response. She pulled back and started over again.

"No time." Roman clamped his hand over the hole in his side, the gauze and tape washed away somewhere in the damn lake. The stitches had torn free, the wound exposed and vulnerable, but he wouldn't let that stop him. Not when it came to Brie. Sweeping Luther's service weapon from the sand, he checked the magazine and loaded a round into the chamber. This wasn't over. He headed toward the lighthouse, a new rush of adrenaline lighting his nerves on fire. He'd trusted Brie with his heart, and he'd fight for her until his last breath. "I going to find my partner."

"Roman," the profiler said from behind, and he turned to meet her light brown gaze. "Someone attacks one of us, they attack all of us. Give her hell."

He nodded then followed the path of wells in the sand to the front door of the gift shop. The gunshot had come from inside the tower, he was sure of it. The team might've been torn to pieces, but he'd been left standing. He'd finish this. Roman cleared the small gift shop filled with trinkets and souvenirs before stepping through the door leading into the lighthouse tower. He scanned the stairs, the platforms, every brick in the wall. No movement. No signs of an ambush. Two steps. Three. Metal scraped against cement as he kicked a long, thin blade across the floor.

A boning knife…covered in blood.

The killer's?

Keeping his back to the wall, he spiraled up the tower step-by-step, his boots squishing with lake water every move he made. She had to be here. Because if she wasn't, if she was already dead… No. Brie was the strongest of them all, the only one who'd managed to bring them together as a team, the only one who'd broken through the haze he'd been lost in for so long. She knew the truth about him, trusted him, wanted him. Not as her knight in shining armor, but as the damaged man he'd always been.

"Roman, no." That voice. Her voice. He'd recognize it anywhere. It'd been part of his dreams—his fantasies—for months, and his nerve endings stood at attention. There. On one of the upper platforms. The edge of her coat draped over the metal, hiding her outline from him initial search of the tower. "It's…trap. Get out."

Son of a bitch. She wasn't moving. Roman pounded up the stairs, heart in his throat. Then he saw her. Back pressed against the wall, she'd managed to sit herself up. Gun tight in his hand, he lowered to his knees beside her and scanned her injuries. Stab wound to the gut, laceration across her arm, and where the hell was the rest of the blood coming from? Her back? Rage exploded through him, but it wouldn't do a damn bit of good. Right now, he had to get her the hell out of here. He framed her face with his free hand, forced her to focus on him. "Baby, tell me what to do."

"Stop the bleeding." A single tear slipped from the corner of her eye. "I shot her, but it wasn't fatal. She went up…the stairs. She…" Brie's throat worked to swallow, her breathing growing shallower with every attempt. "She wants…to kill you in order to punish…me. Stop the bleeding then go. I'll…finish this."

"I told you before." He swiped blood crusted hair from her face. Hell, she was too damn pale, and she still hadn't moved. They were running out of time. "I'm not going anywhere. I chose you. I took you to my bed. That means something to me."

"It means something…to me, too." Her weak smile only tightened the vise around his heart. Brie stretched her hand toward him, tremors wracking through her as she took the gun from his hand. "You're my weakness, and I can't…watch you die."

A second gunshot echoed off the walls.

Shock washed over him as he stared down at the flow of blood coming from his chest. His ears rang, vision going blurry. What the hell just happened? The pain set in then, and he fell back.

Brie's scream echoed through his mind. "Roman!"

CHAPTER THIRTY-FIVE

SHE COULDN'T STOP THE BLEEDING.

Brie had caught her partner's before he'd hit the platform and pressed her hand to Roman's wound as he fell back. No. No, no, no, no. His breathing shallowed as seconds—minutes—ticked by. She wasn't going to watch him die. Footsteps sounded off the tower's walls. The shot had come from another platform above, from Brie's own service weapon when Tabitha had taken it off of her. They had to move. "Get up, Roman. Come on. We can do this. We have to do this."

Her own wound protested as she forced him to sit up. She bit back the scream clawing up her throat. The sun hadn't fully risen. If they moved fast enough, she could use the shadows along the walls to their advantage. Just as their killer had. Safety. She had to get him to safety, stop her own bleeding, and regroup. She'd told him the truth before. He'd become her weakness, but she wouldn't let Tabitha use him against her.

"I've taken down your team, you're bleeding out, and the partner you've sworn to protect is dying." The killer's voice grew louder as she advanced. "There's nothing you can do to beat me, Agent McKinney. I've already won. The only lives you've managed to save are the victims the Dream Catcher won't be able to hunt now. The women who escaped, who left me behind to suffer, who betrayed me? They're all going to die. Because of you."

No. Brie wrapped her hand around the gun she'd taken from Roman. Moaning through the pain in her gut, she forced him to his feet. She'd gotten him through the woods under heavy fire and a gunshot wound in her shoulder. What was a knife wound compared to a bullet? His weight unbalanced her, and she fell into the side railing. Bruising pressure dug into her hip, but she forced herself to dig deep, to rely on the strength she'd built over the last few years to power her through. One level of stairs. That was all that stood between them and potential cover. Well, that and the armed homicidal maniac two platforms above. "Go to hell."

"I'll see you there," Tabitha said.

Two more gunshots ricocheted off the metal under her feet. Faster than she thought possible, Roman hauled Brie back into the wall, covering her with his body in an attempt to protect her. Air pushed from her lungs, and pain bolted down her spine, but they couldn't stop. Sliding his arm across her low back, he pulled her into his chest as she took aim over his left shoulder and fired. Tabitha's outline disappeared from the platform above, presumably to take cover, and Brie seized the advantage. She took the majority of her partner's weight against her side and headed for the stairs. He stumbled, gripping the outside railing tight, but she kept him on his feet. Forty feet. Thirty. They could make it.

A third bullet slammed into the back of her right thigh, and Brie went down hard. She couldn't hold back her scream as her leg gave out and lost balance, taking Roman with her. The tower, Tabitha, everything blurred as they tumbled down the metal stairs. Metal cut into her then cold cement as she landed face first at the bottom of the stairs. She exhaled hard, kicking up dust from the floor as she gathered the strength to get up. Her hand brushed Roman's arm. She'd been shot, stabbed, beaten, her body at the edge of shutting down from blood loss, but Brie fisted his shirt collar and pulled him to his feet. She'd spent the last twenty years hiding behind the armor she'd built, believing she was strongest on her own, only relying on herself. But it'd all been a lie, an excuse to keep her distance. And it'd only taken nearly dying—twice—for her to realize it.

She was stronger because of him. She'd survived because of him.

Roman pulled her close, the scent of water and sand clinging to his skin, but this time, her stomach didn't revolt. "I've got you...baby. Lean...on me."

"I know." He'd always had her back, put her needs first, and trusted her instincts. He led her forward. Huddled under the protection of his arm, Brie shifted her weight off her injured leg, but it wouldn't be enough. Her leg was useless, and she'd already lost too much blood. If Roman hadn't come for her, she'd never made it out of the lighthouse alive. Two steps. Three. A fourth bullet embedded in the brick beside her head, and Brie automatically ducked. They reached the door leading into the gift shop and slammed it closed behind them.

Roman positioned her against the nearest wall and disappeared, and she slid down until her butt hit the floor. In seconds, he'd wedged a chair from behind one of the counters under the doorknob to keep the door from opening. It wouldn't hold Tabitha off forever, but it was a start. They had to find cover, a place they could lay low to regroup until neither of them were bleeding out. Somewhere no one would find them. Not even the rest of their team. This case had already taken enough lives. She couldn't stand to lose anyone else today. The doorknob rattled, then fists pounded against the door. He brushed a strand of sticky hair away from her face, his fingertips careful of the stinging cut on her cheek, and settled his gaze on hers. "We've got to move. That door isn't going to hold her for long."

She nodded, out of energy to do anything more. How had she gotten so lucky to be assigned a partner like him? Committed, loyal, selfless. Roman Bradford embodied everything that was right with their team, everything she hadn't known she'd been missing in her life. There was nothing he could do, nothing he could say, that would make her believe he wasn't exactly what'd she needed to fill the hollowness inside. Did he know that? Did he know how much she needed him? That he'd become the one bright light in a life filled with darkness and evil? A cough ripped up her throat, something salty and hot coating her mouth. She covered her face in the crook of her arm and came away with specks of blood on her coat. "The…dunes."

Color drained from his face as he studied her. "Brie, your mouth—"

"I need you to tie something around my leg to slow…the bleeding. We don't…have time to extract the bullet." He turned back into the gift shop, and she doubled over against the pain ripping through her midsection. A wave of dizziness increased the pull on her body as he searched the small store for something they could use as a tourniquet. But the slug in his right pectoral muscle… There was nothing they could do for that here. Banging persisted from behind the door. She'd find them cover, then inspect his wound. Her heart pulsed hard below her ears as he returned with what looked like a dog harness and leash. She couldn't stop the laugh escaping past her lips as delirium set in. "You know, it's not that kind of walk."

His smile chased back the agony burning through her—for just a moment—as he separated the harness from the leash and circled the length around her thigh. "Smart ass."

"We can lose…her in the marshlands long enough to come up with a plan. And hopefully not die from blood loss on the way…there." She fisted his shirt as he pulled the leash tighter, cutting off most of the blood flow through her leg. It wasn't permanent, but it'd work for now. The door holding back the killer and the chair slid forward an inch. They had to move. Using Roman to pull herself up, she led him to the back of the store, her left leg stiff with the tourniquet wrapped around her thigh, toes dragging on the floor. She pushed through the secondary exit, his arm around her lower back, hers draped across his wide shoulders. A perfect fit.

"Which way?" His labored breathing turned watery as they treaded through the sand. Damn it. Could the bullet have nicked his lung? His groan penetrated deep into her, and in that moment, she wanted nothing more than to take away the pain tearing through him.

"Over that hill." A small dirt trail filled the space between the lake's shore and the start of the dunes, but they headed straight for the knee-high grass blocking the view of the marshes beyond the nearest hill. Tourists avoided the area, vehicles were forbidden this far inland, but Brie had memorized the layout of this area years ago. Tabitha wouldn't find them here. Not until they wanted to be found. She just had to keep Roman focused, conscious—alive—and they'd make it. Any other outcome... And she didn't know what she'd do. "I know it doesn't seem like it, but we're winning."

"We've both been shot, you've been stabbed, and our team got blown up less than thirty minutes ago along with the evidence the crime scene unit wasn't able to pull off that boat in time." He dug his toes into the hill, plunging his free hand into the sand to help them over the peak. "How on earth could we possibly be winning?"

"Tabitha hasn't killed us yet. That's got to count for...something, right? By the way, the psychopath who's been posing as my sister...her name is Tabitha." After everything they'd been through, they still had each other. That was all that mattered. Brie led them around the edge of the first shallow marshland, swiping grass out of the way, but each step took a toll. Exhaustion, blood loss, hell, maybe a head injury thrown in, all it of it stole the energy she'd been running off of for the past two hours. Her body couldn't take anymore. Just a little further. A tingling sensation had climbed down her injured leg as the tourniquet did its job, but it wasn't enough. Blood had seeped into the waistband of her slacks, crusted along her midsection. Her vision darkened despite the piercing rays of sunrise coming through the thick tree line ahead. No. She had to keep going. Sand and wetlands turned to dirt and dead foliage as they took cover behind the tree line. Almost there. Almost there. She'd been through this part of the state park before. She could've sworn there'd been a ranger station here. Right here. Brie slowed her pace, her fingers aching as she forced herself to keep hold of him, and she blinked to clear the sweat dripping into her eyes. It had to be around here somewhere. Because if it wasn't, they were dead. "When this is over...you owe me a box of...cupcakes and as many romantic comedies as I want to watch...however many times I want to watch them."

"You're going to make me watch A Christmas Prince, aren't you?" His weight increased on her right side, and she battled to keep her balance. "Even though I have a policy not to watch a movie more than once."

The laugh escaping up her throat broke through the eerie silence around them.

"You watched…it?" There. The ranger station. They'd found it. A flood of relief wrestled with the internal damage determined to tear her apart. Places like this had been set up around the entire park to support back country hikers and rangers on patrol. Medical supplies, food, water, gasoline. The small logged structure was flanked by two large trees, their branches brushing against the light gray shingled rooftop. A single door promised a bottleneck if the killer tracked them this far. No vehicle waiting outside, which meant they had the station to themselves.

"Had to see what you liked about it so much." The undercurrent of pain deepened every word out of his mouth. "The snowball fight scene was my favorite part."

"I think you've lost too…much blood." The station's wooden steps protested under their combined weight. She twisted the doorknob and fell inside. The breath knocked from her lungs as she collapsed against the floor, Roman landing beside her. They'd made it. Her eyelids closed slowly. She couldn't feel her fingers, her toes numb from the cold or shock, she didn't know. She didn't care. They were safe. For now. "The part where she comes…down the stairs is obviously the best part of the whole…movie."

"Brie, you have to open your eyes. Stay with me." The sound of fabric tearing reached through the ringing in her ears. Heat feathered over stomach. Roman's hand? "Shit. There's too much blood. I can't see the wound clearly." Heavy footsteps vibrated through her from the old planked floor, his breathing labored and deep. "Okay, I'm going to have to strip you down to see the damage. Hang on, baby. You're going to be okay. I promise."

"I'm going to…have a scar, aren't…I?" Tired. She was so tired, but Brie used her last reserves of strength to open her eyes. Above her, Roman dove into the first aid kit that'd materialized beside her and extracted a pair of medical scissors from inside. He cut through her blouse, exposing the wound in her stomach, then did the same with her slacks. She couldn't feel the cold as she raised her hand to his chest. The bleeding across his shirt had slowed. Was he going to make it?

"I'm glad…you're my partner."

Darkness closed in.

CHAPTER THIRTY-SIX

Roman threaded the last stitch through the newest hole in his chest as she slept. He'd been lucky. The bullet hadn't gone very deep and the killer had missed anything major. He'd been able to pull it out himself. The lake water hanging out at the back of his throat wouldn't clear out, but if that was the worst thing after everything they'd been through, he'd take it. Cleaning the area a second time with an alcohol wash, he used fresh gauze and tape from the station's first aid kit to dress both of his wounds. Just as he had with Brie's. He studied her tucked in the only bed in the place, her face bruised, cut, and pale. She'd lost a lot of blood—too much—and only time would tell if she woke up. His stomach knotted. No. Not if. *When.*

They'd taken cover in the ranger's station an hour ago. No telling where the killer was, if Tabitha had tracked them here, but his instincts said she'd try for Brie again. Soon. His partner was one of the Dream Catcher's survivors, and the killer had gone out of her way to ensure every single one of those survivors had been punished. Only this time, he'd be ready.

Roman stretched his T-shirt over his head, locking his teeth against the pull of new stitches, as he maneuvered to Brie's bedside. Tugging the quilt he'd laid over her toward her knees, he checked the dressing taped across her lower abdominals. Minimal bleeding. The stitches were holding. He covered her back up, tracing her brow bone with the pad of his thumb. He'd almost lost her. Twice.

Finding her bleeding out on that platform—barely able to move—had scared him to death. His entire life had flashed before his eyes. Swinging that damn bat as hard as could to defend his mother, graduating basic training, the HRT selection process, operation after operation in the line of fire, the moment he'd pulled the trigger and brought down his former partner. The memories had played in rapid succession, one after the other. Then stopped. Leaving only Brie. The first time he'd set sights on her back at headquarters. Shaking her hand when SAC Haynes had introduced them and the electric jolt that shot through him at her touch. The very first time he'd heard her laugh at some joke he couldn't even remember. The kiss they'd shared in her room at the beach house. Her calling his name in the dark. Heat rushed through him, and he reached for the plastic water bottle he'd found from the storage room. She didn't just cross his mind. She lived in it, had become part of him. Maybe from the first time they'd been in the same room together.

Unscrewing the plastic lid, Roman placed the bottle at her mouth. And waited. One minute. Two. No response. The steady rise and fall of her chest kept his hopes high, but she had yet to wake after slipping into unconsciousness more than an hour ago. Shot twice, stabbed, beaten, abducted, and drugged within the last four days. It was a damn miracle she hadn't given up before now. She was fierce, and strong, and full of a fire he couldn't resist. And no one—not even death—would take her from him. "Take a drink, sweetheart. You've lost a lot of blood."

Her lips parted at his command, and his heart jerked in his chest. Water breached the seal of her mouth. The muscles in her throat constricted as she swallowed, and he shifted closer. Blue-green eyes peaked through long black lashes and struggled to focus on him. "You look like hell."

A single laugh escaped his chest. "Can't imagine why."

"Might have something to do with the very determined serial killer who wants us dead, but what do I know?" Her words were strained, groggy. She scanned the ranger's station then attempted to sit up. Pain flashed across her expression before she hiked further up the bed. "You said she blew up the rest of the team. Any word?"

"I tried hailing them using an old CB radio I found in the back, but I haven't heard anything yet. Last I saw of Luther, she'd called in back up while trying to resuscitate Holloway." Dread pooled at the base of his spine. He'd been so concerned with getting to Brie, he hadn't stopped to wonder if their profiler had been able to save Holloway. "I pulled him out of the water after the explosion, but I'm not sure if he made it."

"And Emma King?" she asked.

"First responders got to her in time," Roman said. "She's going to pull through."

"We can't let Tabitha get away." She struggled to sit up and pushed back the quilt. A line of blood had stained the fresh gauze over the wound in her gut, but Roman knew better than to get in her way. "I'm not the only one left on her list of survivors. There are more out there, living their lives, and they have no idea they're targets. We have to stop her. We have to end this." Running her hands through her hair, she took in the rest of the ranger station. "How long was I out?"

"An hour. Took me twenty minutes and over two hundred stitches to stop the bleeding." Roman slid his hand into hers, massaging the pressure point between her index and thumb. "You scared the hell out of me."

"You're not the only one." Her gaze lowered to their hands. "When Tabitha pressed that detonator, I thought I'd lost you. It felt like she'd reached into my chest and pulled my heart out with her bare hand." She skimmed her hand over his shirt collar, tugging it lower to expose the dressing underneath. Her fingertips grazed the edges of the tape. "That's the most fear I've ever experienced. And that includes waking up on a stranger's boat and realizing I might die there."

"I told you. I'm not going anywhere." Roman leaned over her, careful of her wounds, and pressed his mouth to hers. Cracked skin softened under pressure as he slipped past the seam of her lips. He kissed her, a deep, haze-inducing kiss, that chased the nightmares of their situation to the back of his mind. The anxiety he'd carried since hearing the gunshot from the lighthouse released as she framed his jawline and urged him closer. His upper body balanced above her, he kissed her again, wilder, more frantic. Desperate. After everything they'd been through, he didn't have the strength to hold back anymore. His heart pounded hard in his chest. He wanted them to have a chance, to have a life, to be happy. Together. She'd spent her entire life being chased by monsters. He could protect her from any threat, he could fight for her. If she gave them a chance. "I love you, Brie. I don't ever want to lose you."

Her sharp exhale stirred goosebumps down his neck. Blue-green eyes studied him from forehead to chin as she brushed her thumb through the bristle along his jaw. Her words shook. "Do you mean that?"

"Every damn word." Hell, did she have any idea how much of his soul she owned? This strong, beautiful, controlled woman had stood up to killers, fought for justice, and brought the missing home, all the while sacrificing her own happiness for fear it'd get taken away again. He wasn't going to let that happen. "I've loved you from the second I laid eyes on you back in Washington. For months, I've wanted nothing more than to prove to you there is something out in the world more than the shadows in your eyes. You deserve to be happy, and I will spend the rest of my life trying to make that a reality for you, if you'll let me."

"Brass won't let us work together if they find out." Her eyes glittered as stared up at him. "We won't be partners anymore."

"The bureau has their rules, I understand that, and I've spent the last decade building my career." Roman shrugged then reached out to catch a stray tear trailing down her face. "But between you and the job, you will always come first, baby. For me, the choice is easy." He leaned in, kissing the mole on the left side of her face softly. "We might not be investigating cases together after this, but you'll always be my partner."

Brie smoothed her thumb across his bottom lip, a smile pulling at the edges of her mouth. Curling her hand around his wrist, she brought his knuckles to her mouth. Her lashes hugged her cheeks as she studied the damage to his knuckles and arms. "In that case, I love you, too. I don't know what's going to happen after we catch Tabitha, but I'm ready to find out. With you." She pressed her hand to his chest. "The bullet missed your heart."

Well, hell. She loved him, too.

"It's going to take a lot more than a slug to keep me from you." He sat back on the edge of the bed. But the nightmare wasn't over yet. There was still a killer on the loose. He'd taken stock of the ranger's station while she'd slept off the shock brought on by the amount of blood she'd lost. No weapons. Made sense. Rangers couldn't have civilian hikers coming across a gun and a few boxes of ammunition, but right now, they were dead in the water. Injured, unarmed, and without backup. If isolating them had been the plan so the killer could get to Brie, then Tabitha had done a damn fine job.

Static reached his ears from the back room, and Roman slid off the thin mattress to follow the sound. The CB radio he'd used to contact the team crackled in sporadic increments. Low words pierced through the interference, and he brought the device back into the main room to get a better signal. Window. Teammate. Kill. He recognized the voice on the other end of the line, and his stomach dropped. Tabitha. Approaching the window, he kept out of direct sight as he scanned the landscape around the station. And froze. Two figures stood less than twenty yards away, one held hostage by the boning knife at her throat. "It's Luther. Tabitha must've taken her straight from the beach after we escaped the lighthouse." Damn it. He'd confiscated the profiler's weapon when he'd lost his after the explosion. He'd left his team unprotected at the slightest chance he'd be able to save his partner. Luther had been working on resuscitating Holloway. Where did that leave her partner? Had emergency personnel made it in time to save him?

Compressing the button, Roman spoke slowly and directly into the radio. The training he'd used in volatile hostage situations overseas kicked in, but this time, he knew today would only end in blood.

"You've made it this far without killing a federal agent, Tabitha. If you kill my teammate, you'll have the entire FBI after you, and I can guarantee her partner will spend every waking second of his life hunting you down."

Tabitha kept her attention on him through the window, forcing her hostage to raise the radio and open the channel. "I don't think your team's interrogator is going to be a problem anymore, Agent Bradford, but you can still save him if you act quickly. Give me what I want, or I will spend every waking second of *my life* hunting down everyone you've ever cared about." She pressed the knife harder against Luther's neck, the profiler lifting onto her toes to counter. "Starting with this one."

Kinsley Luther's argument died as the killer slammed the butt of the blade into the side of the profiler's head.

Rage exploded through him. Son of a bitch. How the hell was he supposed to trade his teammates for the woman he'd fallen in love with, the woman he wanted to spend the rest of his life with? He compressed the button once again. "I don't trade lives."

"Even when it could save so many others?" Tabitha asked.

He tossed the radio on the end of the bed, turning to Brie, for once, not seeing the answer.

"Tabitha tortured all those women to get my attention. She wanted me here in Ludington to punish me for escaping the Dream Catcher. I don't think she's going to stop until she gets what she wants, and she'll kill anyone who gets in her way, whether they're innocent or not." Brie locked her gaze on his. "She's trained, she's planned for every contingency, and she's smart. She knows we're injured and alone, and she's going to take advantage as soon as she sees the opportunity."

Damn it.

"You want to give her one." He'd read her mind before she'd opened her mouth. Brie wanted to offer herself up. Just as Haynes had suggested they do before they'd known about all the players in the investigation. Roman hadn't liked the idea then, and he sure as hell didn't like it now. "You're recovering from a stab wound, a gunshot, and a handful of other injuries, and you want to walk out there and offer yourself up in exchange." He ran a hand through his hair and spun away from the window. He'd just gotten her back, gotten a promise of a future together, and she wanted to walk out the front door with her hands up? He couldn't lose her. Not again. Not after they'd decided to give this—whatever this was between them—a shot. The desperation that'd closed through him as he'd kissed her bled into his voice. "She'll kill you."

"I'm not going to let anyone else die because I survived." Brie attempted to lock down the groan escaping up her throat as she maneuvered to the edge of the bed, and he twisted toward her before she had the chance of undoing all the work it'd taken to save her life. He helped her to her feet. She stared up at him, setting her hand over his heart. "Do you trust me?"

"Yes." There was no hesitation. She'd proven time and time again he could count on her. She was nothing like the partner he'd taken down. She'd always have his back, always side with justice.

"Then help me get my clothes back on so we can end this," she said. "Together."

CHAPTER THIRTY-SEVEN

BRIE STEPPED OUT THE STATION'S FRONT DOOR, MORNING LIGHT piercing through the haze of exhaustion and blood loss. Gravel and a thin layer of snow crunched under her boots as she limped to close the distance between her and the killer. Crystalized puffs of air formed in front of her mouth. Her heart beat steadily behind her ears. This was it. This was where twenty years of nightmares, trauma, and death ended. This was what her entire life had been building to since the night she'd escaped her killer. No weapons. Just her and the psychopath who'd set out to destroy everything she cared about. "Agent Luther has nothing to do with this. Let her go, and I'm yours."

Less than thirty feet away, Tabitha shifted her weight between both feet, the blade still at Kinsley's throat. Blood spread across the profiler's collar from the small nick in her skin. An evil smile pulled the killer's lips into a thin line. "You're trying to distract me. Pretending to give me what I want in order to protect your team." Tabitha shook her head. "It won't work, Special Agent McKinney."

"You've tried to kill me twice now. Almost succeeded, too, so I think we're past formalities." Brie ignored pain spearing through her. She could do this. She had to do this. "You want me. This is the only chance you're going to get. Come and take it."

"This agent and I are the only ones who know where your interrogator is. We die, he dies. I'm sure your partner told you all about how he'd left your teammate's life in her hands, but Special Agent Luther here couldn't fight me off and protect him at the same time. And here I thought you federal agents were trained to deal with every threat. Apparently, not so much." Tabitha lowered the knife from Kinsley's neck, but the tension wouldn't drain from Brie's shoulders. Not until Roman was in position. In the next moment, Tabitha raised the weapon back up and swiped the knife toward the profiler's throat. Kinsley wedged her hands between the blade and her neck, crying out as it sliced into the palms of her hands. The killer raised the weapon again, and Kinsley lunged out of the way.

"Roman, now!" Brie rushed Tabitha, drawing the killer's attention away from her partner breaching the tree line from behind. He headed straight for Kinsley as Brie targeted her uninjured shoulder at the killer's ribcage. Hefting her off the ground, she slammed Tabitha onto her back, knocking the boning knife into nearby brush. She fisted the killer's shirt in both hands to haul her up but didn't get the chance as Tabitha slammed both hands down on her forearms. Her attacker rocketed a fist into the wound in Brie's gut, and she fell back, a scream tearing from her throat. Roman reached Kinsley in her peripheral vision and hauled the profiler to her feet. He'd get her to safety.

And Brie would finish this once and for all.

She struggled to straighten, testing the blood seeping through her clothing with her fingertips, and stood. Her partner wouldn't be too happy she'd torn the brand new stitches open, but what was a little blood when she'd already been through the worst pain in her life? The minutes she'd believed Roman hadn't survived the explosion had almost killed her.

Tabitha got to her feet, breath heaving in her chest.

"You never intended to let Aiden and Kinsley go. You planned to tie up every loose end, planned for everything in case law enforcement caught your trail." Brie swiped her hair out of her face. "Then there'd be no one left to hunt you down once you disappeared."

"Not just for law enforcement. For you. Because of everyone who escaped, of everyone I've killed, you're the one who deserved to die the most. You left your sister to die and I was the only one who could make you pay, but I couldn't come at you directly. I had to break you first. Making you believe I was your long-lost sister by cutting off my own finger and killing Kirk Marshall in self-defense was the perfect plan to get inside your head, but you had to pull her out of the lake. You ruined everything!" The killer threw a wide punch aimed at the side of Brie's head.

Brie threw her arm up to block. Another hit came in fast, and she blocked again. She followed up with a swift uppercut aimed at Tabitha's chin, and knocked the woman's head back onto her shoulders. Pain seared through her arm as she hauled her other fist into Tabitha's kidney, but wasn't fast enough to block the bloodied knuckles connecting with her jaw. The tree line, the ground, the ranger's station, everything blurred as momentum twisted her around. Dizziness unbalanced her and she collapsed onto her side. A groan registered from her attacker as Tabitha stumbled to keep her footing. Dirt and fresh air overwhelmed the scent of blood as Brie got back up. She raised her fists. A humorless laugh rushed past her lips. "There's only one person I've ever let break me. And you don't have his smile."

A ferocious growl echoed around her as Tabitha charged. Rage, hatred, and unleashed fury contorted the woman's face into something unrecognizable. The killer arced her arm wide, taking aim at the laceration in Brie's shoulder, but Brie wrapped her hand around Tabitha's wrist. She hauled it over her head and wrenched hard, landing her elbow directly into the killer's spine. A sharp gasp filled her ears a split second before Brie crouched fast and applied as much pressure as she could to the back of her attacker's knee. The sickening sound of bones breaking was overshadowed by Tabitha's guttural scream, but the killer didn't go down. Landing on one knee, Tabitha turned in time for Brie to launch her fist directly into the assailant's right cheekbone, and they both fell to the ground from the combined momentum.

Out of breath, bleeding, Brie struggled to regain her strength to stand. As long as Tabitha was free, every woman who'd survived the Dream Catcher was still at risk.

"Is that all you've got?" A glint of metal caught sunlight, and Brie wrenched out of the way as Tabitha swung a second blade at her. The tip of the knife sank into dirt as Brie pushed to her feet, but the killer was faster. Hobbling toward her on one leg, Tabitha brought the weapon down, barely missing Brie's shoulder.

Pivoting, Brie secured her attacker's wrist in her grip and moved to knock the blade from Tabitha's hand. Another swing missed cutting into her sternum, but she didn't see the fist coming at her until it was too late. Agony burst through the side of her face as bone met flesh. Lightning shot across her vision. Brie struggled to stay upright, but gravity pulled at every cell in her body. Moving in close, the killer aimed the blade for Brie's throat. She stopped the knife's progression by launching both hands out and securing Tabitha's arm then ripped the weapon from the killer's hand. One strong kick to Tabitha's shin brought the killer face down into the dirt. Brie kicked the knife away, launching it into the underbrush. Wiping the blood from her mouth, she doubled over as adrenaline slowly drained from her veins. "It's over, Tabitha. You're under arrest for the murder of Ashlee Carr, Lisa Knowles, Kara Holmes, and Jessica McKinney, and for the attempted murder of three federal agents, as well as Emma King—"

"I've been a prisoner almost my entire life, Special Agent McKinney. I've lived through things you couldn't even dream about." A low, light rumble shook through Tabitha. The laughing grew louder as the killer pushed back onto her haunches and locked one blue eye and one brown eye on her. The contacts. One of them must've fallen out, revealing the true monster beneath the mask. "Because you escaped, Kirk Marshall took his rage out on every single victim that came after you. They suffered longer and more violently because of you. Do you want to know what he did to Jessica?"

Nausea churned in her gut.

"Do you want to know how many times she screamed your name while he was hurting her? How she begged him to kill her so the torment could end?" Tabitha shot her hand out to her side, into the underbrush, and wrapped her fingers around something Brie didn't recognize until the killer had already started charging toward her. The boning knife.

Brie raised her hands in self-defense as someone broke through the trees off to her right. "Roman, no!"

His mountainous shoulders made contact with the killer's body, and they slammed into the ground together in a violent blur. Dust and snow kicked up around them as Brie scrambled forward. The breath emptied from her lungs as they stilled, her partner straddled over Tabitha's hips. Roman wrapped one large hand around the killer's neck, his voice dropping into dangerous territory. "Give me one reason not to squeeze the life out of you."

"Roman." Brie froze as the dust cleared, her body heavy as she caught sight of the blade protruding from her partner's abdominals. No. No, no, no, no. Not Roman. Not after she'd just gotten him back. She had to think. As long as the blade stayed in place, it would keep the bleeding at bay. He'd have a chance. He'd survive—

Tabitha twisted the boning knife deeper, eliciting a groan from Roman's chest before he collapsed onto his side. The killer pressed a hand over the seeping bullet wound in her shoulder as she pushed Roman off of her and stood, a wound almost identical to the one the Dream Catcher had given Brie. "I'll never know what you see in him."

"No!" Brie curled numb fingers into her palms and lunged. Kicking out, she made contact with Tabitha's sternum and knocked the woman back. She'd spent years learning to control the rage and anger that'd become so deeply engrained, become part of her, but the moment that blade had gone into Roman's body, the dam had broken. It spilled out as she attacked again, throwing a fist into the killer's face while she was down. Tabitha's head snapped back against the ground, the blade seemingly forgotten in her hand. Brie put everything she had into the next hit and targeted the bullet wound in the killer's shoulder. Her attacker launched her hips upward, and they rolled together down a slight slope toward the tree line.

Dizziness held onto her as she struggled to stand, and she failed to block the blow to her gut. Then the next. Pain ripped through her as she felt the rest of the stitches tear, but in that moment, her purpose outranked her pain. Catching Tabitha's wrist as she arced the long, slim blade down toward Brie's chest, she caught the woman's other hand before the killer had a chance to make another move. The muscles in her jaw jerked against the exertion to keep herself from getting stabbed. Sweat slid into her eyes despite the below freezing temperatures. She pried the weapon from the killer's hand, tightening her grip around the handle.

She locked her gaze with Tabitha's. Even facing into the sun, Brie could see the woman's internal pain, the years of torture and uncertainty that'd built her into the killer standing in front of her. She could see the hopelessness. And the truth. As long as Tabitha was breathing, the women she'd targeted would always be in danger. Even with their hunter behind bars. "It didn't have to be like this. I could've helped you. Sooner or later, I would've found Kirk Marshall on my own."

"You're so busy protecting everyone else, Briohny," Tabitha said. "Who's going to protect you?"

"My partner." Brie let go of the boning knife that'd brought so much pain and agony to so many. Rolling her opposite wrist out of Tabitha's grip, she caught the blade before it hit the ground, and drove it straight into the killer's heart. Surprise fluttered over Tabitha's expression then smoothed as Brie let her attacker collapse to the ground.

She staggered back, the blood-stained blade in her hand. The tip reached for the earth, and she watched as it fell end over end until it hit the ground. The Dream Catcher's partner lay at her feet, dead. It was over. She pushed her dirt-crusted hair from her face, exhaling every sip of breath she'd been holding since stepping out of the ranger station, and searched for her partner. "Roman."

She sprinted to his side as fast as her body carried her, careful to avoid his injuries as she rolled him onto his back. Cold worked through her slacks and down into her bones as she studied the blood soaked through his button-down shirt. Framing his jawline, she slid to fingers lower to test his pulse. Thready but there. He was still alive. Tears burned in her lower lash line. There was so much blood. "Don't even think about dying on me. You owe me an entire box of cupcakes."

Terror ricocheted through her as webs of black crept in from the edges of her vision. The pain in her gut and back of her thigh returned, and she shot her hand to his arm to hold back the sob bursting from her throat. She had to stay awake. Had to get him help before he bled out, but her body had given everything it could. Brie fell onto her side, staring up into the trees before she was dragged into unconsciousness.

CHAPTER THIRTY-EIGHT

Roman felt like shit.

"I hear you're the one I need to thank for saving my life," a familiar voice said.

He battled the heaviness running through his system to open his eyes. Over-exposed white blurs died to a dull brightness as florescent lighting came into view. Soft beeps registered from the machines beside his bed, crisp white sheets and a heavy top blanket weighing him down. The hospital. Bandages had been placed all over his chest and stomach. His throat had been rubbed raw as though someone had shoved something down into his stomach. Hell, maybe they had. Roman focused on the agent leveraging his elbows onto his knees beside the bed. Aiden Holloway. But where was Brie? The last thing he remembered was her scream when Tabitha had twisted the boning knife in his gut. He tried to swallow around the dryness in his mouth. In vain. Wrapping his hand around the bed railing to haul himself up, he scanned the room. But it was empty aside from Holloway. "Where is she?"

Had she taken down Tabitha? Was she alive?

"She's in the next room over recovering from surgery." Holloway shook his head, bruises darkening all along the man's forearms and neck. Judging from how far the agent had been thrown into the lake, Roman guessed Holloway had been furthest from the blast. Any closer and the team would have lost one of their own. "The woman who'd tried murdering us all—Tabitha Gray—did a number on her, but Brie's too stubborn to not pull through. You know that. Kinsley's with her now."

Roman couldn't ignore the body-wide ache every time he moved. "Is Kinsley okay? Her hands—"

"She's lost about ninety percent feeling so far." Holloway's expression darkened as he lowered his attention to the linoleum flooring. "The surgeon did what he could, but the blade sliced through the major nerves in her palms, and they aren't sure she'll ever be able to get back into the field if she can't pass her weapons test." Wiping his hands down his jeans, the interrogator leaned back in his chair. "She's strong, and she's about as stubborn as Brie. She'll work through this. It's just going to take some time."

Time. That wasn't a commodity the victims Kinsley Luther had helped them find had. How many perpetrators were out there right now that they'd need the profiler's help to find? Hell. The work they did, the people they were assigned to find… They didn't have time. And Roman wasn't going to waste any more of it in this bed. He dropped his head back onto the pillow, the IV in his arm pinching hard. He grabbed for the tubing and pulled it free. The machines went wild, but there was nothing that was going to stop him from—

"Roman?" His name on her lips settled the erratic beat of his pulse. He twisted his head toward the door. Brie. She was standing there, in nothing but a hospital gown with bruises on her beautiful skin and concern etched into her expression. And hell she was a sight for sore eyes.

"I have a feeling this is about to get awkward for me." Holloway vacated his chair, maneuvering past Brie in the doorframe. "Good to see you awake, McKinney."

"Thanks. I'm glad you're not dead," she said, all the while never taking her attention off Roman. Blood trickled down her inner arm, and he realized she'd removed her IV, too. To get to him?

"Tell me you're okay. Then tell me what happened." He couldn't make the pieces fit. After he'd gotten Luther to safety and bandaged her wounds as quickly as he could, he'd gone back to the ranger station and found Brie in a violent, gritty fight to the death with the killer. He'd attacked Tabitha, gotten stabbed then…nothing.

"I'm alive. Thanks to you." Brie closed the distance between them. "And Tabitha is dead. I stabbed her with the same knife she used on all of her victims. Then I went back to save you, and I passed out. Next thing I knew, I woke up here. Kinsley told me she'd used the radio in the ranger's station to call for a medical chopper. We were both airlifted and rushed into surgery." A weak smile played across her perfect mouth, and he wanted nothing more than to feel her lips under his to prove she wasn't a figment of his drugged imagination.

He curled his hand around her wrist, reveling in her body heat, in the softness of her skin, and the tension that his body had held onto for the last few days disappeared. Because of her. His Brie. "You okay?"

"Yeah. For the first time, I feel…free." Her shoulders dropped away from her ears. "After everything that's happened, after so much has been blood spilled, I realized…it's not my fault. I couldn't have beaten the Dream Catcher as a girl, and if I hadn't escaped, I would've have been able to bring him and Tabitha down now. I wouldn't have been able to get all those families the closure and justice they deserved. Tabitha and I were in the exact same situation, but she chose her path, and I chose mine." Roman pulled her closer and wiped at the tear carving a path down her cheeks. "None of those lives are on me." She smoothed her fingers across his hairline, and he closed his eyes as she trailed a path down through his beard. Hell, he loved this woman. "You were supposed to get Kinsley to safety. Why did you come back?"

He opened his eyes, locking on the blue-green depths of hers.

"We're partners. I'm never going to leave you to fight alone." Roman leveraged his weight into the hospital bed, trying to sit straighter, but the pain from the wounds on both sides of his abdominals stole the small about of energy he'd saved. "And I want us to stay that way. I don't have a ring, and I can't get down on one knee right now, but…" He cleared his throat, taking her bruised hand in his. "Brie

McKinney, you are everything I didn't know was missing. In just a few short months, you've filled a hollowness I've carried around my entire life, and there's no way in hell I could ever repay you for that. But, if you'll give me the chance, I'll spend the rest of my life trying. Whether it's here in Ludington, back in Washington, or with one of us working for another agency altogether, I want us to be together. I want you to be my wife. Not just partners on the job but forever."

"You are one smooth negotiator, Special Agent Bradford." Her bottom lip parted from the top. One breath. Two. "But a hospital proposal won't get you out of watching romantic comedies with me until I've made you memorize every single one forwards and backwards." She lifted her index finger. "And I want cupcakes."

"Baby, I'll buy you as many cupcakes as you can handle every damn day if that's what would make you happy." He curved his thumb over the back of her hand, his chest constricting from a new kind of anticipation he hadn't felt in a long time. "All you have to do is marry me."

Lowering herself onto the bed, she leaned into him, watching out for the bandages across his stomach. That gut-wrenching smile of hers flashed wide, and the case, the fear, the blood, it all disappeared to the back of his mind. "Marrying you would make me happy." She leveled her mouth with his then pulled back. "In case that wasn't clear, my answer is 'yes.'"

"Good." He crushed his mouth to hers, ignoring the pain as he pulled her completely onto the bed beside him. Her perfume washed over him as she trapped them under the sheets together. Monitors registered the frantic beat of his heart, but he didn't give a damn. He notched her chin higher with his finger, leveling her gaze with his, and planted a soft kiss on her mouth. "I love you, Brie."

This, right here, being with Brie. This was all that mattered. They'd survived the darkness—together—and would if it ever came calling again. She deserved a happy ending, and he'd fight until his dying breath to give it to her.

EPILOGUE

HER HEELS SANK INTO THE GRASS AS SHE LIMPED HER WAY TOWARD THE small podium at the head of the casket. A pattern of white long-stemmed roses crisscrossed across the gleaming surface. Sea gulls pierced through the silence as she stared out over the large uniformed gathering, but only one stood out among the many. Roman. Her fiancé. His encouraging smile settled the conflict battling inside of her. Curling her fingers at the edge of the wooden surface, she studied the man in the photo on the easel beside her, confidence and love and understanding filling her voice.

"The officer we're burying today has been called a lot of things. Captain, neighbor, friend, protector. Father,"—Brie squared her shoulders—"and, at the end, a traitor. But the fact you're here to pay respects to a man who's protected and served this city for more than twenty years tells me you know the truth about him. That he loved his job, this city, and everyone in it. That he was killed in the line of duty doing the right thing, no matter the personal risk and sacrifice it would take." Brie forced herself to take a deep, cleansing breath as tears welled in her eyes. "Greg Hobbs was there for me when nobody else was, when I thought my life was over, but it was only recently I realized, it was because of him that my life had just begun. He helped me see that I could be more than the things that had happened to me, and I will always be thankful for that. We've lost one of our own, but Captain Greg Hobbs will never be forgotten. Least of all by me."

Uniformed officers raised white-gloved hands in salute as Brie stepped down the small platform and made her way back to her seat. Roman stood and threaded his hand between her elbow and ribcage to give her the added support, but the pain in her thigh was nothing compared to the joy spreading through her. The city had given Greg Hobbs an officer's funeral, where he'd be buried beside the men and women who'd given their lives to protect the city she'd left behind.

"I'm sure Hobbs appreciated everything you said." Roman wrapped his arm at her lower back, pressing his lips to her temple, and her insides fluttered in response.

The medical examiner had matched Tabitha's boning knife to the lacerations and stab wounds on all seven victims, including Captain Hobbs's. After having gone back in the federal database to track down the rest of the Dream Catcher's former victims, she and Roman had come up with only one theory as to why the nomad witness statements hadn't been deleted with their main files. Hobbs had wanted Brie to find her abductor, to bring down the killer threatening to take her away from him all those years. With their identities safe and both killers dead, the case was officially closed. And she could move on. With Roman.

"Special Agent McKinney?" a familiar voice broke through the solemn chaos as parishioners filed down the aisles between gravesites, and Brie turned to face Ted and Glenda McKinney. Tears brimmed her parents' eyes as they stopped short. Seconds ticked in silence, a full minute, before Ted unwrapped his arm from around his wife and offered his hand. "We wanted to thank you for having Jessica's body released so we could bury her properly. Without your help, we're not sure we ever would've gotten the chance to see her again."

"Of course." Brie nodded, the sling making it hard to do much else. "She deserved to come home after all these years. I'm happy you were able to get your daughter back."

"We haven't." Glenda shot her hand out, latching onto Brie's wrist, and tension climbed into her chest at the touch. A knowing light chased back the tears in her mother's blue-green eyes the longer she studied Brie. "At least, not the daughter we abandoned the night Jessica went missing. And we want her back."

Roman squeezed her hip as he settled her mouth against her ear. "I'll give you a few minutes."

Brie couldn't think. Couldn't breathe as her partner walked away. She cleared her throat, parted her lips to say something—anything—but she didn't have the words.

"Briohny." Her father stepped into her, arms outstretched before placing his large hands on either of her shoulders. "We thought we made the worst mistake in our lives leaving you with Greg Hobbs, but seeing the strong, independent woman you've turned into has never made us prouder to be your parents."

Her parents. They weren't her parents. Hobbs had raised her, given her a home, made sure she ate her vegetables and washed behind her ears. Ted and Glenda McKinney, they were… She didn't know what they were. Who they were.

"We have no idea what you've been up to or what you've been through all these years, but we'd like the chance to find out. To show you how much we've missed you, and how much we regret what we did that night. If you'll let us." Glenda McKinney gave a tentative smile as she wrapped her fingers around Brie's uninjured hand. "Oh, Brie, we're so sorry. Can you ever forgive us?"

"I don't know." Ringing filled her ears, and her attention slid to the casket behind her parents. Years of trauma, bitterness, and betrayal had forged her into a woman strong enough to survive not one but two serial killers. As much as she wanted to deny it, she had to give some of that credit to the two people standing in front of her. The rest belonged to Hobbs. "But I'm willing to try." Pressure released from behind her sternum. "My partner and I are due back in Washington to start our new assignments tomorrow." Because, as they'd expected, SAC Haynes had separated them the moment they'd come forward with their relationship, but they hadn't been demoted or reassigned from the missing persons division. "Maybe we could all have breakfast before we leave for the airport."

"We're looking forward to it." Ted McKinney brought her into a quick hug before stepping back. A few seconds later, her parents were carving a path through the cemetery toward their car.

"You okay?" Roman tugged her close, right where she needed to be.

Seven riflemen shouted orders before aiming their rifles into the air and pulling the triggers three times. Each reverberation of shots punctured through the doubt, anger, and emotions she'd held close to the vest all these years. She was better than okay. She was free. From the killer from her past, the guilt she'd carried to the present, free from the bitterness toward her parents, and free to love the man beside her into the future. Free to be happy. She kissed her partner with everything she had. "I am now."

***

Thank you so much for reading this exclusive release of TAKEN!

ABOUT THE AUTHOR

"First class romantic suspense!"
- Cynthia Eden, NYT Bestselling Author

Nichole Severn writes mind-twisting suspense and bullet-proof romance with strong heroines, heroes who dare challenge them, and cases you won't be able to forget. She graduated from Utah Valley University with a degree in Psychology, is a member of International Thriller Writers, and a founding member of the Addicted to Danger Facebook group.

She resides with her very supportive and patient husband, as well as her demon spawn, in Utah. When she's not writing, she's constantly injuring herself running, rock climbing, practicing yoga, and snowboarding.

ALSO BY NICHOLE SEVERN

COLD GROUNDS SERIES
Taken

HUNTING GROUNDS SERIES
Run, Run, Seek

Over the Flames

Into the Veins

Bits and Pieces

View from Above

Study in Color

Art in Blood

Dirt is Thicker (2023)

DEFENDERS OF BATTLE MOUNTAIN
Grave Danger

Dead Giveaway

Dead on Arrival

Presumed Dead

Over Her Dead Body (2023)

Dead Again (2023)

Hunt for a Killer (2023)

BLACKHAWK SECURITY SERIES
Rules in Revenge (free short story)

Rules in Blackmail

Rules in Rescue

Rules in Deceit

Rules in Defiance

Caught in the Crossfire

The Line of Duty

Survival on the Summit

SEARCH AND RESCUE

Search and Rescue

Search and Protect

Search and Defend

Search and Pursue

Search and Destroy

Fatal Rescue boxset

MARSHAL LAW

The Search

The Fugitive

The Witness

The Prosecutor

The Suspect

TACTICAL CRIME DIVISION

Midnight Abduction

BEHAVIORAL ANALYSIS UNIT

Caging a Copycat (free short story)

Profiling a Killer

Printed in Great Britain
by Amazon